Dear Reader,

I'm still celebrating your response to my debut for MIRA Books. *Where the Road Ends* was out last summer, and I can hardly believe it's time for another release.

I bring you *Street Smart* with a bit of trepidation and a whole lot of heart. The trepidation comes from your expectations, which I don't want, ever, to disappoint. This is not like any other book I've written. It explores topics I have not explored before and never thought I would. And yet, as with every single story I tell, it comes from within me. My work seems to happen on its own, almost in spite of me. The people, their lives come from somewhere deep inside. How they get there, I don't question. What to do with them, I don't ask. I sit. I think and feel. I type. And I give them—my characters—to you.

I offer you *Street Smart* with my very best wishes.

*Tara Taylor Quinn*

I love to hear from readers. You can reach me at P.O. Box 15065, Scottsdale, AZ 85267 or check out my Web site: www.tarataylorquinn.com.

# Street Smart
## TARA TAYLOR QUINN

MIRA

ISBN 0-7783-2060-X

STREET SMART

Copyright © 2004 by Tara Taylor Quinn.

All rights reserved. Except for use in any review, the reproduction or
utilization of this work in whole or in part in any form by any electronic,
mechanical or other means, now known or hereafter invented, including
xerography, photocopying and recording, or in any information storage or
retrieval system, is forbidden without the written permission of the publisher,
MIRA Books, 225 Duncan Mill Road, Don Mills, Ontario, Canada M3B 3K9.

All characters in this book have no existence outside the imagination of the
author and have no relation whatsoever to anyone bearing the same name
or names. They are not even distantly inspired by any individual known or
unknown to the author, and all incidents are pure invention.

MIRA and the Star Colophon are trademarks used under license and registered
in Australia, New Zealand, Philippines, United States Patent and Trademark
Office and in other countries.

www.MIRABooks.com

**Printed in U.S.A.**

To the coolest girls I know—
Patricia Potter, Carol Prescott, Lynn Kerstan
and Mary Strand. I'm a lot smarter because
of the four of you. And looking forward to
how much smarter I'm going to get!

# 1

She pushed as hard as she could. Pushed until her insides felt as though they were ripping away from her bones. There was supposed to be time in between. Time to breathe. To maintain sanity. Instead, one wave of mind-altering pain followed another.

How long she'd been lying there, Francesca Witting had no idea. She'd lost track of time during the night. It was all a blur to her now. Pain. Despair. Determination.

And fear.

Something was wrong. She didn't have to see the worried expressions on the faces of the medical personnel as they examined her, measured, watched screens, to know that. If her instincts weren't insistent enough, her body was telling her that this son of hers was not coming into the world as nature had intended. He wasn't helping enough. Or she wasn't. Instead of sliding down the birth canal, he was tearing her apart from the inside out.

Terrified, she rode the pains, accepted them, for they meant she was still alive—and that maybe he was.

Most of the time speech flew around her, over her.

Tense, staccato words—orders she couldn't understand. In a language she knew only peripherally.

Francesca was used to being alone. Was in Italy now, alone, by her own choice.

She'd just never thought she'd die this way.

Never thought she'd die without seeing Autumn again. Without knowing that her runaway half sister who'd been missing for more than two years was safe and well.

People she'd never seen before—and didn't really see now—came and went from the little gray-walled room. Touching her. Mostly she couldn't feel them. The searing pain from within left no room for other sensation. When she could focus, she saw them, all moving quickly in their green scrubs, their hair covered, their features serious. Intensely engaged. Most were wearing thin plastic gloves. Or pushing fingers into them. Or peeling them off.

Few paid attention to the American woman's face. Their concern was lower down, inside the tented sheet, on the miracle that was becoming a tragedy.

Francesca's legs had been spread in stirrups beneath that sheet for so long the position felt permanent. A lot more permanent than her life, or the tiny life that she prayed was still alive, struggling inside her.

"Aahh." She heard the wail, but didn't immediately identify it as her own. As she'd been doing for hours, she stared at a green light ticking off seconds on a monitor to one side of her left knee.

For the past hours she'd alternated between sweating and getting chills from wet skin touched by the room's cool air.

A nurse adjusted the IV connected to her right hand. Probably because the excruciating pain in her lower abdomen was on the downward slope of its current wave, Francesca was aware as the IV needle moved beneath her skin. It hurt.

Another nurse, a fairly young one, stepped up to Francesca's shoulder, offering her ice chips and indistinguishable Italian words in a kind voice. The woman's mouth was pinched, her eyes carefully guarded.

Francesca barely had the energy to shake her head. If she had to swallow, she'd choke. Gripping the bedsheet with clenched fists, she turned her head on the soaking-wet pillow they'd changed more than once. Her short damp hair stuck to the side of her face.

The woman tried again, bringing a spoonful of chips to Francesca's parched lips, her tone encouraging. With a breath she hoped would be deep enough to get her through the next seconds of pain, Francesca allowed the chips to rest against her closed lips. The ice was cold, on the left side of her bottom lip and the right side of her top. Very cold. Cold enough for her to feel. She thought about those cold spots. Concentrated on them. As hard as she could. Until nothing existed but those tiny sensations of cold.

In that split second of relief a vision of Antonio's compelling face flashed before her eyes. His coal-black hair. Eyes that were almost black in color and yet so full of warmth—of intelligent compassion—that they drew her relentlessly.

Oh, God, Antonio. She hadn't told him... Couldn't. His life was elsewhere. Irrevocably tied to another woman. A disabled woman. But it seemed as if, somehow, he'd come here, to this place.

Her face aching with the smile that was attempting to force its way through tight cracked skin, Francesca blinked, hoping to bring his face into clearer focus. His face, with its permanent shadow of a beard that would be thick and full were it permitted to grow longer than twelve hours.

Had someone found out? Called him from halfway around the world? Because she was dying? Or his baby was?

Another pain rose to unbearable levels and she couldn't hold on to his image.

*Don't leave, my love. Stay. Just for a few minutes.*

Blinking the sweat and tears from her eyes, Francesca sought out her only remaining source of strength. Antonio's smile. And saw, instead, a younger face in glaring light. A concerned gaze. A few escaped tendrils of brown hair sticking out from beneath a light green, tied-on cap. A female face.

She blinked again. The pain wasn't subsiding at all.

"Antonio!" The word was a scream inside her mind. In the room, it sounded more like a harsh whisper.

Antonio.

Her biggest sin.

He was one of the few people who'd managed to

penetrate the defenses she'd wrapped around herself after she'd left home and the stepfather who'd hit her and the mother who'd been too emotionally battered to help her. Defenses that had served her well as she became the determined Italian-American photojournalist who'd managed to make a name for herself with her pictures and accompanying text by the time she was thirty.

The nurse was leaning over her, placing her face so close to Francesca's, Francesca could hardly breathe, let alone make out what the woman was trying to say.

Turning her head to the side as her lower stomach twisted inside out, ripping away from her spine, Francesca took one last breath.

"Antonio!"

His face was there again. Just his face this time. Floating above her.

And then everything was dark.


*Gian* was a popular name for Italian boys. But that wasn't why the little guy's mother named him that. Gian meant "God is gracious." And that was the reason Francesca had bestowed the name on her little son. Because the powers that be had been gracious that morning two and a half months ago and preserved the life of the infant who'd been almost strangled by the umbilical cord in his mother's womb.

Francesca was trying to be quiet so as to not wake her paternal grandmother. Sancia Witting, the current matriarch of an old Italian family that had immigrated to Italy from Wales centuries before, needed her afternoon siesta. Rolling up a dozen summer-weight sleepers Francesca stuffed them into the far corner of the second of two oversize dark green duffels on the double bed in Sancia's guest room. Gian, who'd been asleep for more than an hour in his portable crib, wasn't a concern. This son of hers could sleep through a minor hurricane, as he'd proved three weeks before when a debilitating storm had hit the coast of Naples, waking all within a hundred-mile radius. But not Gian.

His washcloth and hooded towels were next. The lotions and powders that left his little body so sweet-smelling already lay secure in a plastic bag in the other duffel, along with a week's worth of disposable diapers padding all her cameras. This late-spring time out of time with her newborn son—and the grandmother she'd just met the month before—had been without doubt the most joyful she'd known since her father's death almost twenty years before. But life was calling on her to begin moving again.

Actually, although she'd never admit as much to her overprotective grandmother, Francesca had done the calling herself. She'd left messages for a couple of magazine editors who were always eager for a Francesca Witting piece.

She'd had calls back from both. And now she and Gian were off to spend June in New York, Boston and San Diego before returning to Sacramento to introduce him to the grandmother who didn't yet know he existed. Francesca had sold the piece she'd come to Italy to do almost a year before—an in-depth look at Italian people through their weathering of disasters. And she'd been asked to do a follow-up piece highlighting the similarities of their character and culture to Italians living in neighborhoods in America. This time she'd have a companion during her travels.

The little guy was sleeping so soundly he hadn't moved since she'd put him down. She'd have to wake him soon or he'd be up all night. Gian's favorite four rattles and a stuffed horse his great-grandmother had given him went in next, beside two pairs of soft-sided shoes.

In the many months since Francesca had left her home in Sacramento, she'd visited families in Sicily who'd lost loved ones in a train crash a couple of years before, those who were affected by Etna's boiling lava spewing forth, and the parents of children who were killed when an earthquake leveled their school. A freelance photojournalist with enough money to follow her artistic inclinations rather than take one of the many job offers she'd received from national magazines and Reuters and newspapers all around the state of California, she'd done the story of her career.

It was while she was visiting Milan, where she'd documented people whose loved ones had died in a plane that had crashed into the top floors of a thirty-story building two years earlier, that Antonio Gillespie, her former boyfriend, had arrived on business from Sacramento. His father-in-law was a retailer with upscale shops all over the states. Antonio, who was second in command, had come to finalize a deal with one of Milan's top designers. And to take a break from the wife he'd described as more of a child than a woman since the car accident that had left her brain-damaged and paralyzed.

Francesca hadn't been able to stay angry with him for having kept the woman a secret during the two years she'd known him, hadn't been able to hold on to feelings of betrayal, because she'd understood. Especially now, glancing over at her tiny son who gave himself as completely to his sleep as he did his play. Her heart was open wide and filled with forgiveness. Gian's father was an admirable man who could not heartlessly send the woman who'd once been his life partner to an institution, in spite of the instant and undeniably rich attachment he and Francesca had shared since she'd first interviewed him for a story she'd done on the debilitating impact of fashion in America. This was the man she'd tell Gian about when he grew up and asked questions about the father he didn't know.

Folding, stuffing, Francesca remembered that last scene in Sacramento. Another retailer had told her that Antonio was married, that the company she'd thought his own actually belonged to his father-in-law. He hadn't tried to deny it. To lie. And in the end, after she'd heard the heart-wrenchingly sad story of a fairy tale gone wrong, she hadn't been angry. Just devastated. And had left the States to get over him. He'd known that. But he'd been as lonely as she....

The sound of dishes rattling in the kitchen across the small villa brought Francesca back to the task at hand. Her grandmother Sancia was up from her siesta and would be expecting Francesca to join her for an afternoon snack. And she still had all her own clothes to pack into the other half of the second duffel.

Although she'd spent more than nine months in Italy before she'd contacted her father's mother, introducing herself to the grandmother she'd never known, Sancia was probably the real reason Francesca had come to this country. Looking back, she could recognize the quest that had driven her halfway around the world at a time when her mother had needed her at home.

Nothing in life had made sense anymore. Nothing, other than her career, had made her happy. She'd begun to question her basic beliefs, her decisions and motivations, even her ability to offer compassionate stories to the world.

So she'd come to Italy with some half-formed hope that she might find what she was missing among the people of her father's land. That the culture, the values, the heart and soul of Italy would give her what she could not seem to provide for herself. A solid sense of self. Of direction.

Almost a year later, contemplating her trip home, she wasn't sure they'd produced anything quite so significant. But these long months had given her Gian.

And he'd given life meaning.

Finished packing, she went to wake her son.

*Five weeks later.*

God, it was sweltering. Carrying a single duffel filled mostly with cameras she hadn't used in more than a month, Francesca climbed the steps of Lucky Seven, an extended-stay motel off the Strip, to the room she'd just rented. Las Vegas in July was hell.

She'd forgotten that.

Just as she'd forgotten anything of value in taking pictures. She hadn't picked up a camera since that last day in Italy, when she'd packed them in the bottom of a bag. Nor did she intend to.

She'd buried any meaning her life held in a little old cemetery a couple of miles from Sancia Witting's home.

The phone was ringing as she pushed her way through the door of her two-room suite.

"Hello?"

A cursory glance told her the room was clean.

"This is José at the front desk, Ms. Witting."

"Yes?" What was he bothering her for? She was tired. Hot. Lacking even an ounce of the capacity it would take to be civil to other human beings.

"I have that number you asked for. The one for the used-car dealer."

She wasn't planning to be in town for more than a week. But she had to get a car now that she was back in the States—she'd sold her Mustang before she'd left for Italy—and figured that, rather than paying for a rental, she'd buy one here. She'd drive Autumn back to Sacramento when they returned together.

"That was quick," she told José now, duffel still on her shoulder as she scribbled the number on the envelope he'd given her downstairs with her receipt.

"My friend's at work tonight. He'll be there all weekend, too."

"Great, thanks," she said, conjuring up enough energy to say a pleasant goodbye and get off the phone. Car-shopping on a Friday night in Vegas. Just what she wanted to do.

But then, she thought, dropping her duffel on the bed, there was nothing in the entire universe that Francesca Witting wanted to do. Except not think about that crib with the too-still infant. That Italian cemetery.

And she wanted to follow up on the phone call her mother had received that week from her younger sister. A runaway, Autumn had been missing for more than two years. Earlier this week, she'd been in Las Vegas. Francesca was going to find her.

And get Autumn's ass home where it belonged.

"Luke, have a seat."

He'd rather stand. But he sat in one of the lushly upholstered high-backed chairs across from his boss and mentor's oversize mahogany desk. The chairs were gold now. The year before they'd been maroon.

Luke preferred the maroon.

"How's your mother?" Amadeo asked.

Fingers steepled at his lips, Luke shrugged. Luke Everson didn't talk about his mother. Amadeo Esposito knew that.

And still, without fail, every time he saw Luke he asked.

Glancing beyond Luke's left shoulder, Amadeo gave a slight nod, dismissing the two "companions" who were never more than a few feet away. Their feet moved soundlessly on the plush maroon carpet that had recently replaced last year's golden brown. Maroon and gold were Esposito's colors. Always had been.

When the heavy wood door clicked shut behind them, Amadeo met Luke's gaze, his dark eyes narrowed. "You want to tell me what's going on at the Bonaparte?"

A lesser man might have been intimidated. Most men who came in contact with the owner and CEO of Biamonte Industries—a conglomerate that owned a tenth of Las Vegas—were intimidated. Italian-born Esposito, while having no Mafia affiliations or connections, was a very rich and sometimes ruthless man who knew how to use his money to get what he wanted.

Amadeo Esposito did many things Luke wouldn't have done—or would've done differently.

But Luke had known the man all his life. He'd seen Amadeo cry at his daughter's funeral fifteen years before. And then again at his wife's.

Amadeo had cried with Luke at Luke's father's funeral three years before.

"There've been too many big wins." Luke told Amadeo what he already knew.

The Bonaparte, one of the Strip's newest and most elite casino-hotels, was Luke's personal responsibility.

Esposito waited. He was not a patient man, something Luke had never respected about him.

Leaning forward, Luke rested his forearms across

his knees. "There's no apparent pattern," he reported. "The winners come from all over. All ages. An eighty-year-old woman from a retirement village in Phoenix, a twenty-two-year-old Wall Street wannabe and everything in between. They hail from no particular part of the country, come at no particular time, stay in no particular hotel, frequent no particular casinos, stay no particular length of time. For some, this is their first time in Vegas. Others are veterans. FaceIt found nothing." Luke named the high-tech surveillance technology that, in conjunction with an Internet security database system, was capable of identifying casino cheaters, card counters and those associated with them.

Esposito's face tightened.

"With the new digital-recording system, plus the incident-reporting and risk-management software, we've been able to call up every aspect of each case individually. We've tracked tape from each dealer down to every single time a drawer opens—and there's absolutely nothing."

"What about dealers?" Esposito demanded. "New technology only means that crooks find new ways to get around it. We're only as good as the people who work for us."

Luke shook his head. "Everyone checks out," he said. "I talked to Jackson, and he vouched for all of them, as well."

Arnold Jackson was not only the best dealer they had, he was the closest thing Luke Everson had to a personal friend. He was as much a part of the family as Luke himself—and one of the handful of people Esposito trusted.

His tanned face creased in a frown beneath dark silver hair, Amadeo leaned forward. "There is one pattern," he said, his voice lowered to the decibel of dangerous. "All the wins are at the Bonaparte."

The back of his neck aching, Luke shook his head. "It's beginning to look like there are at least two others." Luke named them both—well-known strip resorts—listing the dates and exact amounts of the wins in question. "And there's no pattern in the locations," he added. "One's new, one's been around for years. One is independently owned, one's part of a corporation.

"And none have any relationship, either past or current, with Biamonte Industries," he said, summing up what they already knew. He added, "I've been working with the security directors to run a check on all current and past employees to look for someone in common to all three—or even to two of us. Nothing significant has turned up."

"I don't believe in coincidence."

Sighing, Luke sat back, running a hand through his blond hair. "I've viewed and reviewed the tapes. Didn't even come up with a case of enlarged pores." Luke wondered how many of the gamblers they caught counting cards every year knew that something as innocuous as their skin could give them away.

Amadeo didn't reply for several moments. Moments that would've seemed endless had Luke not been fully aware of the older man's habit of focusing silently when he had something to ponder.

"There is one pattern here." Esposito's usually nonexistent Italian accent slipped into his speech.

Raised brows were Luke's only response.

"No two wins took place at the same time."

"Anything else would just be stupid," Luke said.

Nodding slowly, Amadeo said, "And it would also allow a person or persons to be at those tables, as a bystander, guiding the potential winners and waiting in the wings to collect a share of the take."

In Luke's opinion, Esposito had underestimated his ex-marine officer protégé.

Luke elaborated. "The operation would have to be large enough to hire a different player for every win. We have two thousand cameras out there, Amadeo, with a several-yard radius around every table. There isn't a single instance of anyone in the vicinity sharing even a slight resemblance with those in the vicinity of the other wins."

"So maybe we're dealing with a damn good makeup artist," the older man shot back, sitting up straight. "For God's sake, man, this is Las Vegas, home of illusion."

"And home of the people who can spot illusion with eyes half shut."

"You've had the films studied by someone who'd know?"

Luke replied with a slow nod. "Three."

"Carson Bova." Esposito named the city's best.

"Of course."

"Follow up on the payout." There was no mistaking his words as anything but an order. "I want to get inside the personal finances of every single winner. I want evidence of increase equal to the full win."

Technically it couldn't be done.

But Luke nodded. He already had someone on it.

"And run another check on every single one of our security staff."

Already done. But he didn't bother telling his boss that. Amadeo needed to be the one giving the orders. Luke stood, his polished black shoes sinking into the carpet.

"How's the baby thing going?" Esposito asked, his voice, his whole demeanor, softer and more compassionate as he asked the question.

It was this side of the man that Luke trusted. His godfather, whom he honored and cared about. He still couldn't stand Amadeo in his business life.

"I filled out the paperwork," he replied. Amadeo Esposito had given Luke this chance—hooked him up with an agency in town that specialized in finding children for families who didn't qualify for regular adoptions. Luke hadn't even known such a place existed.

Coming around his desk, Amadeo stood mere inches from Luke, his eyes warm and personal. "What's the next step?"

Luke glanced at his watch. He was on the clock. Had work to do. "A series of checks into everything from my medical history to grades in elementary school, by the sound of things," he muttered, stepping toward the door.

"Luke?"

He turned back.

"You'll have your son."

Anticipation filled Luke's chest, but only for a brief instant. Still, after he'd passed Amadeo's current thugs in the outer office, he couldn't help a satisfied nod.

If Amadeo said he'd get his son, he would.

## 2

She had her car—a "used though still in excellent condition" Grand Cherokee. A single woman on her own didn't need anything so big, but Francesca didn't know how much stuff Autumn had accumulated in the two years she'd been gone. A shopping cart full?

Her half sister had called her mother from a pay phone. For anonymity? Or because that phone on the street was her home phone?

Just before eight on Saturday morning, Francesca drove slowly down the Strip, only minimally distracted by the visual cacophony of fantasyland elite mixed with the gutteresque. The opulent signs and landscaping stood beside parking lots filled with potholes and garishly lighted marquees advertising souvenir mugs for ninety-nine cents, beer and three T-shirts for twelve dollars.

Already older couples strolled the sidewalks hand in hand, stepping aside periodically as the occasional man hurried from one casino to the next, exuding an air of desperation—and the desperate hope of someone who's broken free.

Did they ever eat, those occasional men? Francesca wondered. Or did they live on anticipation and the free cocktails offered so readily at the blackjack tables?

Traffic wasn't too bad, but she moved slowly, taking in as many loitering places as she could. Autumn had made that call just a few blocks from here.

Spring Mountain Road. Sands Avenue. The streets followed one after another, just as her map had indicated they would. It all had a "Twilight Zone" feel to Francesca, not only unfamiliar but completely outside the bounds of reality. Was this surrealistic place her sister's stamping ground?

The thought of her beautiful now-seventeen-year-old sister living somewhere on these streets was just too painful to hold on to. Francesca glanced once more at the written directions and highlighted map on the console at her right elbow. The police had said there was nothing they could do with the phone lead. There'd been nothing to trace. Francesca understood that runaways were a dime a dozen in their fine city. And the police had a hell of a lot more to do than Francesca did.

She could sit by that pay phone booth all day every day for the next year if that was what it took to get a lead on her sister's whereabouts. Sit there holding the camera she'd unpacked that morning and tossed in the back seat just so she'd look as though she had some purpose, something to do.

One more intersection and she had to turn right. And then take an immediate left. She'd been in the city a little more than twelve hours. Long enough to buy the car and get some much-needed sleep—via the help of potent prescription sleeping pills given to her by a sympathetic Italian doctor who'd been unable to ease her pain. He'd offered the escape of powerful drugs instead.

There were nights when Francesca cried out of sheer gratitude to him.

Her first impulse was to ignore the ringing of the cell phone plugged into the car's power outlet. But there was only one person who'd be calling. And as much as she didn't want to talk…

"Hi, Mom," she said, without looking at the caller ID on the phone's display.

"What did you find?"

She should've kept her number private.

"It's barely past dawn, Mom," she said, her eyes filling with tears for the sad woman who, living all alone, had aged ten years in the one Francesca had been away. After the death of her first husband, Francesca's father, Kay Stevens's life had gone inexorably downhill. The sudden heart-attack death eighteen months before of the bastard who'd been her second husband—Autumn's father—should've made things at least more bearable.

But it hadn't.

"You don't sleep a lot," Kay said softly, but with the barest hint of the steel she'd instilled in her older daughter sometime before her second husband had come on the scene and attempted to beat it out of both of them. "In the three weeks you were home, you never slept more than four hours a night. Something happened in Italy. I know it did. Why won't you tell me about it?"

A bus stop caught Francesca's eye—an uncom-

fortable-looking bench with a couple of panels over-
head, to block out rain, maybe. It certainly didn't
offer much shade.

No one was sleeping on it. Had Autumn ever?

"There's nothing to tell." The response drained
her, but not nearly as much as the truth would have.

As much as she craved her mother's nurturing
hand, she just didn't have the capacity to talk about
the year in Italy that had changed her life forever.
Not her brief time in Milan with Antonio. Not the
long, slow and frightening birth of her son. And most
especially not the moment she'd reached into his crib
that last afternoon at Sancia's, not the autopsy, nor
the grandmother she'd left behind.

Nor did she believe her mother any longer had the
wherewithal to offer a nurturing hand.

"I think you should at least try to call Antonio,"
her mother said again—a suggestion she'd made
many times in the month since Francesca's return.
"Let him know you're back in town."

"No," she said, as she had every single time. "I
went to Italy because I found out he'd been married
the entire two years I dated him. Why on earth would
I look him up on my return?" Other than these re-
minders from her mother, she didn't think about the
man who'd fathered her child. Not anymore. He'd
been buried right along with the rest of her heart.

"You said his wife was brain-damaged from that
accident...."

"Which doesn't make him any less obligated. Any
less married. And if we're going to continue to dis-
cuss this, I'm hanging up."

Kay's sigh was heavy. ''Will you call me as soon as you get to the phone booth? Let me know what you find?''

''Unless Autumn left a calling card or some graffiti on the side of the booth, a vacant piece of property owned by Sprint isn't going to tell us much.''

''I just thought there might be some homeless person around who'd know—'' Kay broke off. Into the silence that followed, she muttered, ''I know, I'm being presumptuous.'' For a brief moment she sounded again like the confident and capable college professor Francesca had known during the first ten years of her life. ''This initial phase is your job. Mine comes when we get her home.''

She'd find her sister. Francesca couldn't think any further than that. If life required more than one step at a time, she'd be paralyzed.

Inching past a red sign with white blinking lights—at eight o'clock on a Saturday morning— proclaiming Welcome to the Candlelight Wedding Chapel, and then, next to it, a big hot-dog placard, Francesca had to wonder if it was an all-in-one deal—nuptials and a wedding supper without leaving the parking lot.

''I'll hang up now,'' her mother said after another pause. ''Call me as soon as you know anything.''

''I will, Mom.'' *I told you I would.*

''Anything,'' Kay repeated. ''Anything at all. I think—''

Francesca's thumb flipped to the off button just before she dropped the phone back to the console. If asked, she could always say they got disconnected.

Circus Circus was offering free chips and salsa with the purchase of a drink. Francesca made her turn, paying more attention as she got closer to her destination. The phone booth, only a few blocks from the Lucky Seven, could have been reached through backstreets if Francesca had known how to navigate them. With all the construction going on around and behind the Strip—another new casino, road repair, a golf course apparently being shoved in somehow— she hadn't bothered to try.

Another block, and there was the phone. Right in front of a billboard advertising the Striptease Gentlemen's Club.

And across the street, a McDonald's—an old-fashioned rendition of the famous hamburger joint with the ground-to-ground golden arches that were hardly seen anymore. A return to yesteryear? A sign that things were going to be okay again?

Shaking her head, she turned off the engine and settled in, staring at the corner across the street. She knew there was no going back. Ever. Not for her.

And not for Autumn. Her sister had been gone for two years. No matter where she'd been, what she'd been doing, there were bound to be irrevocable changes.

Francesca understood that.

She wasn't sure her mother did.

Fifty-five-year-old Sheila Miller, blackjack dealer extraordinaire, sat at the kitchen table in her little breakfast nook Sunday morning, phone in hand. She'd dialed three times.

And just as often, pushed the disconnect button.

She had to call. If anyone would know who was behind the recent series of big wins at the tables, Arnold Jackson would.

Stomach growling, Sheila gave a cursory glance at the mass of notes and bills strewn across her table where breakfast would've been if she weren't so desperate to lose weight. No matter how she looked at it, she was in deep shit.

With sweaty fingers, Sheila slowly pushed in the numbers she knew by heart.

Her friend and co-worker, Angie Madden, had asked all up and down the Strip for information on the wins. It had to be an inside scam, but no one was talking. That would make sense if Sheila'd been the one asking. She was the straitlaced fuddy-duddy among them. But not Angie. She'd been the queen of scam for years—someone another scammer would trust—or want to brag to.

The home Angie owned didn't come from her ten-year-old divorce the way most people thought. It had been purchased, instead, with money she'd slowly siphoned off her table—and from the cut she took helping others do the same. She'd developed a solid reputation among the old-timers. Most of them had either used her help or were friends with someone who had. They didn't take a lot. And only when they were really in a bind. The well would dry up if they got too greedy.

Most times the take wasn't much at all by casino-loss standards—an electric bill here, an engagement ring there. More often than anything else, it covered the huge medical deductible on their health plan.

The silver-haired Angie Madden had helped more dealers on the Strip than Sheila could count, and not a single one of them was talking.

Just Sheila's luck. The first time in thirty years she wanted to know about the seedier side of a blackjack dealer's life, and she was coming up empty.

Arnold answered on the fourth ring, his voice more gravelly than usual.

She paused long enough to swallow. "I'm sorry, did I wake you?"

"Who is this?"

Feeling the heat come up her face, Sheila stared at the floor. Though Arnold had only been around a few years, he'd quickly become known as the most sought-after bachelor among the dealers. He was smart. Good-looking. And completely true-blue honest.

Which was what made Sheila crazy for him in a way she hadn't been crazy for a man since the end of her disastrous first marriage thirty years before.

She might be attracted to Arnold, but she wasn't ready to deal with that. She still had ten pounds to lose.

"Oh, sorry." She tried for a chuckle and ended up with a cough that probably made her sound as embarrassed as she was. "It's Sheila Miller. We served together on the dealers' continuing education committee last year."

It had been shortly after the holidays. She'd been good and fat then.

"Sheila. Yes, I remember. You were the one who came up with the final justification that clinched our funding."

He had a good memory. That probably meant he remembered the fat, too.

"I was just calling to find out what you know about this series of big wins. My friends and I are getting concerned. Until we know who's behind them we're all suspect. I figured you'd make it your business to find out, especially since most of them are happening at the Bonaparte."

"All I know is that they're happening," the man said. She heard some rustling, wondered if he was getting out of bed. If he slept in the nude. Or if he'd just snuggled deeper beneath the covers.

Alone?

"I've been at this job for thirty years," Sheila told him, folding back the corner of her most recent financial analysis—the one that had kept her up most of the night. If she didn't figure out who was behind this scam—and get in on it—she was going to lose everything. "And not once in all that time was a series of wins this big *ever* a coincidence."

So it had been stupid to use her entire life savings to buy some land outside the city and contract to build a little house on it. She'd thought she could afford it. And after thirty years of sucking up rich jerks' smoke and developing varicose veins standing at a blackjack table, she deserved something more for herself.

"I'm not happy about the situation," Arnold said.

"As you said, whether it's an inside job or not, it makes us all look bad."

And every single night when she came home there were more messages from her builder letting her know about additional expenses. Permit fees and truss calcs and engineering expenses. She'd borrowed—twice—against the condo she'd bought twenty years before, hit up every friend and almost-friend she knew.

"At the Bonaparte they're running extra security checks on all of us," Arnold continued.

Shit. Just what she needed. If the Bonaparte was running checks, so would all the casinos. Her debt was going to turn up and she'd be a prime suspect. Double shit. How could she get in on the scam, assuming she found the source, if she was a prime suspect at the same time?

Sweat trickled between her breasts, gathering uncomfortably at the under-wire of her D-cup bra beneath the white blouse she wore to work.

For years she'd watched the others run scams with absolutely no accountability. *But the moment I even think about it, they're suddenly running extra security checks.*

Her rotten luck.

Which was why she was a fifty-five-year-old, slightly plump single dealer in Las Vegas with the reputation of being straitlaced and definitely not up for a game.

"You want to have dinner tomorrow night?" What the hell. She was in debt. She was fat. If the wins were an inside job, Jackson would eventually find out. And for the first time in thirty years, she had the hots for a guy.

"I'm working tomorrow night."

Yeah, well, it was as good excuse as any. At least the man was nice enough to preserve her pride.

Hanging up the phone, Sheila went over to the counter to cut up some fruit.

Sunday night, when the darkness had grown to the point that the strangers she approached on the street corner could no longer see the picture she had to show them, Francesca gave up for another day. Gave up, but couldn't go back to the Lucky Seven as she had the previous two nights. The black spots on the walls were beginning to take on the image of climbing bugs. She had to keep getting up to make sure they hadn't really moved, that she didn't have to kill them. And she was wearing socks at all times in case the stains on the carpet were from something gross.

Socks in 105° F temperature.

How she ended up at the Bonaparte, Las Vegas's newest casino, and touted as the most opulent, Francesca didn't know. It was a fantasyland. And she needed to escape.

She'd been in the casino almost an hour, no longer aware of all the loud and unfamiliar sounds consuming her brain. She'd found a nickel video slot she was slowly beginning to figure out as she continued to spend two dollars and twenty-five cents with each push of the button. She still wasn't sure how she kept racking up credits, but she knew now that when the genie said "yes!" three times in a row, that was a good thing.

Bells rang around her. A recorded voice periodically called out "Wheel of Fortune!" not too far away. She was pretty sure she kept hearing Alex Trebek call out his famous "Let's play Jeopardy." Another slot machine based on a TV show?

"Cocktails?" asked a waitress whose breasts were falling out of the purple piece of fabric that was supposed to be a top. It was the fourth time she'd been around.

Instead of politely declining as she had previously, Francesca requested a bottle of water and was relieved when the scantily clad woman responded cheerfully as though the request was quite normal.

Wondering how much the water would cost in a place that had marble casements for its slot machines, Francesca pushed the button again and jumped back, heart pounding, as a siren went off and a light on top of the machine started to flash.

Great. Her first time gambling, first time in a casino, and she'd screwed up the machine.

Could you go to jail for that?

*Of course not,* she immediately answered herself, fighting back her automatic sense of gloom and doom. But you didn't have to be in Las Vegas for more than a couple of hours to know that the city took its security seriously.

In the two seconds it took her to consider slipping away, a distinguished-looking man, wearing a three-piece navy suit with a navy-and-white-striped tie that had to be real silk, was by her side, blocking her escape.

"Congratulations!" he said, sticking a card into the machine after which the alarming noise immediately ceased. "Eighteen thousand coins. Not a bad win!"

*Eighteen thousand coins? How much was that in nickel land?*

"Someone will be here shortly to take care of this for you."

His voice was pleasant, reassuring, though his smile was as empty as her heart.

"Take care of it?" she asked, wishing now that she'd stopped back at the motel to change out of the tight skirt and skimpy top and knee-high black leather boots she'd worn that day as an attempt to blend into her corner.

"Any win above a thousand coins is paid by an attendant," he explained.

Francesca was still trying to figure out how much money eighteen thousand nickels really was.

She kept coming up with nine hundred dollars. But that couldn't be right. She'd only been playing nickels.

"I'm Luke Everson," the man said, his smile a bit more genuine. "I'm the head of security here. If you have any problems, don't hesitate to let us know."

"Problems?" Had she just won nine hundred dollars?

"You looked scared to death when that machine went off."

"It was a siren." And the genie hadn't even said "yes" once.

"I take it you haven't done this much before."

*He's not much older than I am.* He'd seemed so much older at first. "Uh, no, this is a first."

"Is it your first time at the Bonaparte, as well?" The conversation was routine, uninvolved, as though she were one of a million of the same cloned human being.

She nodded.

"Well then, I'm glad we've given you such a warm welcome. I hope you'll be back to visit us often."

There was nothing personal about the invitation. Nothing personal about his manner. Despite his blond good looks, the man somehow managed to exude absolutely nothing. Did he have that much control, or was he just as empty inside as she was?

Either way, his reticence put her more at ease than she'd been in a month.

"Thanks," she said. Relaxing against the high back of her stool, she glanced up at him. "Did I just win nine hundred dollars?"

"Yes," he said, grinning down at her in a way that left her confused. He was empty. So was she. This wasn't supposed to have happened. "And I have to tell you," he added, "you've got to be the least excited winner I've ever seen. Doesn't make for great PR, you know?"

She might have apologized if people hadn't descended on them. The waitress with her water—turned out it was free—and the attendant with her money. Before she noticed, Luke Everson, head of security, was gone.

And she'd won nine hundred dollars. As she headed out into the brightly lit night with her money she wondered if the stack of bills in her shoulder bag meant her luck was changing. Did this mean she'd find Autumn tomorrow?

Or had she just wasted what little luck was coming her way?

If so, she wanted to give the money back.

All those steps to climb. Autumn Stevens started up the six flights of concrete steps Sunday night, viewing the task as good exercise. She had to. If she allowed even one second of negative thought, she'd never make it up them at all.

And she had to get up there. Her bathroom was in the apartment on the sixth floor and she had to puke. Praying she'd make it in time, dying at the thought of having to clean up her own barf again, especially through six flights of open stairs, she tried to calm her stomach as she lifted one foot and then the other.

As always, calming thoughts rested on her big sister. Francesca was her knight in shining armor, never mind that she wasn't a man. She was strong. Resilient. She could do anything. Or at least, that was how Autumn had viewed her when she was younger.

Hadn't Francesca proved her knighthood by getting away from the bastard who'd fathered Autumn—and then proceeded to beat the crap out of all three of the women in his care?

Bile rose to her throat and Autumn quickly

switched focus. Last she'd heard, Francesca was in Italy. Antonio had told her. Back when she'd thought him dear and sweet. When she'd felt certain there'd never been a kinder man. Or one more in love.

With the same woman Autumn adored above all others. Her big sister.

God, she missed Cesca. It had been the worst part of leaving the hellhole she'd grown up in—missing her sister's occasional visits.

If she wasn't such a chickenshit she'd ask Antonio if he knew of a way to contact her, if she was allowed to do so. Life looked pretty damned hopeless at the moment, but Cesca would know what to do.

Autumn reached the fifth flight. Had to stop for a second to swallow. Rub her stomach. Calm herself. As soon as she got upstairs, she'd be alone, in her own space, with no need to keep up appearances or tell half truths. No need to lie.

She started up the last flight with the contents of her stomach still in place. There was no point in calling Cesca; Autumn wouldn't tell her anything.

She couldn't.

Not if she wanted to live.

And so far, in spite of everything, that was the choice she'd made.

And continued to make…

# 3

The imprint of four-by-eight-inch bricks against her back was a more familiar sensation than the mattress on her bed at the Lucky Seven. In the past seventy-two hours, Francesca had spent most of her time leaning against that brick wall behind what had to be the least used phone booth in all of Las Vegas. The second day on this corner she'd stood with one foot crossed over the other, dressed in a short, tight denim skirt with four-inch black heels and a skimpy spaghetti-strapped black tank top. The next, she'd planted her shoulder blades against that wall, her rump on the ground and her head lolling back, dressed in rags she'd scavenged in trash Dumpsters. She'd washed them until they were almost too threadbare to wear and then dirtied them up again.

And on Tuesday evening she was there again, leaning one shoulder, her butt and the sole of one thick-soled black boot against the now-familiar wall. This time she was in jeans shorts, a T-shirt that left her belly bare and some black leather wristbands. Looking, she hoped, the way Autumn might have looked when she'd been there.

In the sweltering one-hundred-plus summer temperatures, her feet were sweating profusely in the an-kle-length boots.

But she'd garnered nothing in her disguise as a prostitute—except a couple of offers that had insulted her with their low amounts. As a homeless woman, she'd been spit at once and had a couple of dollars thrown her way.

Both characters had attracted more attention than the photographer she'd pretended to be the first few hours she'd staked out the corner her little sister had visited less than two weeks before. Of course, if she'd bothered to take the lens cap off her camera, she might've drawn some interest. As a general rule people liked to have their picture taken.

As a nonnegotiable rule, Francesca was through with taking pictures.

A couple of businessmen, dressed all in black from their shiny wing-tip shoes to the suit jackets on their backs, passed by, their sunglasses a bit suspect in the gray evening dusk. But then, this was Las Vegas. It hadn't taken her a day to figure out that it took one hell of a lot of street smarts to live in this town.

For once, Francesca let the passersby go without question or comment. They couldn't have any knowledge of her little sister. They just couldn't.

*Derek, call me. Bobbee loves Tom. For a good time call*… She stared at the graffiti scribbled in pen, black marker, even pencil on the metal sides of the phone booth. There was much more scribbled inside, bits and pieces of which she randomly recited during her sleep—and to her mother when she called, just so she'd have something to say. After the third day, she'd managed to convince Kay that those calls were doing neither of them any good and she'd phone her as soon as she had news to report. Francesca hoped she wouldn't hear from her again for at least a few days.

Cars sped around the corner. Others slowed, stopped as the light changed, and still she stood there, leaning nonchalantly, as though she had nowhere to be, nor a care in the world.

She could play this role relatively well. The first part of it was completely true.

A small group of teenagers walked by, young men decked out in black leather and boots, with spiked hair of varying colors and body rings. A couple of them eyed her up, down and back up again. Her stomach tensed but this was what she'd hoped for. Attention from the young crowd.

"Hey, you guys from around here?"

They stopped. Glanced at her with hooded eyes. "Yeah, maybe."

"You ever seen this girl?" She passed over a two-year-old photo of her sister. It had been taken right before Autumn left home. Francesca had been shocked when she'd first seen it. The pink hair, the piercing at the corner of her sister's lip, the leather choker were all completely foreign to her.

"Nah, but I wouldn't mind meeting her," the tallest guy said.

"Yeah," echoed the shorter fat one. "You know where she hangs?"

They were nothing but a bunch of tough-acting little kids. Francesca turned away without another word.

Talking in short spurts, the group passed. Five minutes later, a homeless woman shuffled by.

She shook her head silently when Francesca showed her the picture. Francesca gave the woman a five dollar bill. Her reward was another sad shake of the head.

And then a couple of men walked by, their hands full of the cards picturing naked women, phone numbers scrolled across them, that were passed out on the Strip every night of the week in this bizarre and twisted town.

It was one of those times she was thankful not to have Autumn recognized.

''Wonder how much they're paid,'' she muttered as they headed toward the Strip. The colorful glittering lights that made that part of town look like day even in the dead of night were beginning to pop on.

A minute later the streetlight changed. A mother hurried across the street with two little children hanging on to the frayed edge of her shorts, a bag of groceries under one arm. The youngest child, a boy, was crying. Judging by the dual streams of grime running down his face, he'd been at it a while. Francesca watched them turn into the rock-strewn drive of the rent-by-the-month apartment building next to where she was standing. The little girl turned back to look at her. Francesca feigned sudden attention to the massage parlor across the street. It was either that or the pawn shop on the opposite corner, and she'd already read their colorful though roughly painted windows more times than she could count.

Or she could cry.

And then, from out of nowhere, a young girl was inside the phone booth. Francesca had no idea where she'd come from. She'd had her head turned for less than a moment.

The girl was maybe seventeen, but probably younger. She dialed a number she appeared to know by heart. She was little, blond, though she had on an oversize T-shirt and shorts that were longer than most girls her age in this town were wearing. Francesca couldn't see her shoes inside the phone booth. Nor could she see her face.

Every nerve in her body stiffened as she waited for the girl to finish. She moved forward slowly, as though waiting to make a call, taking deep breaths to calm the tension in her chest. She was a journalist, albeit usually one who hid behind a lens. Still, on more than one occasion, she'd collected some pretty hard-to-come-by information to complete a story.

Francesca was right there at the door of the phone booth just as the girl emerged.

"I'm sorry, were you waiting to make a call?" the girl asked. Her smile was sweet. The look in her eyes made her seem older than Francesca's mother. And she was at least six months pregnant.

With no ring on her finger.

Choking back the animal wail that rose to her throat as she stared at the girl's belly, Francesca detached herself. She was a professional—and nothing but. It was a trick that had become habit years ago.

For the first time since…well, for the first time in many weeks, Francesca almost wished she had a camera. This girl was a story that needed to be told.

Just a story. Not a person.

"Uh, yeah," she said, watching the girl. "I, uh, need to call a cab."

The girl, standing just outside the booth, smiled again. Her petite features would have been beautiful if life hadn't tampered with them far too early. Her unlined skin was rough where it should've revealed the freshness of youth. And those eyes…

Would her little sister have eyes like that? Could Francesca bear to find out? Could she look in Autumn's eyes and not lose what little hold she had on any desire to live?

She could only look at the girl's eyes. Not her belly.

"Well, if that's all you need, save yourself the fifty cents and just walk a block up there," the girl was saying, pointing toward the Strip. "There're always a ton of them milling around."

"Thanks." Francesca wondered what someone her sister's age would say. It had been less than fifteen years since she was a teenager, but it seemed like fifty. She'd felt more confident as a prostitute. "You need a ride?" she asked. "We could share."

"Nah," the girl said. "My ride's coming."

On a street corner? Was that the call the girl had made?

"I had an appointment up the street. They're picking me up there."

And she hadn't been able to use the phone at her

appointment? The reporter in Francesca asked questions while the big sister prayed this child could help her. She'd talked to more than a hundred people in three days.

But before she could haul out her picture, an unmistakable look of fear appeared on the younger girl's face. "I gotta go," she called as she turned, and ran across the street—against the light. She'd been watching a navy sedan stopped at the corner of the Strip, waiting to turn toward them.

If she hadn't had only one mission left in life—to find Autumn—Francesca would have followed her. Followed the blue sedan to see if the girl climbed inside. And to see who was driving.

Could've been her mother, of course. And maybe the girl had sneaked away to call her boyfriend.

But somehow Francesca didn't think so.

This girl had seen too much of life to be afraid of a little parental displeasure. And the fear on her face had been more than concern about being grounded.

Sliding down the familiar brick wall, welcoming the heat against her back and ignoring the light scrape of brick against skin, Francesca wondered, not for the first time, if she had the stomach for what might lie ahead.

Or, more accurately, if she had the heart.

Because she'd figured something out during these days on the streets. If Autumn was more than a passerby, if she'd been living in this town, finding her means of survival here, she wasn't going to be anything like the young girl Francesca remembered.

And chances were, she'd done things, seen things,

her older sister had never, in all her travels, done or seen.

Deciding to give the dinner she'd packed in her satchel to the next homeless person who passed, Francesca leaned her head against the wall and closed her eyes. She'd covered some pretty brutal things during her career. Natural disasters. Murders. Fires. Crime scenes.

Those she could handle.

The death of innocence she could not.

"You have today off, don't you, Luke?"

Finishing the toaster waffle and coffee he'd fixed himself before dawn Thursday morning, Luke didn't even lift his glance from the morning paper as he nodded. But the muscles in the back of his neck, and everywhere else he could possibly feel tension, stiffened. He'd hoped to be gone before she got up.

With things growing more tense at work every day that an explanation for the big wins eluded him, and no news on the baby front, he'd made plans for a little stress relief.

"What are you going to do?"

*Be free. Out. Away from you.*

"Jump." He spoke almost belligerently, hating himself for doing it even while he deliberately chose the word.

She sank into the chair next to him, her short gray hair askew, her lined face bare and ancient. "Please, son," she said, watery blue eyes filling with tears. "Please don't." She took a deep breath, looking down at the table, one shaky hand clutching the other. "Not ever again," she said, her voice stronger as her gaze turned on him. "I can't stand it," she said. "I can't sit here knowing that you're up there, jumping out of planes, falling to your death. I just can't stand it."

He'd known his announcement would upset her. He hadn't expected the shrill voice, the panic in her eyes. He'd been skydiving for years. Had honors packed away in a box from his years as a marine, when he'd been one of the best jumpers they'd had.

It was the one thing he did on a regular basis, just for himself.

"Mom," he said, his voice softening even as his chest constricted. "You know I'm not going to fall to my death." He'd expected a fight today—about her wanting him to spend his day off at home, with her. He'd assumed that if she'd caught him before he left, their argument would've been about his leaving the house. Not this.

"Luke, no!" Her translucent, bony hand clutched his forearm. "You have to promise me! You'll never go up there again. You can't! If you jump, you'll die. I just know it!" She was sobbing, screaming. He didn't have to look at her to know the lost, glazed look that would've come to Carol Everson's eyes.

"Mom," he said, trying to emulate the calm but firm tone his father had always used. Trying, and— as always—failing. "I've been jumping since I was sixteen. You've watched many times—as recently as last month. Dad explained it all to you, remember?" Turning from the table he leaned forward, holding both of her cold hands between his own warm fingers. "You're okay with this," he reminded her.

Jumping was the only thing that had kept him sane during his years as a teenager in this house. He'd joined a club at school and, with the help of his father, had managed to hide it from his mom until he knew for sure he was going to like it. Then they'd had to convince her he was perfectly safe doing this.

"No, Luke!" Her eyes glistened wildly, her entire body starting to shake in the long flannel nightgown she was wearing in spite of the fact that it was summer and she lived in the desert. "I can't allow it! Please, Luke! I saw a documentary on deaths from skydiving on television last week. Please tell me you won't go! Not ever again!"

Tears streamed down her face as Luke looked helplessly on.

"The documentary was about the teams that perform aerial tricks. I don't do any trick jumping," he said slowly, softly. "I always wear a backup chute. I don't take any unnecessary chances. I don't even free-fall very far anymore." He mentally crossed his fingers on that last one. Free-falling was the best part of the jump and he held the state record.

"No!" She choked. Luke handed her the half-drunk glass of water he'd poured for himself. She didn't even see it. "Drink," he said, raising it to her lips.

The glass lay against her lower lip, but he didn't tip it. Her mouth hung open, unresponsive, and he knew what would happen if he attempted to force the liquid into her. It would dribble down her chin to her chest while she remained completely unaware.

"Oh, God," she moaned. "Oh, God." She was rocking back and forth, shaking her head.

Setting the glass on the table, Luke stood, frowning as he stared down at her. She wasn't going to take skydiving from him, too. Anxiety disorders or not, she just wasn't.

"Mom." He tried again, squatting down, meeting her at eye level. He lifted a hand to her face, drying the tears, cupping her cheek. "It's okay. Shh, it's okay."

"It's not okay, Luke," she said, her voice trembling with emotions he would never, in a million lifetimes, understand. "It's not okay. You have no idea what you're talking about."

With a heavy sigh he dropped his hand. Straightened. "I'm here, aren't I?" Shame warmed his skin as he heard the resentment he spent his life trying not to feel. Or at least to hide.

"It's not okay!" she screamed, rocking, crying, this small pitiful creature who'd borne him.

"I'll stay home today." He heard the words, uttered a thousand times before, as if from a distance. Mostly he felt the familiar and deadening weight of obligation and debilitating resentment. Only thoughts of the life that was coming, the son he'd soon have, kept him calm.

"No!" she screamed again. "Tell me, Luke! Promise me!" Head raised, exposing a neck that was so thin, so frail-looking, he could hardly believe it. "You won't ever jump again!"

Staring at her, Luke couldn't make the words come. It had been this way for as long as he could remember. It had started with birthday parties. If his father was home he'd been able to go, but as an executive with Biamonte Industries—a position he'd needed to hold to pay his wife's medical expenses and to keep her world contained enough to allow her to live outside a professional facility—Marshall Everson had had to put in ungodly hours, which also included a fair amount of travel. In later years there'd been dates, games, even a senior trip that Luke had to give up. He'd never been able to sustain membership on a team, be on student council, run for class president, join a club. He'd skydived. It was something he could do privately. On his own time or, rather, the time his father arranged for him.

"Mom…"

It was going to be different with his son. He was going to hire a nanny, ten nannies if he had to, to ensure that his son had all the opportunities he had not.

"Say it, Luke!" Falling forward with the force of the sob that followed, she lay there, chest to her knees, moaning. "Oh, God. I'm going to be…"

Luke grabbed the kitchen trash, put it in front of her and turned his back. When she was finished he handed her a wet cloth, wordlessly waiting while she wiped her face.

She'd be calmer now, at least for a while. She'd be able to swallow her medication and give it time to work.

But this wasn't the end of it. He knew that.

Just as he knew the woman was slowly sucking the life out of him.

He needed his son, a boy to teach all the things he loved, to play ball with, explore with, watch horror movies with. A boy to bring vibrancy and enthusiasm and messy science experiments into his home.

A son to carry on the Everson name.

A child to give hope and purpose to his future.

A reason to live.

On Thursday evening, just before dusk, Francesca was sitting on her corner, dressed like a teenage homeless person, holding a battered McDonald's cup out to passersby with a hand that was gloved—even in the July heat—although her glove was fingerless. She'd been observing others for five days and, if nothing else, had a pretty clear idea how to portray any number of characters. For some reason, a lot of the homeless folks covered their hands in some fashion.

Perhaps for trash-digging?

It was a story she'd have wanted to do were she living in another lifetime. With another heart.

She wasn't showing around the picture as much, though it was always close at hand, securely tucked into the waistband of her torn-and-dirty pair of too-tight jeans. A lot of the same people were coming by. And were starting to notice her.

So she was now permanently homeless—at least in the role she played. It was the only reason she could think of that would allow her to hang out continuously at the same corner. Homeless people seemed to pick a place and stake it out as their own personal property. Probably some kind of homing instinct.

A cop stopped at the corner. She and her mother were in contact with the Las Vegas police and she knew her presence could be explained in a sixty-second phone call if necessary. Still, she'd noticed that a lot of homeless people tended to avoid the eye of anyone in authority. Francesca studied the once-white tennis shoes on her feet.

Did they avoid those glances out of shame? Or fear of punishment? She shrugged the thought away. Everyone had problems. Heartaches. Hard lives. Some were just more obvious than others.

The job she'd done on those shoes wasn't half bad. She'd had to rub them against the cement in the parking lot outside the Lucky Seven for more than an hour to get that ragged hole in the toe. She'd thrown away the laces and then she'd tossed the shoes around in a big bag with dinner leftovers, shaken them off and left them outside to dry.

For all that, they were the most comfortable pair of shoes she'd had on all week.

The door of the phone booth creaked. Forcing herself to stay in character, to appear disinterested, Francesca slowly turned her gaze toward it. She felt as if she now knew that small booth more intimately than she knew her own body. After five days, she really didn't expect much. She just didn't have anything else to do. Anywhere else to go, to look.

She had nowhere to be. Not that week. Not for the rest of her life. Until she ran out of money and needed to eat. But with the savings she'd amassed, that wouldn't be for a long time. And it wasn't something she particularly cared about one way or the other, anyway.

A woman stood in the booth, her back to Francesca, dialing quickly.

Francesca had no idea how she was going to earn money when she needed it again. She had no desire to pick up a camera. No inner voice guiding her to the perfect picture. Though she had a few of her cameras in her bag at the Lucky Seven, she hadn't touched them since that first day in town.

She watched the short brunette, of indeterminate age, as she talked. And then the woman turned.

She couldn't be more than twenty. If that.

And she was pregnant.

That made the seventh pregnant woman this week. Seven times she'd lost her breath as the sight slammed into her. With practice it was supposed to get easier.

It didn't.

And this one was so young, barely a child herself. How could she possibly cope? Birth was hard.

And mothering so much harder. What would she do if she went to her baby's crib one afternoon, reached for him, expecting to pull that tiny warm body into her arms and found it limp and—

No. Forget it. Just forget.

Professional detachment was slow in descending, but as it came Francesca was reminded of the pregnant girl she'd seen in that same phone booth a couple of days before. The girl who'd inadvertently turned up in Francesca's dream last night.

In the old days that had meant a story for sure.

Today, Francesca was only irritated by the distraction from what mattered. There was no anticipation, no "aha" moment, no real vision of what would be. Just a nagging idea that if she'd had anything left in her, she could have done something. Taken photographs. Told a story...

Still, as the girl finished her conversation, Francesca approached her, holding Autumn's picture. Her gaze remained at eye level.

"Excuse me," she said, "I'm looking for my friend. She told me to look her up when I got to town but she moved. The last address I had for her was in those apartments." She nodded toward the rent-by-the-month place next door. "You wouldn't happen to have seen her, would you?"

It was one of the lies she'd perfected over the week.

The brunette glanced at the picture. And away.

Another dead end. Francesca wasn't surprised. She knew she'd have to turn over a lot of nonessential pieces before she found the right one.

And then she realized the girl hadn't said no. She was looking at the picture again.

"Do you know her?"

Shaking her head, the girl studied Francesca—obviously taking in her tattered clothes, dirty hair, lack of makeup. Even the shoes she'd so carefully aged.

"You hungry?" she asked instead.

No. Not for a long time. "A little."

"I'll bet it's been a while since you had a good meal."

She shrugged, leaving her shoulders hunched defensively as she'd seen a twenty-something homeless guy do the other day on her way home. He seemed to pretty much hang out in an alleyway between the Lucky Seven and a tattoo parlor.

The girl dropped a buck in the tattered McDonald's cup. "There's a discount food mart the next block over. You can get a lot there."

"Thanks."

Apparently the gaunt cheeks she'd seen in the bathroom mirror at the Lucky Seven that morning added credibility to the part she was playing. Good to know her lack of desire for any kind of food had paid off somewhere.

"Where you staying?" the young woman asked.

"Around."

The girl looked at the photo again. She was withholding information. Francesca's deadened instincts surged for the briefest of seconds.

"You sure you haven't seen her?" she asked, scuffing her feet. "I could really use a turn of luck."

"Maybe I have," the girl said. "I'm not sure."

Maybe. Those dormant instincts became a little more sharply honed. "Do you have any idea where that might've been? Or when?"

The girl, staring at the photo one more time, shook her head. "I don't know. I'm probably wrong." She laughed a little nervously. "I'm always thinking I've met people before when I haven't."

*No way, babe. You aren't getting me this close and then backing up on me.* "If there's a chance you've seen her, ever, can you think where it might've been?''

With a hand hovering protectively over her extended belly the girl peered down the street, back at the photo and then once again glanced at Francesca's attire.

Francesca couldn't take her eyes off that hand. Or breathe.

''You from Sacramento?'' the girl asked.

*Oh, my God.* Eyes raised, Francesca gasped. Coughed. *She knows her.*

Pain gave way to an excitement that challenged her dormant emotions. Francesca nodded slowly.

The girl nodded, too. Looked back down the street. And then said, ''If I've seen her, it was probably at Guido's.''

*Guido's.*

Trembling, Francesca scuffed her feet again. ''Where's that?''

The girl gestured toward Las Vegas Boulevard. ''Not far,'' she said, backing away. ''It's just on the other side of the Strip.'' She named a street Francesca had never heard of. ''You can walk from here, easy.'' She was at the corner by then, and as the light changed, she turned and hurried across the street, heading in the same direction the girl of Francesca's dream had taken earlier in the week.

Guido's. An Italian name.

# 4

It took her fifteen minutes to find Guido's. But only because she had to walk back to the Lucky Seven and get her car. And then it was another twenty before she actually approached the door. After having seen the place, she'd gone to the motel to change before going in. The crowd seemed too ''young adult.''

In her short but not too short denim skirt and tight green T-shirt, she figured she'd blend in just fine. So long as no one looked too closely at the newly acquired lines of strain adorning the corners of her mouth and eyes.

As far as she could tell, if you ignored the thrift store across the street that had so much stacked inside you could hardly see through the window, Guido's was an almost-nice neighborhood hangout, with a pizza and sandwich sign above the door, in addition to the requisite Vegas marquee with glittering lights—this one proclaiming that the city's best pool and dart games could be found inside. Sitting in the parking lot, she'd actually been relieved. It didn't seem like a place where her sister would've gone to turn tricks. Or model for any of those millions of cards that people used for sidewalk decor each night.

It felt good to think that Autumn had frequented a place as normal-looking as this.

With a deep breath for luck, or strength, or just enough air to endure, she pulled open the darkened glass door. For all she knew, Autumn was in there right now, sharing a pizza with a friend, throwing darts—although her sister had never been the sporty type—waiting tables, even. Anything. Just there.

Francesca panicked. What if she didn't recognize her? Kids changed a lot from fifteen to seventeen. And the police had warned her that runaways, because most didn't want to be found, often drastically changed their appearances.

She jumped as pool balls clacked to her left, followed by the sound of at least two dropping into pockets. Voices were little more than white noise, all blending together until she couldn't make out a single conversation. A strange mixture of New Age and rock music played in the background, but not as loudly as she would've figured for a young adult hangout.

As her eyes adjusted slowly from the bright Vegas sun to the track-lighted room with its dark paneling and wood floors, Francesca couldn't breathe. She wasn't ready for this. Wasn't ready to *feel* again.

Not yet.

Maybe never.

Thoughts of crawling into bed, hiding under the covers and being thankful that her baby sister was alive while she slept away the next ten years consumed her. Ten years from now Autumn would be an adult. With a real life. In control of that life. She'd come back then.

Except if the cops were to be believed, her sister could be involved with all kinds of dangerous people, just to survive. If she wasn't rescued she could well be dead before ten years were up. Las Vegas runaways had a relatively short life span.

"You coming or going?" The voice was male. Appreciative. And right in front of her.

"Sorry." Francesca tried to smile at him. "I don't know," she answered. He looked Italian. Somehow that made a difference. "I, uh, I'm hoping to meet a friend of mine."

"You new to town?"

"Yeah."

He was older than she would've expected. Older than she was. Midthirties, she'd guess. Dark hair, tall, broad, nice brown eyes. A friendly smile.

His presence calmed her—unlike the feeling that had haunted her on and off since meeting her own empty future in the eyes of the man at the Bonaparte the other night.

"If you want to wait for your friend, you can have a seat at the bar," this man said, walking toward the long, polished dark wood counter with padded leather stools. It ran along the entire length of the building, completely dominating the back wall. "We're a family-owned place," he added. "No one will bother you."

Walking with him toward the bar, Francesca wondered if he was included in that *no one*. Or if this

was just one of the nicer pickup lines she'd heard.
Mostly she wondered if any of the girls in the room
would turn out to be Autumn. Since she had no idea
what to expect, she couldn't be certain that her sister
wasn't there.

"You work here?" she asked her companion, sliding onto a stool about halfway down the bar. There
were quite a few people milling around, but the
stools on either side of her were vacant.

"My pop owned the place," he surprised her by
saying, meeting her on the opposite side of the bar.
"What can I get you?"

"A diet cola?"

He grinned. "You sure about that? I make a
prickly pear margarita that I'm rather proud of."

"In a pizza place?"

"It's Vegas." His smile was contagious. With a
white towel he wiped down the space in front of her.

"Okay, one margarita." Any more than that and
she wouldn't be able to take her sleeping pill.

Glancing around, she was pretty sure Autumn
wasn't there. Her sister could disguise a lot of
things—like hair color or style—but, even in the
town of illusion, she couldn't make herself shorter
than five-five or change her delicate bone structure.

"By the way." He set down the glass he'd pulled
from a rack above his head, wiped his hand and held
it out to her. "I'm Carlo Fucilla. My friends call me
Carl."

"Carlo," she repeated. "A good Italian name."
Not that she'd necessarily have known that—or noticed—a year ago.

His handshake was warm, firm, but no stronger than her own. "My grandparents came to the States to get married," he said. Glass in hand, he stood directly in front of her, although with the bar between them all she could see was his white, short-sleeved polo shirt from the waist up. "My grandfather had been married before and the Catholic Church wouldn't sanction his second marriage. Neither would their families. So they came here to start a new family."

"And how'd they do?" The voice belonged to Francesca Witting, photojournalist, who'd recently returned from a year spent traveling all over Italy forming a composite of the challenges and strengths of its people. Francesca Witting, who was supposed to have done a follow-up story on Italian families in the United States. The voice was misplaced.

"They were married for sixty-five years," he told her as he backed away.

Exactly the type of family she would've been looking for a month ago. If life hadn't changed the rules so drastically.

As she sat there today, her shutter finger didn't itch even a little bit. And she couldn't care less how Carlo would look on film.

When her drink appeared Francesca sipped greedily, grateful that the man—who hadn't oversold himself in the margarita department—hung around in between serving his other customers. Although, it didn't take her long to figure out that she wasn't the only one he was friendly with. He seemed to truly like people.

Enough to remember his customers after they left? To remember Autumn? And how did she find out without raising his suspicions? Without having to explain more than she wanted to?

"You said your father owned this place, past tense. He doesn't anymore?" she asked when he was once again standing in front of her. He did seem to be stopping there more often than anywhere else. She'd noticed a while ago that he wasn't wearing a wedding ring.

"He died a couple of years ago."

Death. Caskets. With lids that slowly closed, choking out any hope that there'd been a mistake. Funerals. Raw earth, freshly shoveled…

"I'm…sorry." He didn't know her, or anything about her. The anonymity was protection.

"It's okay." He shrugged, called out to some other customers, asking if they were ready, and excused himself as he moved down to pour beer into frosted mugs from one of the six or eight taps across from the cash register.

Ten minutes passed. Then twenty. Thirty. Carl had been right when he'd told her no one would bother her. Besides an occasional smile sent her way, she was left completely alone. People came. And went. And every single time the door opened, Francesca's heart skipped a beat. And then settled into the familiar plod of disappointment. She was thinking more and more about showing Carl Autumn's picture.

But why would she be asking questions about the friend she'd supposedly come there to meet? This was different from a street corner.

There was no way she was getting this close only to have someone tip off Autumn and have her run again. The setback would be too much. She'd become obsessed with finding Autumn. Her sister's unexpected phone call to Sacramento had pulled Francesca out of a dark and dangerous place. Autumn had become a reason to live.

Second margarita in hand, she was glad she'd come. It felt good to be around people. To be no one in no man's land, with nothing to do but let the alcohol numb what little was left of her ability to feel.

"So is this bar still in your family?" she asked the only person she knew in Las Vegas, if she didn't count José at the front desk at the Lucky Seven. Or the head of security at the Bonaparte.

Carl, filling some bowls with snack mix, nodded. "Technically my brothers and I own it together, but they all had different interests, so I run it."

She liked his shrug. And his grin.

"How many brothers do you have?"

"Three."

"And you all share the profits?"

"Nah." He grinned. "There wouldn't be enough to go around. They've got pretty expensive tastes. I take a manager's salary. The rest goes to Mom for as long as she's alive."

"Does she work here?" It didn't matter. None of this mattered, Italian family or not.

He waved toward a side door leading to a back

room. "Try taking a step into the kitchen and you'll find out."

A strong woman. Francesca liked that. And thought, for the brief moment before the pain descended, about Sancia. Loving, brokenhearted Sancia. Francesca would never have looked up the elderly woman, introduced herself, if she'd had any idea of the agony she'd bring with her.

She'd called her once since returning to the States, but neither of them had been able to speak through their tears, and she hadn't repeated the experience. Later, when she was better, she'd visit Sancia again. Maybe.

"Looks like your friend's a no-show," Carl said after she'd been there for more than an hour.

"Yeah."

It was an opening. She just wasn't sure she wanted to take it yet. Didn't want to risk blowing her cover. Not many people handed around pictures of their friends, asking if anyone had seen them or knew anything about them.

She wanted to be able to come back to Guido's. Waiting was much more pleasant there.

"So…" He hesitated, looking a little sheepish. "Is this the first time you've been stood up?"

His assumption was kind of nice. But then, he couldn't know what life was like for a woman who'd loved a man who was married to someone else.

"I wasn't stood up," she said now. "I was meeting a girlfriend…."

His obvious pleasure in that news was gratifying. To her ego at least. The rest of her couldn't care less.

There were a lot of young girls hanging around. Dressed-for-dates young women. They were a friendly bunch. Autumn wasn't among them.

She had a third margarita. Might have gone for a fourth if her car hadn't been in the parking lot. While the trade-off—a possible night in a jail cell for DUI—would in some ways be worth the numb and almost peaceful oblivion she was finding, she couldn't let herself lose even a day on the hunt for Autumn. It would just make the trail that much longer. Provide that much more opportunity for the rains to pour down and wash away Autumn's tracks. Because come they would. They always did.

"You sure you're okay to drive?" Carl asked her just before midnight as he walked her to the door.

Most of the crowd had disappeared, although there were still a couple of twenty-something guys shooting pool, a few friends sitting at the bar, and a table or two occupied in the corners of the room. All these people were younger than the real Francesca Witting.

"Positive. Three's my limit."

"So, you think the margaritas might be good enough to bring you back for seconds?"

Was the next night too soon? "Is that an invitation?"

"Well..." He shrugged again, though not with any lack of confidence. "I'd probably have taken my chances on a dinner date, but it's a little tough for a guy in my position to date much, since I work almost every night of the week."

She tried hard—harder than she'd known she could—to overcome her immediate defensiveness.

"I'm sorry," she told him, wishing she could feel the sentiment. "I don't date."

"Not at all?"

"No." Unequivocally.

He studied her for several seconds. "Well, then," he started slowly. "Are friends out of the question, too?"

"Um, I don't think I'll be in town long," she said.

"So, you aren't coming back?"

*Yes! She had to.* "I'm not leaving yet."

"How about tomorrow, then?"

The invitation played right into her hands. Francesca nodded.

His grin made her wonder if she'd made a big mistake. But she *had* to be back tomorrow night. And every night after that until she found her sister. Or got another lead that took her to the next waiting place.

The street corner by day.

Guido's by night.

Life could be worse.


The woman was beautiful. Tall. Slender. Wavy blond hair. And compassionate. It was that last quality that captivated Luke. Sure, he liked his women gorgeous, but in this town of tinsel and illusion, what attracted him most was real softness. Inside softness.

Las Vegas was filled with beautiful women. They could be found—and had—anywhere, anytime, at any age, for anything a guy wanted.

"Let's take a picnic out to the desert," Melissa

Thomas suggested when Luke picked her up early Saturday evening.

He'd met the social worker while coaching basketball at the local crisis center and quickly found that she was unlike any woman he knew. Ambitious, driven, and motivated completely by her compassion for the underprivileged children she worked twelve-hour days serving.

"Sounds great," he told her, rounding the car to open her door. He'd missed his jump again that morning, and a sojourn with nature sounded almost as good as the time alone with Melissa. "I've got a blanket in the trunk and we can run by the deli for the rest of it."

"Including a bottle of Italian wine?"

It was a taste he'd introduced her to, compliments of the tutelage he'd received growing up at the knee of Amadeo. A little-known sparkling wine from the region of Campania, rather than the more famous wines from Tuscany and Napoli. The deli wouldn't have his favorite, but there'd be a decent choice.

"You got it." Luke took her hand as he backed his Jaguar out of her driveway. She was giving him an evening of freedom, an evening away from bustling restaurants with waiters and managers whose friendliness was professional. Impersonal. Away from glittering people and traffic and city noise. There was very little he wouldn't give her in return.

Melissa had been married once. In college. All Luke knew about it was that her young husband had been unfaithful and the marriage had ended abruptly. She'd been living alone for almost ten years. Owned a small home in one of Las Vegas's gated communities.

Luke had been dating her for six months. They didn't see each other all that often. They both worked a lot. And he had his ever-increasing responsibilities at home—responsibilities about which Melissa knew nothing. Still, they'd fallen into a state of being comfortably exclusive.

He checked his cell phone while she was at the deli counter making her choices, relaxing when there were no calls. The Allens, old friends of his parents who lived in the same gated community as Luke and his mother, had invited Carol over for dinner and a movie. They'd been planning to pick her up fifteen minutes ago, but there was always the chance she'd refused to go with them. Which often meant the onset of an episode that required Luke's attention. The Allens could handle it, of course. But Luke didn't like to accept their help for his own leisure purposes. He needed to be able to call upon them when he was at work and just couldn't get home.

"All set." Melissa joined him, carrying several containers. Pocketing his phone, Luke took them from her and got in line to pay.

"Work?" she asked with a disappointed frown. Carol, work—it was all one and the same as far as Melissa knew.

"Nope," he told her with an easy smile. He was looking forward to the hours ahead.

"Well, thank goodness." Luke loved the way she cuddled up to his side, both her arms wrapped around one of his. "Not that I ever like it when we have to cut a date short, but it would be particularly hard tonight.''

He grinned down at her. ''Why's that?'' Was she feeling the same anticipation—and need—that he was? They hadn't made love in a couple of weeks, and while ordinarily he'd take that in stride, since he'd started seeing Melissa, he had sex on his mind a lot.

She was an incredible lover. Wild without being too wild, tender, wanton. She made the most incredible noises when she came. And she was funny. Luke had never associated sex with laughter before. Would've thought the one would detract from the other. It didn't.

''Because I have something I want to talk to you about.''

*Huh?* ''Okay, good,'' Luke said, briefly wondering what he'd missed. He felt her arms wrapped around his middle, her palms under his T-shirt, against the bare skin of his belly. Funny how such a casual touch could be so erotic.

Yes, he was looking forward to the evening. And to her.

He was a lucky man.

Sheila Miller was going to get lucky tonight. A waitress friend of hers in the high-stakes room at the Bonaparte had assured her that Arnold Jackson would be off at nine.

''Could you take Spring Mountain Road, please?'' She tried to ease back on the authoritative tone that came so naturally and had lost her more than one relationship as she addressed the cabbie. "There's less traffic there this time of night."

The man, who apparently had little mastery of the English language, nodded wordlessly. She hoped he'd understood her.

On the freeway, with cars traveling much faster than the speed limit, they were in the slowest lane. Sheila wanted to scream. To take over. She sat forward, peeling her bare back from the vinyl upholstery in the back seat of the ten-year-old sedan. And chewed on the end of her tongue to keep it silent.

It wasn't the guy's fault that she was nervous, had to pee and should've driven her own car. But then she would've had to drive herself home in order to get to work in the morning.

Home. Where, on her table, lay the envelope she'd received in the mail that afternoon, threatening foreclosure and worse....

"Tell me, fella, you think—" Sheila started and then shut up. She couldn't believe she'd almost asked the cabbie if he thought she was overdressed. She really was losing it. Anyway, if the black, knee-length halter dress was too much, it was too late to do anything about it. And she looked damned good in it. Especially for a fifty-five-year-old woman. The thirty-five pounds she'd lost had left behind a waist that accentuated her breasts; unlike most of her friends, hers hadn't drooped after menopause.

Arnold *had* to notice. She couldn't get the man off her mind. For the first time in thirty years, she'd fallen for a guy. Hard. And she was also running out of time. If she didn't find out who was behind the streak of wins that was causing such a ruckus up and down the Strip, she could very well end up in jail for misrepresentation. When extra building costs on her dream home kept popping up—to the tune of thousands each time—she'd promised her condo to a loan shark as collateral on a twenty-five-percent-interest loan. With her salary eaten up by daily expenses, she was about to miss her first payment. And the condo was already mortgaged to the hilt. To two different banks.

Word on the street said the scam was an inside job. That meant Arnold was going to find out about it. In a business where employer trust was paramount, he protected his integrity above all else. She recognized that because she'd always been just like him.

And like him, she was determined to find out what was going on. Pronto.

But unlike him, it wasn't to protect her integrity. Not this time. She valued honesty above all else—except her freedom. She could go to jail for misrepresentation because she'd put her condo up for collateral twice. The only chance she had was to get in on the Strip scam before it was over. As soon as the perpetrators got wind that the other side was close, they'd shut down. They always did.

Her biggest fear was that the scam would be history before she could cash in. She had absolutely no idea what she'd do then.

# 5

By the time Carl took his break shortly after ten on Saturday night, Francesca had already reached her margarita limit.

A third night without sleeping pills. She had to get to bed before the buzz wore off.

"You aren't leaving, are you?" he asked Francesca. She stood just after Rebecca, the young woman who'd been waiting tables all evening, had gone behind the bar to relieve him.

As had happened the night before, and the night before that, the place had been filled with young people earlier, mostly young women calling greetings to others who came in the door. But slowly the crowd had thinned to some guys shooting pool and throwing darts at one end of the room, with people at a few scattered tables here and there. For the past half hour, the door had only opened as someone left.

Autumn wasn't coming.

"Yeah, I should get back." It was light before six in the morning these days. She had an appointment with a phone booth.

Hands in the pockets of his jeans, Carl nodded. "You can't spare another fifteen minutes to sit with me?" His dark eyes were warm, welcoming.

She'd refused the night before. But three shots of tequila weren't going to wear off in fifteen minutes. And her room at the Lucky Seven was so…empty. "I guess I can."

*What am I doing?* There was no place in her schedule for friends. And no life in her heart.

Still, when he asked if she'd like to share his tomato-and-basil pizza, she didn't say no.

She shouldn't have stayed. Sitting alone with Carl at a table in the comfortable back corner of his bar was very different from sharing casual hit-and-miss conversation as he worked. More intimate.

He wanted to know too much.

She'd almost prefer talking to her mother.

The information she offered him—that she was from Sacramento, that she was a photojournalist taking some time off, even that she was half Italian—wasn't enough to satisfy him. He wanted to know why she wasn't married, but that wasn't up for discussion.

"Who's your artist?" she asked, pointing to the wall across from them instead of answering his question. She'd noticed the watercolors the night before—various depictions of wine bottles with muted purple flower backgrounds. She'd described them to her mother when she'd called to tell Kay about the fairly positive identification of Autumn at Guido's. She'd had a hard time convincing her to stay in Sacramento and let Francesca find out what they needed to know. Only the threat that Autumn was more likely to run again if she found out Kay was in town had ultimately worked. Francesca had hated using it.

"I don't know the artist. Are you currently involved with anyone?"

He'd pushed the last piece of uneaten pizza aside, his forearms resting on the table as he peered at her.

"You don't give up, do you?"

He grinned, spread his hands. "You're a woman. I'm Italian."

"Yeah, right." Head bent, Francesca half smiled. "I've been watching you for two days, buster. And a womanizer you're not."

Sitting back, he narrowed his eyes. She hadn't seen him look so serious before. "That's true," he told her quietly. "But you intrigue me, Francesca. You hide so much more than you show."

Longing for her sunken mattress at the Lucky Seven, Francesca moved around some crumbs on the dark wooden table. "You've got an impressive imagination."

"No, I've got an uncanny ability to read people." If the words had carried even a hint of bravado, a hint of anything other than sincerity, she'd have had no problem getting up and walking out.

Instead, she sat there, unfocused and quietly panicking. She *couldn't* like him. Didn't want to feel anything.

She only wanted to find Autumn.

And her sister had been at Guido's.

"I'm a little disappointed my friend didn't show this weekend," she said, working hard to concentrate through the fog of exhaustion she'd brought upon herself. "I was really looking forward to seeing her."

"Did you call her?"

She shook her head. And then wished she hadn't as the thickness inside her skull didn't keep up with the movement. "I tried. There was no answer."

"You think something happened to her?"

Holding her head perfectly still, Francesca shrugged. "She moves a lot. Not being able to reach her for weeks on end isn't all that unusual." An understatement if ever she'd heard one.

"Still," he said, leaning on the table again, bringing his face with its kind brown eyes closer to hers. "She must be pretty special if you came all the way from Sacramento just to see her."

"Like I said, I'm taking some time off, anyway, and hadn't seen Vegas in more than twenty years. It sounded like fun."

Or might have if fun wasn't so far removed from what her life had become.

And then, because she couldn't wait any longer, Francesca pulled out Autumn's picture. "But you're right, she is special," she said. "See?" Instead of the photo with the pink hair and the lip ring, this was an age progression of Francesca's favorite portrait of her sister. Autumn was one of those girls whose guileless beauty, even as a child, caused people to take a second look.

The lighting in the bar was more atmospheric than illuminating and Carl sat back, holding up the photo as he studied it.

"I've seen her." His words made her heart pound—

and brought an unexpected and instant rush of tears.
Francesca camouflaged them by bending down to her
bag on the floor, rustling for her car keys. She
clutched them as she slowly sat back up.

"In here?" she asked when she could trust herself.
He nodded. "I'm pretty sure."

"Recently?"

He shook his head. "I don't think so, or I'd remember better. But I know she's been in. Seems to
me she was here all the time a while back. Hanging
out with a bunch of girls. And then she quit coming
in."

Damn. It was the first in a string of words that
Francesca screamed silently. And, had she been in
her room, would've said out loud.

"That's the way it is with them," Carl continued,
his gaze on a couple who'd just approached the bar.
"One by one they seem to drop out of sight."

"What's that about?" she asked, with no possible
solutions of her own to offer. She frowned, wishing
her head was clearer. That was it for margaritas. Period.

"I'm not sure." He handed the picture back to her
as they stood. His break was over, which no doubt
explained his preoccupation. "They're young and
they're female," he said. "I figure it's either the result of hurt feelings or finding a boyfriend. Girls that
age seem to forget they ever had girlfriends when
they find a steady guy. My job is just to provide a
relatively safe place for them if they choose to come
here."

Didn't paint a pretty picture of her sex, but remembering back to her own teen years, Francesca had to admit Carl was at least partially right.

So did that mean Autumn had a boyfriend? Hurt feelings? Or had her sister dropped out of sight for other reasons? Like needing to pay the rent?

According to the Vegas police, too many runaways ended up working the streets to stay alive. The city abounded in prostitution opportunities. The younger the prostitute, the better, as far as some johns were concerned.

"What do those girls do?" she asked Carl, afraid to hear the answer. They walked to the door together, and she liked how he felt beside her, strong, reassuring. As though no matter how bad his answer, it would still be okay.

An illusion in the town of illusions.

"I have no idea." Not a great answer, but better than the one she'd feared.

"How do they all know one another?"

Standing in front of her at the door, blocking the bar from her view, he shrugged. "I'm not even sure they do know one another before they start hanging out here," he said, his focus fully on her again. "I run a clean, safe place. Word about that kind of thing tends to spread in a town like this. Someone meets someone in line someplace and mentions coming here sometime...." His voice trailed off.

"You're probably right," she said, her hand on the door. Other than their initial handshake, he'd never touched her. But Francesca felt as though she'd been hugged. It had been a long time. "While I'm in town, would you mind if I hang out here a bit? See if I hear anything about my friend?''

Carl grinned. ''I'd be happy to have you....''

Carl's words had been more than acquiescence to her request. They'd contained a not-too-subtly-veiled invitation.

If she came back, she'd be encouraging him.

He was a nice guy. A man comfortable in his own skin. And gorgeous skin it was, too.

He brought comfort to a life bereft of human intimacy.

Out in the darkened parking lot, she slid into her car, a new weight added to emotions that were already overburdened.

The flicker of candle flames reflected in Melissa's eyes, adding dimension to an evening already beyond the realm of everyday life. Sitting on a blanket in the Nevada desert, lighted votives along the edges of their little clearing, Luke knew a peace he'd hardly ever found in his life. A sense of well-being.

''A perfect moment.''

The surprise in Melissa's eyes matched what he felt as he heard himself say the words out loud. Luke Everson wasn't prone to fanciful thoughts. To anything that he couldn't completely control.

''A perfect moment,'' she repeated softly, her gaze, only inches from his own, alight with things he couldn't describe—yet knew he recognized.

Leaning forward, he touched his lips to hers, lightly. Once. Twice. Passion flowed around them, between them, inside him. Yet passion wasn't all....

"Luke?"

"Mmm-hmm?"

She pulled his hand onto her lap, cradling it between hers, smiling at him. A womanly smile that blended with the charged atmosphere.

"Can we talk about something?"

"Of course." They'd been talking all night. About anything. Everything. She was a great conversationalist.

"I mean really talk."

"Certainly." Focusing on her serious expression, he banked all passion for now. "What's up?"

"Well…" She looked down, giggled.

*Giggled?* Melissa didn't giggle.

"I, uh…" Meeting his gaze, she was completely serious again. "I don't quite know how to start."

"I didn't realize we had a problem communicating," he said, frowning, curious about what Melissa would say. He wasn't used to seeing her embarrassed.

But the news wasn't bad. He could tell by looking at her.

"I want to adopt a little girl."

Wow. What an unexpected thing. Coincidental. He and Melissa really did think alike.

"Say something."

"I'm not sure what *to* say." They could exchange names of adoption agencies.

Her brows drew together, her eyes filling with concern made sharper by the candlelight. "Are you mad?"

"Of course not! Why would I be mad?"

"It'll be a major change."

"Change is inevitable." He'd known it was coming for them, eventually. If not before, it would happen when he got his son. He'd have a lot less time to spend with her then.

"Luke?" She moved closer, her legs resting on top of his. "You *are* mad, aren't you?"

She was beautiful. It felt damn good to spend time with her like this. "No," he said, looking into her eyes. "I'm not mad at all."

"So, what do you think?"

"Girls are nice." Sounded inane, but he meant it. Nice for a family. Or a single woman. Not for a single man to raise alone. A girl had needs that only a mother could meet. "Do you have an agency in mind?"

He thought about mentioning Colter, but considering the fees the agency charged—due to their specialty in successfully maneuvering hard-to-complete adoptions—he decided not to. He didn't want to steer her wrong. Being a woman, Melissa wouldn't have to spend that kind of money. From what he'd learned during his frustrating rounds of applications in the past couple of years, adopting a child appeared to be much easier for a single woman, rather than a single man.

"No, but I have a child in mind," she said, a sweet smile, an excited smile, spreading over her face. "Jenny came into the system a couple of months ago for counseling. Yesterday her parents' rights were severed, making her eligible for adoption, and the foster parents don't want to adopt."

"How old is she?"

"Three." The enthusiasm the single word carried told its own story.

"It's a great age." Of course, these days, to Luke any age wās a good age.

"So, you think I should pursue this?"

"Absolutely."

"And you'll be okay with it?"

Running a finger along her cheek, down to her neck, he moved aside a lock of hair that had fallen forward. "Why wouldn't I be?"

"We-ell…" She was frowning again. Holding his gaze but frowning. "It's going to affect you, too," she said slowly. "At least I hope it is."

He caressed her neck slowly, just beneath her ear where she was most sensitive. "You're worried that we aren't going to have alone time."

"Well, yeah…" The frown didn't dissipate. If anything it grew. "But…Luke, I thought we were building something here."

"I agree!" There was no reason to frown. "What we've built is great. The best I've ever had. I wasn't speaking lightly when I said the moment was perfect. I haven't had a lot of that in my life."

She pulled away. Emotionally more than physically, although there was nothing tangible to show him that. "What we've built," she repeated. "Not what we're building? You think our relationship is…static? That we can't build it any further?"

"What? You're upset because I'm happy with where we are?"

The ground was hard beneath his butt.

"I'm upset because I thought we were on our way to something more."

"And we are," he told her. "We always are, every single day that we wake up alive." It was hot. Especially with all the candles around them. Damned hot.

What kind of bullshit was he spouting?

How long would it take the Jag to cool down when he turned on the air? Halfway back to the city? Three-quarters of the way?

"I thought we were moving toward a lifetime together."

There was wine left in the bottle. He couldn't take it in the Jag like that. It might tip over. He'd split the cork. He hated to waste it, but he supposed he could pour it out. Get a snake drunk.

"I have every hope of knowing you for many years," he said, even though he knew the reply had been too long in coming.

"Uh-huh, I'm beginning to understand what that means." Her tone was different than anything he'd heard from her before.

She was packing up the remains of their picnic, putting the bread back in its plastic bag, wrapping up the cheese, throwing used napkins in a separate bag. They'd finished off the roasted-chicken-and-rice salad.

"Beginning to understand what?" he asked, arms resting lightly on raised knees. Ordinarily he'd be helping her clean up, but she seemed to want to do it all herself.

"That you have no intention of having this relationship go anywhere but where it is. Like to the altar, for instance.''

He grabbed the wine. Dumped it out. Then wished he hadn't. He could've used some to pour down his throat. That feeling was coming again. The one where he felt as if he was stuffed in a tube, his arms and legs cramped against his body, a constricting tube sealed top and bottom.

It happened every time.

''I grew up an only child.'' Those were more words he hadn't meant to say. It was a testament to Melissa's importance to him. ''My father was a great guy—a hero to me not just while I was a kid but until the day he died.''

She was watching him, her expression open. And somehow, under the protection of the dark desert night, he spoke of things he'd never before put into words.

''And my mother...'' Luke stopped as shame spread through him. ''My mother was—is—needier than a newborn babe.''

''Needy how?'' Her words were like whispers of wind, encouraging him, without judgment, to continue.

''There've been various diagnoses over the years—pretty much every time a new professional was consulted—and the new medications or treatments that accompanied them. My father tried everything, from the purely scientific to the holistic, and even saw a medical intuitive for a while. But the upshot is that she suffers from several different anxiety disorders that, taken together, cripple her. The experts are pretty solid on panic and obsessive-compulsive disorders, plus agoraphobia, which comes from severe social-anxiety disorder. All I know is that emotionally she's about as stable as a rotted-out, three-legged wooden chair.''

''That's pretty unstable.'' Melissa moved closer. She didn't touch him, almost as though she sensed that doing so would be too much for him. With *that* feeling there, invading him, her touch wouldn't be helpful.

It was over between them. He knew it. Just as he knew that he owed her this explanation. Something he'd given none of the other women he'd dated.

''She should have been hospitalized—or at least could've been, very easily—but my father would have no part of that. My whole life I watched him give first consideration to her emotional health in every decision he had to make. He tolerated her clinging, her dependency on him. From canceled trips, missed parties, to having to uninvite friends he'd asked over, my father just took it all in stride with a cheeriness that never seemed to falter.''

The man was unbelievable. Everything Luke was not.

''Why?''

''He loved her.'' He'd never gotten why that meant his father had to be a prisoner. ''He said her condition was part of who she was and he accepted that. He got her the best help money could buy. And the rest, he just…accepted.''

''Must've been hard for you, growing up with that.''

Yeah. It *had* been. Until sometimes he'd wondered if he was going to join his mother in her inability to handle life.

But he'd made it through. He just wished he could have done it the way his father had, with heroism intact.

"I resented the hell out of her."

"I'm not surprised."

He glanced at her, read the understanding in her eyes. With raised brows he asked a silent question he'd never voice.

"It's a natural reaction, Luke. You'd have to be pretty much inhuman *not* to resent her. It sounds like her illness robbed you of a good deal of your childhood."

"I had to step in when my father's promotions required some business travel and late-night meetings. My plans were always subject to cancellation based on her mental state."

That was why—about two minutes after his father's retirement—Luke had joined the marines for the sole purpose of getting out of Las Vegas as fast as he could.

"Like I said, you'd have to be inhuman not to resent that."

"My father didn't."

"Your father was an adult when he took on that responsibility. He'd already had his formative years. Had a chance to be *formed* into a man."

Luke grinned at her, though he didn't feel at all lighthearted. "You sound like a juvenile counselor."

"I am one." She played along with his pitiful attempt to introduce a little levity into an evening gone to hell. "So…I'm fairly certain there's a reason you chose to tell me all of this now." She sat with crossed legs, her hands resting behind her.

"I was in the marines during my twenties and when I dated, it was with some vague idea of escaping my childhood, my family, by marrying and starting a family of my own. On terms I could live with."

Raising her knees, she rested her arms on them.

"And every single time I developed an intimate relationship with a woman, I'd start to feel trapped." There, the truth was out. Hurting her was hell. Worse than hell.

He met her gaze, braced for whatever anger she might send his way. Although he hadn't meant to mislead her, he'd obviously done so, and he'd take the full blame. A little smile tilted her lips.

"How could you expect anything else?" she asked. "You were trapping yourself. Trying to control things that aren't meant to be controlled. Trying to fit life and love into a box into which it couldn't possibly fit."

She was good. He'd give her that. He also trusted her. "How so?"

"You were going about the whole process for the wrong reasons with the wrong goal in mind. There was no possible way for your heart to find peace."

He was sure she was right. But what, exactly, was she trying to tell him? What should he do? What should he have done differently?

"Dating—marriage—isn't supposed to be an escape," she said softly. "And love can't be forced.

From what you describe, you were looking at each woman you dated, not for who she was, but as a means of escaping your mother. You wanted escape, but what you were attempting to do would only have trapped you further. In a loveless marriage you didn't really want.''

Maybe.

''You know what gave your father the ability to remain cheerful despite the stress of coping with your mother's situation?''

He shook his head. Lord knew he'd tried. Sober. Drunk. Sick. Healthy. He'd tried. He'd tried figuring it out while floating in the sky all by himself after he'd jumped out of a plane at twenty thousand feet. He'd tried praying. He'd even gone to a psychic once.

''It was *love.*'' Melissa's whisper pierced the warm night. ''All you have to do is fall in love.''

He wished he could pull her into his arms, make his life, his problems, disappear. And knew that kissing her at this point would be cruel.

''You got that trapped feeling tonight.'' It was more statement than question.

He answered her, anyway. ''Yes.''

''Take me home?''

She was trying not to cry. Luke had never felt more like a jerk than he did at that moment. And vowed, as he tried not to notice the quiet sniffles and the surreptitious wiping of her eyes on the way home, that he was not ever, *ever,* doing this to a woman again.

He'd realized long ago that he wasn't a marrying

man. At least not unless, by some miracle, a cure was found for emotional claustrophobia. One of his mother's doctors had once suggested that some of her anxiety disorders were genetic. If so, perhaps Luke had inherited one.

And even if he did get beyond the "trapped" stage of a relationship, the chances of finding a woman capable of taking on his mother were pretty slim. One thing was for sure: as long as Carol Everson was alive she'd always be a part of Luke's daily life, always living with him. It was an obligation he'd inherited from his father—the need to create a secure and protected world for his mother. Luke loved her, but there were times he couldn't stand her. How could he ever ask a stranger to sign on for the same thing?

And, at sixty-eight, Carol Everson was in perfect physical health.

He'd just have to find a way to take care of her— keep her home like his father wanted—and not let her affect his son's life as his own was affected. He was going to do things differently than his father had.

Somehow.

Even the presence of trained professionals in her home gave Carol panic attacks. But if it came to hiring someone or having his son suffer, he'd hire someone. It was still better than institutionalizing her.

After an uncomfortably long drive, Luke pulled up to Melissa's house. He got out to walk her to her door.

"No, please…" Her voice broke. "I'd rather you just went."

*Or tell me I was wrong, that I don't make you feel trapped.* He heard the unspoken qualifier.

He almost told her that. And knew, as he climbed back into his car and watched her shoulders shake as she let herself into her house, that she was the last woman he was going to hurt this way. No more serious, long-term relationships for him.

# 6

Homeless by day. A well-dressed young woman hanging out by night. And—when the pressure inside started to scare her—a tourist finding escape amid the cacophony of lights and loud noises and frenetic energy of one of the Strip casinos. This was Francesca's life.

There was nothing traditional about it, perhaps, but during that next week the routine of it all took on a sense of normalcy. If nothing else, losing herself in this illusion of a life in the glittery city was making it a little easier to run from the pain that haunted her. She had a home—her bed at the Lucky Seven. A friend—the bartender at Guido's. A job—her search for Autumn. And a hobby—nickel video machines. She had purpose.

And that was enough.

In deference to the heat, she'd started a tear in each of the legs of her daytime jeans, ripping them off so that she now had ragged shorts—with a hole in the back just below her waist. Everything else about her daily outfit was the same. A T-shirt she'd torn at the midriff allowed her shoulders protection from the sun while giving her a bit of "air-conditioning." Looking at the toes of her multistained and ripped, once-white tennis shoes on Wednesday afternoon, she decided she rather liked them. They had character. And were comfortable. They were her friends.

Okay, not a thought she'd share with anyone. But true just the same. They felt like home.

As did the dirty beige fingerless gloves. They might make her palms sweat, but they offered an odd kind of protection.

Protection from what, she had no idea. But if she sat there long enough, she'd figure it out.

She always did.

It was part of what had made her so successful in her former life. Her ability to get inside a story, inside the people, and depict things that most people would never have seen on their own.

A couple of girls sauntered down the street from the north—the direction in which both her pregnant "friends" had gone. They weren't at all pregnant. Just young, pretty, wearing too much makeup and clothes that were too obvious in their flashiness. Even for Las Vegas. It was painful to see these young girls trying so hard.

For the wrong things.

The girls crossed the street. Looked at Francesca. And then looked again. When one of them smiled at her, she stood up.

From her experience the past week, most people looked away when they saw a homeless person.

"You hungry?" the shorter of the two asked, chomping on a wad of gum.

It was the same question the pregnant girl had asked her the week before.

"A little," Francesca said, rattling her almost empty McDonald's cup.

The girls each dropped in some change.

Francesca hated to take it. "Business has been slow," she said, imitating the careless shrug and half smile she'd witnessed the other night when she'd passed a homeless woman on the Strip.

In appreciation of the inadvertent lesson, she'd dropped a twenty in the woman's cracked casino cup.

"You new to town?" the taller girl asked. They were both blond—whether naturally or not she couldn't tell—both slender, and both promising real beauty if they'd take some of the crap off their faces. And neither seemed to be disgusted by Francesca's seemingly unwashed, unkempt state.

She shrugged again. Living in a foreign culture, she tried not to say too much. She didn't know how much information homeless people offered. Especially homeless runaways, which was how she'd prefer to appear. "I'm hoping to find a friend of mine," she said. "She told me to look her up when I got to town but she moved. She used to live right there." She aimed a shoulder at the motel-turned-apartment building next door and then pulled out Autumn's photo—the one with pink hair and the lip ring. "You wouldn't have seen her, would you?"

With bent heads the girls studied the photo. Glanced at each other and then at Francesca. "Joy's a friend of yours?" the shorter of the two asked.

*Joy?* Francesca nodded, her heart beating so frantically she could hardly breathe. Didn't even try to speak.

*They knew Autumn. After all this time, she was standing with two girls who knew her baby sister! They'd seen her. They'd know if she was okay. What she was doing...*

"Well..." The two girls exchanged another glance and Francesca fought the urge to grab them and shake the information out of them.

"We know where she works."

*Oh, God.* Okay. Steady. "Where?"

The taller girl nodded up the street. "Place called Biamonte Industries."

"*B-i-a-m-o-n-t-e?*" She spelled it out, confirming the information. It was hard to concentrate. To slow down enough to remember that she was a homeless person who didn't care about much of anything.

The girls nodded. And told her the place was just a couple of blocks up the street.

"What's she do there?"

*Does she look healthy? Happy? Normal?*

"We don't know," the shorter one said. "She hasn't told us." The girl didn't sound too happy about that.

Or all that fond of Autumn, either.

Francesca frowned, nervous energy causing her to jiggle her cup of coins—until she saw the girls staring and forced herself to stop. "Doesn't sound like...Joy."

"We used to hang out with her some," the tall girl said. She seemed the more cautious but also more compassionate of the two. "One day she and another friend of ours showed up bragging 'cause they got these new jobs."

Francesca's heart pulled as it occurred to her that these two girls might be runaways, too. They didn't look down and out, but...

God, don't let them make their living walking Las Vegas Boulevard dressed like that at three in the morning.

With cell phones glued to their ears.

"We all asked, but they refused to tell us what they were doing," the shorter one said, flicking her hair, still chomping.

Francesca had seen the slew of young prostitutes who coursed the Boulevard long after they should've been in bed each night, all on cell phones, no doubt making "business calls" and accepting assignations. A couple of different nights since she'd come to town, after Guido's closed and before she could reasonably hope to sleep, she'd been on the Strip. An hour or two at a casino usually calmed her. And then she'd driven herself crazy wondering if her sister was out there, among those girls.

"But suddenly they have these new clothes, a place to live. They're really making it, you know?" The taller girl reminded Francesca of a friend she'd had in high school. Sweet. Too pretty for her own good. And permanently bewildered by a life that had hurt her in ways young girls aren't supposed to be hurt.

Looking from one to the other, keeping her face neutral, Francesca nodded.

"So one day when they left for work, I followed them," the shorter one said, gazing up the street, past

Francesca, as though there was something more interesting there. "They went into Biamonte."

"We've been going back every week for a year and a half," the taller girl said, "applying for jobs, but so far, nothing."

"Did you ask for Joy?"

"Yeah, but the receptionist just plays dumb," said the girl Francesca liked the least. "Joy probably told her to."

Francesca doubted that. She hadn't seen her sister in two years, granted, but Autumn had never been one to hide behind others. If she had a problem with these two, she'd have handled it face-to-face.

"You said you've been applying for a year and a half?" she asked the taller, less blatantly sexy girl.

"Yeah, 'bout that."

"So she's been working there a long time."

"Yeah, and she didn't mention it to you, either, huh?" This short girl was really getting on Francesca's nerves.

Francesca gravitated a little closer to the taller girl, wishing she had her alone. She might have an ally there. "You guys seen her lately?" she asked.

The girl shook her head. "Not since February. March, maybe."

Disappointment stung, but maybe not as sharply as it had when Guido's hadn't turned up any recent evidence.

Besides, she still had Biamonte to infiltrate. And she wasn't a novice at getting information, the way these two were.

"You have any idea where she went?" she asked, careful to sound discouraged—not excited.

As the shorter girl turned to follow the progress of a middle-aged businessman across the street, the other one shook her head. "She did this once before." She shifted her weight from foot to foot. "Dropped out of sight for months and then suddenly turned up again. Never said where she'd been."

"Did she seem...different?" It was only when both girls sent her an odd glance that she realized she was sounding more like a reporter—or a desperate older sister—than a homeless friend.

"Nah," the smaller one said.

"She did have a new hangout that she turned us on to, though."

"Where? Maybe I can find her there."

The gum-chewer shook her head. "I doubt it. I haven't been there in a couple weeks, but she hadn't been in for a lot longer than that." A cell phone in her purse started to ring, and she quickly dug inside, pushing the button to answer her phone before she had it fully to her ear.

"It's a place called Guido's if you want to check it out, anyway," the other girl offered, half paying attention to her friend's call. "If she's not around, maybe someone there has seen her."

*Guido's again.* To a journalist, a repeated source was nothing but good news. Validation that she was on the right track.

"Is it far?" she asked with hesitation. "I don't have cab fare."

"You can walk it, easy." The compassion in the taller girl's smile touched Francesca. As her friend hung up and told her they had to go, the girl rattled off directions.

"You can always check at Biamonte, too," the friendlier girl said as her companion pulled her away. "They're closed for today, but they'll be open at seven in the morning."

"Thanks," Francesca said, walking beside her. "Maybe we'll meet up again sometime," she said. "At Guido's or something."

"Sure," the girl said. Her friend nodded, as well, but her attention was clearly elsewhere. They were heading toward the Strip.

"Mind telling me your names?" she called as she slowed. "In case I find Joy? I can tell her I met you."

"I'm Molly." The tall girl turned toward Francesca, walking backward for a moment. "She's Sunshine."

An unlikely name for the frosty girl. The girls turned onto the Boulevard, their movement changing from hurried to suggestive, and Francesca revised the thought. If she were a young girl allowing strange men to do whatever they wanted to her naked body, she'd put up a cold front, too.

Back at her post, she waited a few more minutes to make sure the girls weren't coming back and then headed for home to change into her Guido's garb, trying not to imagine what possible atrocious acts the name *Joy* was meant to cover up.

* * *

"Matteo, I love you so much." Naked, Autumn laid her head on his tanned shoulder Wednesday evening, shifting her leg to rest between his. The thick dark hair on his thigh tickled her in places he'd just caressed so delicately. Places that were still ultrasensitive from the unbelievably sweet touch of his fingers.

*Matteo.* Her own special name for him, the Italian version of his American name, Matthew.

"I love you, too, Golden Girl," he said, his voice husky because she'd touched him in that particular way.

She still couldn't believe they were doing this. That he'd honored her completely when she'd told him that while she wanted to make love with him, she couldn't have intercourse because she wanted to be a virgin when she married.

Lying to Matteo killed her. Not that she didn't want to wait for marriage to have sex with him. She still had dreams of the long white gown, a real church, and God smiling down on her union.

It just wasn't the *only* reason she couldn't have intercourse with him.

His fingers moved slowly up and down her arm as he cradled her against him. "Do you have any idea how often I've thanked God that you ran into my garage last February?"

She laughed, burying her face. "It was pouring! I looked like a rat." Or worse. She'd only been out of the hospital a few days and had been so upset she'd jumped out of Antonio's car, paying no attention to the weather.

He'd just told her he'd scheduled her next project. Made an appointment for her to see Dr. Bishop.

Matteo lifted her chin, kissed her softly. "You were the most beautiful thing I'd ever seen."

He kissed her again. And then again. And somehow, although she'd assumed they were finished, he was making her feel that way again—blasting every other thought from her mind.

"I can't believe how good it is without really, you know, doing it," she said a while later.

"You make it good, *cara,*" he said, chuckling deep in his throat. For being only twenty-one, Matteo was one of the most mature men she'd ever met.

"Sometimes I worry that you're going to get bored with me, you know, just doing that…" She moved her mouth on his chest, emulating the way she'd moved against him down lower just a few minutes before. "That you'll go find someone who's ready to do it all."

"I don't want to 'do it all' with anyone else." He mimicked her but with such a loving tone that she smiled along with him. "I want *you.* And I don't mind waiting. Our wedding night will be something very, very special."

Oh, God. She was going to throw up.

*Not now.* She begged her stomach. She couldn't get sick in front of Matteo.

"Golden Girl?"

"Yeah?" She thought of cool breezes. Blue skies. A meadow of soft flowing grass.

"I don't want you to feel you have to do this," he said, so tenderly she fell in love with him all over again. And started to cry. "I mean, don't get me wrong, I loved tonight. It was something I'll never forget. But if this is the only time, I'm really okay with that."

She struggled not to cry. Because he'd ask questions she couldn't—*shouldn't*—answer. And she wasn't sure she could trust herself not to answer him.

Soon she wasn't going to be able to do this with him, even if she wanted to. And not long after that, she wouldn't even be able to see him.

"I'm going to remember this night forever," she whispered, knowing that if she tried to talk more loudly he'd realize what an emotional mess she was.

Was this how Cesca felt when she'd had to leave Antonio? Or had her sister already known what it had taken Autumn months to figure out? That Antonio Gillespie wasn't worth wasting thought on.

She pulled Matteo's hand onto her stomach and was surprised at how immediately the nausea quieted.

And then his hand slid lower and she wanted to spread her legs for him again. Shocking for a girl who'd grown to detest spreading her legs.

Not that she'd ever done it for *this* reason.

But she wouldn't have time.

Pulling away from him would've been impossible had she not known the consequences of disobeying the rules. She had to be home at the apartment and resting by ten o'clock every night. And be home napping for an hour every afternoon, as well. Not that anyone really checked, but if they did, and she wasn't there…

That morning Antonio had stopped by the apartment unexpectedly. She hadn't even known he was in town. He'd reminded her that she'd agreed to this. Had signed on willingly.

But that had been before she'd met Matteo.

"Oh, my God, Joy!"

"What?" Turning her head, she saw what he was looking at. The moonlight shining on her bare back.

How could she have forgotten? Not once, in all this time, had she forgotten.

She jumped up so quickly her head spun, but she didn't let the dizziness stop her from grabbing her shirt, pulling it on.

"Hey!" He grabbed her hand, pulled her back down to the mattress. He was up on one elbow, the sheet over his hips.

"What?" She couldn't look at him.

"There are scars all over your back!"

"I'm sorry. I know they're ugly." If she hadn't already understood how much this man affected her, she knew now.

She wanted to die more than she ever had before. She'd promised herself Matteo would never see how ugly she was.

"Who did this to you?"

She tried to stand. He held her wrist, not bruising her, but making it very clear he wasn't going to let her go.

"I have to get home."

"Not until you tell me who did this to you."

Turning, she stared at him. "I have to go, Matt.

I'll be in trouble.'' It was something he always respected without question.

"In trouble with whom?"

He'd never asked that before. Things were getting way too complicated. "My guardian," she said, a reply she'd heard Chancey give once. A lie.

"You're a ward of the state." He knew she was only seventeen. He was one of the few people in Vegas who knew the truth about that.

It hurt to nod, to confirm another falsehood. But it wasn't that far from the truth. She *was* a ward. And in this state.

"I have to go," she said again. She needed her pants.

"I wasn't kidding, Joy," he said now, frowning, his voice firmer than she'd ever heard it—even the one time he'd yelled at his little sister for running into the street to get her ball. "You aren't going until you tell me who did that to you."

Autumn wasn't one to cower. Or to be strong-armed. She yanked against his hold on her. "Let me go!"

He did. And slid his legs off the other side of the bed, pulling on his jeans. Frozen on the bed, she asked, "What are you doing?"

"I'm going to follow you home and have a talk with this guardian of yours."

"No!" Not that anyone would be there, but she knew Matt wouldn't give up. Eventually he'd find out about Antonio or her "project manager" and she couldn't let that happen. Not ever. She wasn't allowed to have a boyfriend. It was one of the major rules. "I told you, they don't know I'm seeing you."

"They think you're too young because you're still a minor and I'm twenty-one," he said without his usual affection and understanding.

He was really pissed.

"Right." She nodded, still sitting there naked. He couldn't go anywhere as long as she was sitting there without her clothes on.

"Well I think it's much worse—and punishable by law—to beat a young girl to within an inch of her life."

Yeah, well, it probably was. In a perfect world.

Head bent, Autumn shuddered. She was only seventeen. Life shouldn't have to be so complicated. Always, other lives rested on her shoulders. Since the day she was born, lives were at stake.

"They didn't do it," she whispered. She could tell him that lie about the barbed wire fence. It had worked before.

"Then tell me who did." The tenderness was back in his tone—and in his touch as he sat next to her, his hand moving lightly at her neck, rubbing away the tension that was always there. He was naked from the waist up.

"My father."

His hand stilled. "And that's why you're a ward of the state?"

She started to nod. The answer was so simple. "No."

There were just too many lies.

"He's a politician. A lawyer, first. Then a judge.

And now the attorney general of California. A powerful man who's far too smart for the world's good. He knows the law and he knows how to work it. He knows how to intimidate. He's friends with every powerful, rich person in the state. And he's charming as hell. Even if I could get someone to listen to me, to believe me over him, they'd be too scared of the retribution that might fall their way if they acted against him.'' She could hardly speak. Her throat was tight, her chest was tight. ''Apparently my mother tried once, calling the police, and ended up with a diagnosis of obsessive-compulsive disorder. The disease warps your perceptions, and the official story was that she'd tripped on the molding at the top of the stairs, fallen, and somehow convinced herself that my father was angry at her and had punched her with his fist. My father got sympathy votes out of that one and came out looking like a hero for standing by her.''

''So what did she do when he hit you?'' His voice was that of a stranger. Cold. Neutral.

His anger almost made her cry again. No one had ever loved her enough to think her father should be punished for his sins. Until now.

''She told me to stay quiet. She promised to keep him away from me.''

''Did she?''

''No.''

He stood. Sat down again. Started to rub her back. Stopped. ''Come on, honey, let's get your pants on.''

She'd forgotten they were still off. Gently he held open her panties, bearing her weight with her hand on his shoulder as she stepped into them. He pulled them up. And then did the same with her jeans.

She shouldn't let him help her. Autumn had to take care of herself. She knew that. She couldn't afford to be weak. Or needy.

Still, she let him.

What could it hurt? He'd be gone soon enough.

"I ran away."

Hands on the button of her jeans, he jerked harder than necessary to pull the sides of the waistband together, his gaze meeting hers.

"You're a runaway?" It changed things for him. She could see that. Matt was the most straitlaced guy she'd ever known.

"Not anymore." She had a job. A home. A life. Even a family—of sorts.

"That's why you're a ward of the state."

This time she took the easy answer. The lie.

Autumn nodded.

# 7

At five after seven on Thursday morning, Francesca, dressed like herself, was at the front door of Biamonte Industries. She wore flat brown leather sandals that barely made a sound, her cotton navy shorts and a lightweight, short-sleeved blouse freshly pressed. She pulled open the door to what she hoped would be a much-awaited and completely successful reunion with her baby sister.

She wasn't dumb enough to count on that, though. As determined as she was to find her sister, Autumn seemed equally determined not to be found. There was absolutely no guarantee the girl was going to be as elated to see Francesca as Francesca would be to see her.

Walking through the ornate lobby, noticing everything from the eight-tiered crystal chandelier to the placard on the wall listing all the businesses housed within the building, she asked the brightly smiling, professionally dressed receptionist for Joy Stevens.

Pulling out what appeared to be a company directory, the woman thumbed through several pages and then shook her head.

"There's no one here by that name."

On a long shot, she tried Autumn Stevens. Not that

she really thought her sister would be using her real name.

"I'm sorry," the woman said, her smile not quite as vibrant as she slid the directory back in its slot.

"I know she works in this building." Francesca wasn't the least bit discouraged by the woman's inability to help her. She hadn't expected this to be easy. "Do you mind if I sit over there and wait for her?"

The slender woman frowned. "Well…"

"Thanks," Francesca said, moving across the lobby to a padded bench along a far wall. She'd already scoped things out. That front door was the only regular access to Biamonte Industries' five floors of offices.

An hour later, she once again approached the eight-foot rounded podium behind which Biamonte's very busy and accomplished receptionist held court.

"Theresa," she said, having paid attention during her vigil, "you've got that directory on disk, don't you? To make changes and print new versions?"

Putting down the phone after an apparently unhappy caller had been giving her a hard time, Theresa nodded.

"Good. Then we can do a first-name search."

"I can't—"

"Sure you can," Francesca said, leaning both arms on the counter with a wistful shrug and a conspiratorial smile. "My friend's obviously gotten married without telling me, but I've been out of the country for a couple of years. I'm only home for a couple of weeks and wanted to surprise her."

"Go to her house."

"She moved."

"Call her."

"Phone's disconnected."

"I can't—"

"Please," Francesca said. "It would take a lot less time for you just to look up the name Joy than you're spending arguing with me. I'm not asking to see your directory, only to have you take a quick peek."

When she saw that the woman's eyes softened, she tried again. "Please. I don't know how long it'll be before I can get home again and she really helped me out at a critical time in my life."

Slowly, the woman nodded. Clicked a few times, stared at the screen in front of her. And shook her head. "No Joy anyplace," she said.

"How—"

"No Autumn, either," Theresa interrupted. "I already looked."

Damn. What the hell was going on? The girls had followed Autumn here.

Eighteen months before.

"Is there any way to check last year's entries?"

"Not here." The woman was becoming impatient again. "I only have the current version."

"Is there anyone who would—"

"Check with Human Resources," Theresa interrupted again, grabbing a big pile of papers and folders from the inbox on top of the counter in front of her. "Third floor."

Theresa was one impatient woman. If she didn't

slow down, she was going to die of stress before she was fifty.

On the third floor, Francesca quickly spotted the office she needed. The words *Human Resources* were painted in big black letters on the paneled window directly across from the elevator.

Ten minutes later she was back in the hall. The people in Human Resources made the receptionist look downright friendly. Biamonte wasn't the most appealing place to work. She wouldn't be surprised if Autumn had quit.

And—in keeping with the rest of her morning—the elevator doors were just closing as she approached. The lone man inside shot his arm out, obviously trying to hold open the door, but it was too late.

She knew that man. Staring at the closed door, she needed a few minutes to place him. She could count on one hand the number of people she knew in this town, but she was sure she'd met him. Had spoken to him.

She remembered that his voice had been calm. Reassuring.

The casino at the Bonaparte! Her nine-hundred-dollar win that first Sunday she'd been in town. He was head of security at the Bonaparte. His name was Luke Everson. She knew a man who had business at Biamonte. When she was through with the day's—and night's—work, she was going to pay him a visit.

A good journalist knew that an ''in'' was all it took. And there was enough of the old Francesca left that she knew she'd just found hers.

Waiting for the next elevator, she tried to shake off the morning's failure, mentally planning the rest of her day. A quick trip back to the Lucky Seven to change into her homeless gear. She'd spent too long at Guido's the night before to rinse out the T-shirt. It hadn't occurred to her to worry about it, considering her plans to visit Biamonte this morning. She'd been so cocky about her ability to glean information where others had failed.

*Come on.* She willed the elevator to arrive before she melted into nothing in the offices of this company who'd apparently hired her sister and then lost all trace of her.

She'd be fine as soon as she got outside and breathed some fresh air. Even sweltering-hot fresh air.

Chilled to the bone, she rubbed her hands over her upper arms. She should've brought a sweater. Every single place she went in Las Vegas, she froze. The state should be sued for the amount of energy it wasted on air-conditioning, she thought irritably.

A couple of men, talking about some board meeting, walked up to the elevator and continued to converse as though she wasn't there. Francesca turned, pretending interest in the black metal board that listed room numbers for that floor.

And came face-to-face with the unobtrusive but elegant gold lettering on a door just down the hall.

*Colter Adoption Agency.*

She had to look. Like someone coming upon a fatal car accident, she was compelled to see who was in there. Prospective parents? Pregnant women? A baby?

And found only one woman behind a desk, talking on the phone.

Francesca backed away. She made it into the elevator and downstairs without conscious thought. She went to the Lucky Seven to change. And on to her street corner. It was routine. Habit. Her life.

And then she looked at the phone booth—and thought of those two young girls. They'd been coming from the direction of Biamonte. Had they been visiting the adoption agency? Giving away their babies?

They'd been sent to torture her. To remind her of what she was trying so desperately to forget. Little Gian. *Oh, God, how could you?*

For the first time since her return to the States she thought about calling Antonio. But there was no point. Nothing he could do. Except perhaps ease the ache for a second for two. And then make it worse when he had to leave her again.

Those girls were giving away their babies. She just knew it.

She'd been a single mother. Alone and pregnant.

Okay, maybe she'd had a successful career. Enough money to provide all the security she and her baby could ever want. Health insurance.

Still, she'd been alone. So alone.

She couldn't imagine being twenty, broke and that alone....

Struck anew by the cruelty of life, Francesca sank to the ground, cup in front of her, no longer playing a part. If home was where the heart was, she *was* homeless.

Women who'd rather be dead than without their babies suffered so much, while others just gave them away. Part of her knew she wasn't being rational, but pain never left much room for concepts like fairness. God, she hurt so badly she didn't know how she was going to stand up, let alone go anywhere when the day was done. Just let her sit there in the heat, head against the brick building, and sleep.

Without end.

"Easy does it, lady."

*Easyduzit.* What did that mean, anyway?

"There you go. Let's just get you inside."

*Go?* She was going somewhere?

"We at the Bonniport?" She didn't think that sounded right, but it was close enough. As long as she got there.

"You said you're staying at the Lucky Seven." The deep voice just kept coming at her.

"Iss ho-o-ome."

"And that's exactly where you need to be."

Oh. For some reason she thought she was supposed to be at the Bonniport. She'd left Guido's. She was pretty sure. And the Bonniport was next.

She had her list. In her head.

But she didn't feel all that great. She'd just get up these stairs he was making her climb and then worry about the list.

"Are you taking me home?" She looked up at the man who had his arm around her waist. "You said if I had more, you wouldn't let me drive.'' She spoke slowly and carefully, a little smug that she'd remembered what he'd told her.

''We are home.''

Uh. Trying really hard to focus, she studied the once-white wood in front of her. ''Yep, thas my do-o-or. And my do-o-or handle, too.''

He unlocked it. Someone else had a key to her room? She hadn't known that.

She stumbled over the threshold and the man's arm kept her from falling. Her head lolled back and as she looked into somewhat amused brown eyes, she started to giggle.

''What so funny?''

''You aren't shomebody, you're Carl.'' Her chin dropped and she wasn't sure she wanted to bother lifting it from her chest.

''Yes, and you're going to bed like all good girls do at this time of night.''

Bed. Alone. Ghosts and nightmares and darkness.

''Are you coming with me?''

''Do you want me to?''

''Yess.'' She nodded, but her chin didn't come back up like it was supposed to. ''Very mush.''

''Then I'd be honored.''

''Okay, go-o-od.'' God, she was dizzy.

''I had more than three mar-ga-ri-tas.'' She pronounced the word very carefully. She knew he was really proud of his drinks.

''Yes, you certainly did.''

''I'm drunk.'' She made extra sure the *k* came out.

''Yep.''

Just so they both knew. That was all right, then.

"Can I lie down?" She'd thought she was going to throw up, but she didn't feel as though she would once he finally stopped holding her upright. Lying on the side of the bed that was usually empty, she smiled and was thankful when he unbuttoned her shirt. She wasn't sure she'd have been able to do that.

He unlaced her high-heeled sandals, too. She heard them thump as they hit the floor. And then he slid her short black skirt over her hips.

Her panties started to come down but he pulled them back up.

"No one was there tonight." Her eyes were closed, but the thoughts hadn't stopped yet.

"It was one of our busiest nights."

"No one I kne-e-ew," she said with enough emphasis so he'd realize what she meant.

"I didn't think you knew anyone in Vegas." He was pulling the sheets down underneath her.

"I have a friend," she said, opening her eyes and then closing them again. She wouldn't throw up if her eyes were closed. "I tol' you that."

"Oh, yes. Your friend who never showed up."

It wasn't nice to remind her.

"People have babies."

"Yes, they do."

She was glad he knew. Did he know how much it hurt, too? She wanted to ask him. But she couldn't think about that. The drinks were supposed to keep her from thinking about that.

"I can't shleep in my bra. Pleashe," she added

when nothing happened. If he didn't help her, she'd start to cry.

She might start, anyway. Having babies hurt even if she drank a lot.

"Um." Carl coughed. "Do you have a nightgown or something?"

"Unner here." She tried to lift the opposite pillow, but only managed to drop the back of her hand against it.

It was a T-shirt, not a nightgown. Hopefully he'd figure that out.

When he sat down next to her, Francesca rolled over onto her side, presenting him with her back where the bra was fastened.

The last thing she remembered was feeling the latch release.

He should have left hours ago. Though he varied his schedule for obvious reasons, Luke had technically been off work for several hours. Had actually gone home to find his mother already in bed asleep, out for the night with aid of a sleeping pill, and he'd turned around and come back.

They'd had another big win in the casino that night.

Amadeo was going to shit bricks.

After spending a few frustrating hours viewing and reviewing tapes, Luke bade his staff good night and left the surveillance booth to head downstairs. Every single win was with a different dealer. The only thing any of the recent episodes had in common was the card tables and the size of the wins.

What was he missing?

Strolling along the carpeted main roadway that wound through the casino, he took occasional detours into various nooks and crannies as though someplace among those machines and tables would be the answer he was seeking.

His only discovery was something he already knew. Even at this time of night, the unbelievably popular Wheel of Fortune machines were occupied. Shaking his head, Luke moved on. He just didn't get it. The allure of gambling passed him by, and those machines were at the top of his list. They were some of the casino's biggest moneymakers. People spent more money trying for a chance to spin that damn wheel and the payoffs were less than with many of the other, less popular machines.

It was the cheap thrill of seeing that spin button appear—feeling you were getting two games for your money. But you spent more money for games that, while they doubled on occasion, paid less than one.

What did that say about human nature?

This late at night, most areas of the casino were populated only by an occasional gambler, the sound effects and blinking lights of the machines quiet. Many of the tables were closed.

Hard to believe that just six or seven hours before, the place had been abuzz with security and officials and bystanders gawking at and cheering the most recent of the Strip's million-dollar winners.

They'd break this up soon. There were just too many experts working on the case, too much high-tech equipment, for it not to happen.

Hands in his pockets, Luke continued to look around. There was something about the casino in the early morning that spoke to him. Like the hours on Christmas Day before people were up and the presents were opened.

It was filled with energy and anticipation of good things to come. And a curious sort of peace. It was a time after the disappointments of past losses, and before the next day's allotment.

"What's up with you?" Arnold Jackson asked as Luke slid onto a stool at the dealer's blackjack table as the Bonaparte's most successful dealer watched the floor person, Steve Wallace, place all the gaming equipment—the shoe or card holder, paddle, signs and cut cards—in the shoe box.

"You're here late, aren't you, boss?" Wallace asked.

Luke shrugged. "It's harder to solve a mystery when you're lying awake in bed."

Wallace was a good guy.

He wanted to talk to Arnold.

He watched, almost dizzy with exhaustion, as Arnold very deliberately removed the cheque-tray lid and placed it right side up on the table.

Luke remembered the first time he'd heard the term *cheque.* He'd been about six, accompanying his father to work, and thought that players at the blackjack tables had to write checks for every single deal. He'd pondered the logistics of that more often than he'd ever want to admit.

It had been a couple of years before he'd found

out that the term referred to the chips that were used for betting.

As he did every single time he closed his table, Arnold took out every single cheque, setting them in rows. The highest denomination was always closest to the tray.

The reverence with which Jackson methodically went through each stack, counting the chips with the same series of movements, impressed Luke. Every man should value his work so much.

Even the way Jackson held the chips was carefully choreographed.

Luke watched the ritual silently, respecting the seriousness of table closure.

Systematically Arnold put all the cheques back into their holder, calling out the count for each denomination, which Wallace recorded on the table inventory slip. Having grown up in Las Vegas, in casinos, Luke appreciated Arnold's efficiency and organization. He went through the entire procedure with never an incorrect finger movement.

In a world of escapism and illusion, Arnold Jackson was a man of complete integrity.

Arnold signed off on the table inventory slip, put one copy in the table drop at his hip and another inside the cheque tray.

''What'd you notice?'' Luke asked the second the closing was complete and Wallace had walked off.

Standing at attention, as though the table was still open, Jackson shook his head. ''Not a damn thing.''

''There was nothing on the tapes,'' Luke reported.

"Millions of dollars in expensive surveillance equipment and it nets a big fat zero."

"I've got word out on the street," Jackson said quietly, brushing lint off his table as though discussing nothing more important than the casino's janitorial service. There was no one else in the vicinity, but Arnold Jackson took no chances. It was one of the things Luke respected so much about the older man. And one of the things that had gained Arnold such a stellar reputation—both in Vegas and in his previous careers.

"If this has any kind of inside mark on it, we'll know soon."

Luke nodded. It was the least of his concerns. And, in many ways, the worst possibility. With insiders, not only did the casino suffer the financial hit, but serious morale issues, as well. Casino employees were often closer to one another than family, thanks to the level of trust required.

"Care for a drink?" Luke asked.

"Chivas on the rocks?"

"You got it."

A loud roar of voices came from a table several yards away. Luke didn't even look over. Someone was celebrating a win. Which probably still amounted to an out-of-pocket loss for the winner if you calculated what was spent to make that win.

"You know, buddy, you really need to lighten up if you're going to work in this place."

"What?" Luke frowned down at the grinning man. "What do you mean?"

"Your disapproval is showing."

"Gambling's asinine and weak."

"It's entertainment."

Luke shook his head. He'd seen so many lives crushed and broken by the gambling disease. You couldn't grow up in this place and miss it.

"Going to a concert's entertainment," he told his gray-haired companion.

As always they settled at the one bar that didn't offer performers, taking the round table in the corner as far away from everyone and everything else as it was possible to be.

They toasted to another night closed, to another day on the job. And with their second drink, to the peace and quiet that had finally descended.

By the third one, they were back to their ongoing argument. The value—or lack of it—in gambling.

"My clients might lose their money, but they're usually having a good time. Even if they lose, they'll remember their vacations with smiles on their faces."

Luke understood how important it was to Arnold to believe that.

"I love ya for the job you do, man," Luke said, enjoying the light alcohol buzz. "You're the best. But you know as well as I do that part of what makes you so damn good is your ability to charm people into stopping at your table, and then getting them to stay there and spend beyond what they might have planned to spend."

"Yeah, well, how much of your concert ticket cost do you leave the theater with?"

With a grin, Luke shook his head. It always ended this way. He knew what was coming next, too.

"Besides," Arnold continued, "all those people at my table are paying for that fancy house you live in, my friend."

He couldn't argue.

It was true. Always had been.

# 8

"Hi, Mom." Eyes closed, Francesca rolled over, cell phone to her ear, as she answered the early-morning call.

Every part of her body ached.

"Yes," she murmured. "I know I said I'd call."

Carl had just left—something she couldn't even think about right now—or she might not even have been awake to hear her phone.

"I didn't have anything to tell you," she said when she garnered, from the gist of her mother's wailings, that Kay was demanding an explanation. "The Biamonte information didn't pan out."

"How do you think I felt?" Kay continued, her voice a few decibels up from normal. "Waiting all night long. Wondering. You could at least have let me know there was no *reason* to wait...." Kay continued to berate her.

This was hard on her mother. Francesca knew that. First, having lost her youngest child to the streets without a trace, and now having to sit in another state, helpless, waiting for her to be found.

Or to call again.

Kay Stevens needed to vent and Francesca was the only one she could do it with.

Still… "I'm not feeling well this morning, Mom," she finally managed. "I think I've caught a bug…."

There were worms in the bottom of tequila bottles. This morning, that counted.

"Probably all those hours sitting on the street with God knows what other diseased homeless people who—"

"It's not like we sit around in bunches breathing on one another," Francesca interrupted. "I have to go, Mom. I need to use the bathroom."

To lie on the cool, if torn, linoleum floor until her body was kind to her and let her throw up.

Not taking any chances, Francesca went to the Bonaparte before showing up at Guido's that evening. She was wearing her usual tight skirt—denim tonight—black sandals with four-inch heels and a ribbed tank top that left about an inch of belly showing every time she moved. The overabundance of makeup she usually wore to make her look like the young adults who hung out at Guido's was still in her purse. So was the chewing gum, big hoop earrings and ponytail clasp.

The last time she'd seen Luke Everson had been fairly late at night, but as head of security surely he worked earlier in the evening, too. Often when she used to make investigative calls for her assignments, she hadn't known what she was going to do until she got there; in this case, she didn't know how she'd find him, but it turned out to be relatively simple.

He was standing on the casino floor speaking with an older gentleman, a dealer judging by the crisp white shirt and pleated black tux slacks he was wearing. Not wanting to take a chance on losing him, she poked around the nearby slot machines until he was finished.

"Excuse me, Mr. Everson?" She wasn't certain he'd be able to hear her over the ringing bells and machine-generated voices and the sounds of coins dropping, but it was as loud as she could manage at the moment. While her stomach had settled some, her head had not become any kinder to her as the day wore on.

Hailing a security employee pushing a change cart, he exchanged a few words. Not many, but enough for Francesca to catch up with him—without losing the contents of her stomach to the dizziness brought on by her sudden movement.

Not that there was much in her stomach.

Unless you counted far too much of yesterday's tequila. She hadn't felt like eating much that day. Especially after falling asleep in the hot sun with her head against a hard brick wall.

"Mr. Everson," she said, touching him on the back of his arm.

He turned, his eyes filled with questions when he saw her.

"You don't remember me."

It had been pretty much a foregone conclusion.

"I'm sorry, no."

"You were here a Sunday or two ago when I won a nine-hundred-dollar jackpot on a nickel slot machine."

"Oh, yes," he said, but she was fairly sure he still

didn't remember. He didn't seem to mind talking to her, though.

"It was my first time in a casino and I didn't know what was happening."

He remembered then. Had she been another woman, or herself in another time, she would've been flattered by the appreciative light in his eyes.

"You thought you'd done something wrong."

"I thought I broke the machine."

"So," he said, arms folded as though he planned to stay around a while. "How much more than that have you fed back into the slot machines?"

"None." She shook her head. And then wanted to kill herself for having done so. "No, Mr. Security Head." She hoped she was pulling off the light tone. "Your town has not made a single dime on me. Or nickel, either."

"Good for you!" he said, obviously impressed.

"Well, at least not in the casinos," she added, unsure why she was continuing with this particular conversation. Except that, in spite of how close to death she felt, she was enjoying it. "I *have* eaten while I've been here."

"And slept, too, I imagine."

"Yeah." But not nearly as much as he probably thought. And not anywhere that put her out much. She could practically pay her bill at the Lucky Seven with what she'd collected in her McDonald's cup.

"Would you like to get a coffee or something?"

Nothing in Francesca's life worked this easily. "If that offer included hot tea, I'd be glad to." Must be the inch of belly she'd caught him peeking at.

"We could have something stronger, if you'd like. I have friends in the bar."

"No, thanks," Francesca said, swallowing carefully. "Tea would be great."

It would go well with the dry toast she'd had at a cheap little grill around the corner from her phone booth that afternoon.

He was a nice man. In Vegas.

After half an hour of chatting with Luke Everson in a relatively quiet lounge, Francesca was surprised by how much she liked him.

In her previous life, she'd made ferreting out the information people didn't want her to know into an art, and had found since her arrival in Vegas that she hadn't completely lost the talent. Which was why she felt so pleased by how genuine Luke Everson appeared.

"I'm sure glad your memory is better than mine," he told her as he sipped cappuccino. "I'd have walked right by you."

"You did."

"Well, there you go, then." He grinned, his gaze focused solely on her. "Thank you for not letting my ignorance stand in your way."

"You don't spare yourself much, do you?"

"What's the point? People's true colors usually come out in time, anyway."

She sat forward, trying not to notice when his eyes dropped to the low-cut cotton-ribbed V of the black shirt she was wearing. "Okay, well, that's an opening if ever I heard one," she said.

"Opening for what?"

"I came here specifically to find you."

Sitting back in the padded leather chair, he unbuttoned the jacket of his charcoal suit. "Should I be flattered?"

"I would be." She grinned. And tried not to grimace as she experienced another stab to her brain.

"Why don't you tell me why, and then I'll decide how I feel about it."

Great-looking. Honest. And a discriminating man, to boot. Who wore a suit with as much ease as most men wore basketball shorts.

Francesca pondered what to tell him to win his empathy and his help—and found herself being unusually candid.

"I'm not here vacationing."

"I doubted that, since you've been here what? Two weeks?"

"Yep, two weeks today."

A waitress came around and Luke ordered an appetizer for them to share and offered her another drink. She made the big leap from tea to diet cola.

"You're not a drinker?"

"Not really." She stopped herself before she shook her head that time. "I mean, I drink. Occasionally. I don't have anything against it. I'm just not a big drinker." She stopped. And then, as his eyes continued to rest on her with an affectionate kind of amusement, she finished, "I had far too many margaritas last night."

His grin widened knowingly. "And today you pay."

More than he knew. She was dreading her trip to Guido's that night. Facing Carl.

She had no idea what they'd done. Or not done. But her braless state that morning hadn't been reassuring. She suspected that, in the condition she'd been, she hadn't managed to get herself out of it. And that meant, at the very least, he'd seen her topless.

Carl was a great guy. She was truly fond of him. But she wasn't planning to have a get-naked relationship with him.

Or with anyone.

"So what was the occasion?" Luke asked. His gaze didn't waver. Despite all the people walking by the lounge to the other establishments inside the hotel, including the casino just across the wide-open walkway that ran through the middle of the entire first floor of the Bonaparte, he didn't get distracted. Even a little.

His attention was…unusual. Though not in a negative way.

"It all has to do with why I'm here," she said. "I'm in town looking for my younger sister." This was a time when playing it straight was her best shot.

He didn't say anything. Just kept paying attention.

"She ran away from home and disappeared without a trace two years ago. We looked everywhere, had posters out, local police forces and the FBI involved. My mother even hired a private investigator."

"And now you think she's here? In Vegas?"

"A little over three weeks ago she called my mother, apparently just to say she was all right."

"An odd thing to do after all this time."

"Yeah. But maybe not. The police say they all get homesick after a while."

"Two years is a pretty long while."

"That's what I thought."

"And when she called, she said she was in Vegas?"

"My mother had a tracer put on our line when she first left. The call came from a phone booth just a few blocks from here."

He whistled. "Definitely a lead, but that isn't necessarily where you'd want to find her."

She almost nodded, and settled for a tiny, sad smile. "I keep asking myself, would I rather she was still out there, lost to us, alone? Or can I deal with what the past two years have done to her? Deal with what she might have done to herself."

"You'd rather deal with it."

Two months ago, she'd have agreed with him, hands down. Tonight she wasn't so sure.

When did people know if they'd reached the limit of what they could endure? Self-pity aside, when was the hurting too much?

Only the thought that Autumn was out there, perhaps feeling the same way Francesca did, overwhelmed by life's pain, kept her pushing ahead. That and the fact that her sister was one of the few people Francesca loved.

For now, as long as she could put one foot in front of the other, she'd be taking steps toward Autumn.

"That's what I think, too," she finally said. "I've spent the past two weeks hanging out at that phone booth on the off chance that she comes to the vicinity regularly. And I've been showing around her picture, asking anyone who'll talk to me if they've seen her." Describing her homeless garb, she got him to laugh, but it didn't distract him from the seriousness of their conversation.

"The heat out there has to be overpowering." He motioned for another beer for himself and a diet cola for her.

"It gets a little hot."

"More like scorching." His look was penetrating as he met her eyes. "I'm surprised you manage to stay conscious."

"Anytime I get too lethargic I duck into the convenience store down the street or cross over to McDonald's." In truth, she was so tightly strung that she almost welcomed the lethargy.

"There aren't too many people who'd put themselves through that for a runaway sibling."

The admiration in his voice embarrassed her. He didn't know the half of it. Like the part where, before her sister had run away, Francesca had been so busy with her own life that she hadn't heard Autumn's very real cries for help as anything more than teenage complaining. Or how, after a year of dead ends in the search for the runaway girl and overwhelmed by her own heartaches, she'd left the country. "I've never been one to follow the crowd."

"The discouragement, especially after two years, has got to take its toll."

Yeah. "It hasn't all been discouraging. I've actually met a few people who think they've seen her."

"And?"

Although she didn't go into detail about the young women she'd met, she told him about Guido's. About Carl who'd befriended her and also recognized Autumn's picture.

"Hearing about it from various different sources is encouraging." His emphasis on that last word validated the hope she'd barely allowed herself to acknowledge.

She might have told him so if they hadn't been interrupted by the arrival of the vegetable quesadilla he'd ordered.

"This is really good," she told him after the first bite. She immediately took a second. It had been a long time since food had given her any real pleasure.

He nodded, taking a large slice. "I was a kid when I first had it—and not really that fond of vegetables. But I learned to make it when I was on my own."

"You make vegetable quesadillas?"

He nodded.

"All the men I've known can't even make toast without burning it."

He shrugged. "I'm a pretty independent guy." There was more to the story. She could feel it. "And I didn't have any intention of being forced to eat out all the time."

So what wasn't he saying? Once, she would have asked; now she couldn't be bothered. She took a sip of diet cola, instead. And another bite of quesadilla.

He wasn't wearing a wedding ring. Not that *that*

meant anything. And whether he lived alone was none of her concern.

"You went to Guido's and didn't find your sister," Luke said when they'd finished off half the quesadilla.

Wiping her mouth with the cloth napkin, she shook her head. "Not yet, anyway." She told him about the crowd of young women who came and went. "I've started dressing to fit in with them, which explains tonight's attire." She was glad to have the opportunity to do that—to explain.

Luke held up the last piece of quesadilla, offering it to her. She shook her head. Funny, Antonio had always assumed the last piece was for him.

"You're on your way to Guido's?"

She nodded. "Every night. Carl thinks I'm looking for a friend. He doesn't know she's my sister. It's a pretty sure bet that no one there would tell me anything if they knew why I wanted to find her. Carl's noticed the girls hanging out, of course, but he doesn't seem to have any idea where they come from, or what they do, other than drink beer at Guido's. He says he's just glad he's giving them a relatively safe place to be."

She shrugged. "I'm hoping to be invited to have a drink or something, be one of them, but so far I haven't been successful."

"My God, woman, you're on the street all day and in a bar all night? When do you rest?"

Usually from about three to five in the morning. "Between midnight and breakfast."

And now would he understand how important it was that he help her?

"I'm here to find Autumn, and I'd much rather be out looking than sitting in a hotel room staring at a television set."

He had to know how serious she was.

Holding his beer bottle by the neck, he brought it to his lips, took a long swig. Francesca envied him that alcoholic relaxation aid, but knew her stomach wouldn't thank her if she imbibed.

"So what does any of this have to do with me?" he asked, pulling lightly at the silver foil label on the bottle.

She took a deep breath. So much rested on this. "I met a couple of young women who knew Autumn," she told him, but didn't say where she'd seen them. "They said she worked at Biamonte Industries."

He blinked. There was no other reaction.

"I went there yesterday morning, and no one seems to have heard of her. But I have to tell you, they didn't put out a lot of effort to find her." She spoke quickly. Before he cut her off with a shake of the head, she had to make him understand that he might be her last hope. "I asked for Autumn Stevens, but I'm pretty sure she's not using her real name. The girls called her Joy. I tried to get Biamonte personnel to do a search for me, but they refused. Nor was I granted permission to show her picture around. If she's working there, they don't want to know. They don't want to be responsible for hiring a runaway."

He wasn't shaking his head. Francesca slowed to a stop.

"How do you think I can help?"

Her steady eyes gave no indication of the waves crashing inside her stomach. "You're a trained detective, aren't you?"

He acknowledged the statement with a lowering of his head. "But from the sound of things there are many trained detectives working on this already."

"I saw you at Biamonte the other day. I was hoping you'd have some kind of 'in' with them."

There. She'd said it. And now it was up to him.

"Biamonte Industries owns the Bonaparte."

"Oh!" Her aching head pounded with possibilities. "I had no idea they had any interests outside that one building!" It could be why no one there had recognized her sister. "So Autumn could be working *here*." She looked around, hope warring with her hangover.

"Not likely." Even frowning he was attractive. "Because we're in the gambling industry here, we screen all our employees too carefully and too often for a runaway's false ID to pass. At least for long. But I can check. We have photos of every employee on file. And computer software that identifies matches."

She sat forward, telling herself to remain calm. "Does Biamonte have other business, too?" Now that she knew they owned a resort hotel, it only made sense.

"A few. And some apartment complexes."

"And you'll help me find her?"

"I can get access to employment records," he told her, frowning again. "I'm not sure how much help they'll be."

Francesca almost started to cry—an indication of how close to the edge she felt. "They'll be all the help I need," she told him. "Even if she's not there anymore."

He nodded, sitting back in the chair, one ankle crossed over his knee, hands linked over his stomach. His golden brown eyebrows were still furrowed, his expression concerned.

"The office opens at seven. If you let me know where I can reach you, I'll call shortly after that."

Grabbing a pen from her bag, Francesca scribbled her cell phone number on the small square paper napkin under her glass, folded it once and handed it to him. She'd given it to Carl, too, in case Autumn showed up at the bar when she wasn't there.

"Thank you," she said, far more emotionally than she might have done a few months earlier.

"Don't get your hopes up—we might not find anything at all. If she's lying about her name, she could be lying about anything else that might identify her."

He was wasting his time telling her that. She refused to hear it. She returned the pen to her bag, preparing to leave.

She had to get to Guido's—to Carl—before she decided she was just too sick to face him tonight and went home.

That meant wasting a night of surveillance because she'd been weak and stupid and looking for oblivion.

The quesadilla had settled her stomach. Facing Carl was going to be the tough part.

"But you said there are pictures…" She pressed Luke, refusing to be daunted as she remembered something she'd seen the day before. "I caught a glimpse of some files on a desk while I was in Human Resources and they had photos attached."

"A hire photo, yes." He nodded, taking another sip from his nearly empty bottle. "And Biamonte has thousands of employees."

Thousands of photos.

"You've agreed to help me, Everson." She laid a twenty on the table. "I'm not going to give up."

"You're also not going to pay for this," he told her. "Put your money away."

"You don't—"

"I won't," he interrupted. And then, "I work here," he reminded her with a lighter tone. "I have a company account."

Which he certainly didn't have to share with her.

She really liked this man.

Almost as much as she liked Carl.

She'd been in Las Vegas for two weeks, had made two new friends.

Her luck must be changing.

# 9

She had to get to Guido's. Luke watched Francesca Witting stand and tried to talk himself out of opening his mouth with anything but a promise to be in touch.

All he wanted was to sit right where he was and have one more beer before signing the tab and heading home.

She'd said Guido's was only a few blocks from the hotel. He'd never heard of the place.

And he didn't expect to find her little sister at Biamonte, either.

"Francesca." She'd thanked him and he hadn't missed her sincerity. She was walking away.

She turned back, that inch of skin at her waist as interesting from the back as it was from the front.

That didn't make a lot of sense. Other than when he had a woman in his arms and her skin was his for the touching, he was pretty much immune to naked female skin. In Las Vegas it was more commonplace than cheap buffets.

She was looking at him, her brow raised in question over dark eyes that intrigued him. All that darkness. Her hair, her eyes. Tanned skin.

"Did you call me?" She'd walked back to the

table, was standing there with that belly almost at eye level.

"I have an idea where you might find her." Damn, when would he ever learn not to take on responsibilities that weren't his? He already had enough of them at work—and at home.

"Where?" Her eyes were huge as she sank back to the edge of the chair.

"Have you looked on the Internet yet?"

"At missing person's sites?" She was frowning. "We put her picture there."

"No." He shook his head, fairly certain that other options hadn't occurred to her. They weren't ones people like her frequented—or probably even knew about. They weren't ones the police frequented, either, at least to his knowledge. And even if they did, it would take someone who knew Autumn Stevens to recognize her. A headshot probably wouldn't do it. "At the Las Vegas 'for hire' sites."

"Want ads? On the Internet? I didn't even know there was such a thing. You think she'd register there?" She dropped her bag to the floor, leaned forward with both arms on the table. "I doubt she'd use her own name, so how would we even know it was her? I suppose I could just start calling them all…."

"Francesca."

She stopped.

"I'm talking about escort sites." Rubbing at the pain in the back of his neck, he added, "There are hundreds of them."

"Escorts or sites?"

"Sites. Thousands of escorts."

"Oh."

She understood what he was saying. Her shoulders drooped. And her eyes lost the light of hope they'd been carrying most of the evening.

While Luke suspected that this side of Vegas was something only people who'd actually seen it would grasp, he could almost see her preparing herself.

Figuring that plain speech was kindest, he said, "There are many different Web sites, many businesses and some independents, too. Girls are ranked by age—or by other interests that may attract their clients...."

"Interests?"

Luke's respect for her went up another notch. She wasn't going to spare herself.

"You know, those who want fantasy, or mature women, or buxom ones...."

Her face expressionless, she gave one small nod of acknowledgement.

"There are pictures and descriptions for every girl who has a listing."

"And you think Autumn's there."

Wishing he still had that beer, Luke looked her straight in the eye. "I think, considering the fact that she's a runaway who's been in this town a long time, obviously using false identification—which means no social security number and thereby eliminating any chance for a legitimate job—it's a possibility."

Chin forward, Francesca nodded again. Very slowly. "I'm not going to find her at Biamonte," she said.

The crowds in the walkway just outside the lounge

were growing larger—their movement more halting. By midevening they'd be at a standstill as people waited just to walk through.

He didn't get the pleasure in that.

"Not unless she used her real name, or had some way to obtain a real social security number for a bogus name. Every single Biamonte employee is verified through the Social Security Administration."

He'd known he couldn't let her go without telling her that. Even though her eyes showed her emotional exhaustion. And, when he'd said he'd help her, she'd smiled a real smile.

"She could have legally changed her name."

He looked at her, certain she knew better than that. "Not while she's a runaway minor. If the law enforcement you've contacted has anything on the ball, the minute she tries to access her social security number the police will be notified."

John, the bartender whom he'd known for years, caught his eye, brow raised in question.

Luke shook his head.

"So how do I find these sites?"

"Get on a search engine and type in Las Vegas prostitutes. You'll have plenty of choices."

Her skin paled. "You sure know a lot about them."

He forgave her the accusation in her voice. He'd probably have handled himself much less circumspectly if it had just been suggested that *his* younger sister—not that he had one—was being used by men like himself who knew exactly where to find them.

"I've never been with an escort or hired a

woman's services in my life,'' he told her quietly. ''But you don't grow up a guy in Las Vegas without hearing about them. Or how to access them. And you don't grow up a guy in Las Vegas without being curious enough to at least have a look.''

Francesca swallowed. Picked up her bag. Hugged it against her.

''I don't have a computer.''

''I have one in my office. You're welcome to use it.''

''Okay.'' She didn't look as if she had the energy to keep her eyes open, much less spend hours staring at a computer screen.

''Tomorrow?''

''If that's the soonest you can do it.''

''It's probably the soonest you can do it,'' he told her, smiling gently. There was nothing about this woman that said ''take care of me.'' On the contrary, she was completely self-sufficient, bruised and battered, yet standing with fists at the ready. Luke found that he *wanted* to help her.

''If I'm not looking at a computer someplace, I'm going to be spending the next few hours at Guido's,'' she said, not moving a muscle.

''I have the evening free,'' Luke heard himself say. ''If you'd like to go up now, we can start checking them out.''

He'd have to call home first, make sure his mother had eaten and was content ensconced in front of the classic-movie channel. He'd spoken to her just before he'd run into Francesca and she'd been having a good day.

"If you're sure you're free…"

He wasn't free. He wasn't ever going to be free. Even after his mother left this world, her influence would remain with Luke—as the episode with Melissa over the weekend had made painfully evident.

But right now, he had the time to help an admirable woman who no longer knew where to turn.

It was the best he could do.

*Fetish?* What, exactly, was that? Francesca didn't want to know, not in this context, anyway. It was the first word she saw on the first page Luke brought up. Before she looked away.

"Have a seat," he said, vacating his chair to give her access to the computer mouse.

"I'd rather just stand if that's okay with you."

He'd shed his suit jacket. His shoulders seemed even broader in the starched white shirt, his blond hair half an inch from touching the collar. And if she stared at those shoulders, she couldn't see the computer screen….

"For that matter, here's her picture. You look." She pulled a copy of the photo from a side pocket of her bag, set it on the desk. But she knew he couldn't do this for her, that she had to look at those photos.

But not until he'd at least seen a picture of the real Autumn Stevens. The one Francesca cried for almost every night lately.

"Chances are she's going to look quite different," he said, although he had to realize it'd been her desperation talking.

"I know," she told him, moving forward once again. "The police already warned me that she'll have changed in any way she can to avoid detection. I'm sure she's cut and dyed her hair."

"On one of these sites she could easily be wearing a wig. And enough makeup to change her eye shape or the shape of her mouth, depending on who did her photos."

Francesca continued to focus on the image of the Autumn she knew while she fought with herself.

*You want to do this.*

No, she really didn't.

*You want to find her.*

Not here. Not like this.

"Okay," she told him. "Let's take them systematically from the top so we're sure we don't miss any."

He moved the blinking cursor arrow to the top of the list. College girls. Francesca held her breath. He clicked.

And the screen filled with a couple of paragraphs claiming that their college girls were the youngest legally available. Firm. And fun. To the left was a list of names.

There was no Joy among them.

With his right hand dropping to the desk, Luke asked, "Now what?"

"Let's do it." The words were sharp. "Start at the top."

*Storm Hunter.*

She couldn't be more than twenty. Had long brown hair that hung down seductively at her side as she lowered her head. Her eyes were big and brown and accentuated with dark makeup. Her mouth slightly open. Moist. Red. And she was completely naked.

Her breasts were huge. In the middle of the computer screen and staring straight out. She was sitting with her legs spread, and while there was a bit of blurring across her crotch, the black hair was obvious. As were her fingers as she touched herself.

If Autumn had ever done that...

If someone had seen her that way, stood before her with a camera...

Tears sprang to her eyes and, as embarrassed as she was, Francesca couldn't seem to blink them away.

Warm fingers threaded through hers, not intimately, just connecting. "It's okay."

She couldn't look at him. Just kept staring at the screen.

"Nope," Francesca said when she could speak. "She's fairly small-busted."

This wasn't her sister they were talking about. It couldn't be. It was a job. *Detach.*

Yes, detach. Take a deep breath. And another. She could do this.

"Don't let that blind you." Luke's voice sounded very loud suddenly. She'd thought he was much farther away. "She could've had them done."

"A runaway? If she had that kind of money she wouldn't need to be here." She was decisive. Professional.

"And if she works for any of these escort companies, they could've paid for it. Like an investment.''

Last night's alcohol took another wrong turn in her stomach. Pain shot through her head, leaving her in a numbed haze.

Jessica was a redhead. She had smaller breasts. Smaller everything. She was cute. And claimed to be soft enough for even the most discriminating man.

Amanda knew every hot spot in Vegas and was always up for a good time.

Lillian loved to travel and would go anywhere.

Francesca took a deep breath as they finished the first list. Autumn wasn't there.

The next link was only one word. *Exotic.*

Luke clicked quickly. And then again. Bringing up several girls in short order before he closed that page.

''They're all Asian,'' he said.

''Guess it would be too much to hope that all these lists would be that easy?''

He turned, glanced up at her with eyes so compassionate she had the urge to hug him. Until she remembered that she was detached. Safe. Distant. Unmoved.

*Buxom* was next.

*Gross* was more like it.

After that were the strippers.

As they moved through the list, she and Luke developed a system. Standing beside him, her brief brush of his upper arm translated into the next click.

When they got to the fantasy screen, she had to look away. And detach herself all over again. The first click showed a guy and a girl.

The girl's name was Joy.

She couldn't have been more than eighteen.

She had short blond hair. Francesca looked away again. None of the photos of this girl were nude. Suggestive, yes. A butt shot in a thong. But not nude.

The hum of the computer's hard drive overwhelmed the room. Luke didn't move. Francesca pulled air into her lungs. Exhaled slowly. Inhaled again.

And went back to work.

The girl's hair was blond. It seemed to be her original color. Was there some comfort to be had in that? Even if nothing else was as it had once been?

"Steady." Luke grabbed her hand as she swayed.

"Sorry," she said, breathing, and he let her go. She had to regulate her breathing. She'd gone overboard on the deep breaths. That was all.

In through the nose. Out through the mouth. Every relaxation technique taught the same thing.

She glanced back again. The hair was still blond. The girl was standing to the side of a pole, holding on with both hands.

Francesca made it to the chin and had to stop but didn't look away. It was a chin. Everyone had them.

The lips were painted and parted in such a seductive expression that their natural shape was unrecognizable.

Which was fine with her. She almost made it to the nose, promising herself she was going to do it, and then, against every bit of determination she had, her gaze jumped up to the hair again.

Shoulders squared, Francesca tried again. And

again. She just could not meet those eyes. They'd tell everything.

Luke said nothing. He didn't rush her. Didn't ask if she was ready to move on. Didn't ask if this Joy was her Joy. Her Autumn.

There was another pose on the page. The girl was standing, hands on knees, with her backside, naked except for a thong, facing the camera. She was peering at the viewer over her left shoulder.

Francesca couldn't look. In her desperation to escape the sight, her gaze landed on the girl's face. On the teasing smile. The pert little nose.

And the eyes.

Once there, Francesca couldn't look away. Heart pounding, she stared. And stared.

The face wasn't Autumn's at all. The cheekbones were too high. The eyes closer together.

"Her eyes are brown."

"Mmm-hmm." She would always remember this man in this moment, staring straight ahead. Giving her the space she needed, the privacy she needed, while staying so close she couldn't possibly feel alone.

"Autumn's eyes are blue."

"Color-tinted contacts are fairly common."

"You can change hair, add plastic to body parts, colorize, lose weight or gain it, but you can't change the person looking out from a woman's eyes. That's not Autumn."

"Should we keep going?"

Oh, God. For that brief moment she'd forgotten. This one photo wasn't all or nothing. It meant simply that they hadn't found Autumn yet. If she left any site unseen, she wouldn't know that her baby sister wasn't there.

She'd have to find out, just so she could rest. The alternatives—finding Autumn's picture or going away wondering—were equally inconceivable to her.

"Ready?" he asked.

She nodded, forgetting that he was facing forward and couldn't see her.

"Yes," she whispered.

He'd said there were hundreds of these pages.

She shouldn't have been so quick to give up her chance to sit.

Brushing his upper arm, Francesca took another couple of deep breaths and went back to work. This was how she survived.

By detaching herself. Pretending, in those moments that were too difficult to bear, that her problems belonged to someone else. Pretending she was on the outside looking in.


"Tell me about yourself."

"What's to know?" Arnold Jackson shrugged, a bit uncomfortable in the less-formal polo shirt and cotton slacks he was wearing.

"If I had the answer to that, I wouldn't have asked." Sheila Miller smiled over her shot of Chivas in the intimate lounge outside town.

He toyed with the rim of his whiskey glass, not unhappy to be there. "I used to be a pretty damn good sky diver."

He'd figured his largely impersonal answer would

disappoint her. Still, as the enthusiasm in her gaze grew dimmer, Arnold knew an unexpected regret.

"Yeah, and I was a ballet dancer," she told him, her strong but slender fingers raising the glass to lips that had appeared in his thoughts a time or two lately. "So, now we've got that out of the way, is there any point in asking again? Or are we just going to skip right back to analyzing possibilities in the big scam?"

That conversation had monopolized their time together the previous Saturday night when she'd surprised him at work. She'd invited him for a drink. He'd had nowhere else to be.

And enjoyed himself far more than he'd expected to. Arnold Jackson had spent so many years loving an ex-wife who no longer wanted him, the idea of being excluded from intimate relationships had become habit.

"What do you want to know?"

Her grin was cute. The fact that it reached her eyes satisfied him.

"You married?"

"No."

"Ever been?"

"Yes."

"And?"

He leaned forward, pinning her with a stare that served him well when a drunk was getting rowdy at his table. "And I'm divorced. Six years. She lives in Arizona and, no, I don't have contact with her."

Not personal contact. That was a little hard to manage these days. He wasn't sure he loved her anymore, either, he'd been shocked to find as he'd done some soul-searching this past week. At least not as anything more than once-close friends.

Sheila had a powerful gaze of her own. And didn't hesitate to use it. "Any children?"

This was territory she wasn't welcome to enter. No matter how many times he'd thought about her recently.

"Nope."

She nodded. "Well fair's fair. What do you want to know about me?"

How soon she'd go to bed with him.

"The same."

"Never been married, so never divorced and consequently no contact with him, either."

"And children?"

She grinned. "Nope."

Arnold motioned for another round of drinks. It was Friday night. Still early. He'd ask for dinner menus, too.

And then, maybe, he'd see about bed.

# 10

Francesca played things a little differently Saturday night. Dressed in a black leather skirt, black ankle boots and a tight silver lamé top—one she'd bought at the mall on the Strip that evening after leaving her "day job"—she chose a table for two along the back wall at Guido's.

"If I were a sensitive guy, I'd think you were avoiding me." Carl showed up at her table, margarita in hand, while she was still perusing the menu.

"I was going to order club soda," she told him, making herself meet that calm, kind gaze.

Which, considering the embarrassment burning through her, wasn't easy.

"It's on the house." He set the glass down. "And will be followed by a soda chaser."

The world didn't have enough men like him. "I wasn't avoiding you. I ran into someone who thought she knew my friend."

She told him about Biamonte's. And the Bonaparte. And wasn't really sure why, when she told him about the head of security at the Bonaparte, she didn't mention that Luke was relatively young and good-looking or that she'd spent hours late at night looking at Web sites with him.

"So did he get back to you this morning regarding your friend's employment?"

"Only to say it would have to wait until Monday."

And to extend an offer to accompany her to Guido's that night. An offer she'd quickly refused.

She couldn't afford to complicate her life.

"And in the meantime, you've decided to join the fray," Carl said, indicating the table she'd chosen right in the middle of the space that, an hour from now, would be crowded with the young girls who regularly hung out at Guido's.

"Watching from afar, looking lost and alone and in need of a friend, hasn't done the trick."

He looked good, solid. His shoulders filling out his polo shirt, hips lean in the close-fitting jeans, had become familiar to her. Even in this short time.

"Drink the margarita slowly," he warned, one foot on the chair opposite her, his round tray resting on the upraised knee. "A soda won't seem as friendly."

Francesca smiled. She just couldn't help it. "Carl, thanks for the other night."

He didn't glance away, but the expression in his eyes was no longer as open.

"I'm really sorry."

"Don't be." Brushing her cheek with the back of his forefinger, he stood. "I'm the one who should apologize. I served you all those drinks."

"Only because I insisted." That much she remembered. "And you didn't let me drive. Thank you."

Free hand sliding into his pocket, Carl looked toward the bar. "No problem. Anytime."

He was going to walk away. She couldn't let him. "Carl."

He turned back with a raised brow, watching her silently.

"If I did anything or—"

"Nothing happened."

"Something did. I was in no state to have undressed myself."

Sinking into the chair, Carl took her hand where it lay on the table. He peered at her from eyes slightly lowered. "Although it took more self-control than I knew I possessed, I didn't look," he told her. And then, as she felt heat moving up her body to burn her face, he continued. "If and when I see you naked, it will be with your full cooperation and participation."

"Okay." She smiled in spite of herself. He had a way of getting that response from her. "That's a deal."

Not that she could imagine a day when she'd be either cooperating or participating. She'd have told him so then, but his gaze was warm again, and if she'd learned anything in the past year, it was that one could never predict the future.

Carl stood, still holding her hand. "There's one thing I saw, though," he told her, the somber look in his dark eyes warning her. Until that moment she'd forgotten—she'd been so drunk, and it'd been years since her stepfather had been an issue. It wasn't like she ever saw the scars herself.

Forcing herself to meet his eyes again, she just shook her head.

He nodded and then said he'd put in an order for pizza.

He was giving her time. But that last look he'd sent her told her he wasn't giving up. And Francesca realized anew why she lived her life alone.

When people got close, things got messy.


"Why aren't you out tonight?"

Luke shrugged, lifting his wineglass to his lips, trying to avoid his mother's eyes as she stared at him across the dining room table. Saturday night, eating lamb chops at home with his mother.

The story of his life.

But not for long. He'd had some news that day. News he wanted to sit and quietly savor.

"What happened to that woman you've been seeing?"

"What woman?" He'd purposely never mentioned Melissa.

"I don't know, you didn't say, but you've been doing something besides working these past months. And you don't shower and shave twice in a day just to go out for a beer."

"How do you know I wasn't volunteering at the center?"

It was something he'd been doing on and off for years. Spending time with young boys at a crisis center in town that temporarily housed youth up to ten years of age when the courts removed them from abusive homes. They came and went so quickly he hardly ever knew their names. He just played basketball.

"Is that where you met her?"

Luke stopped, glass in midair, peering across at the woman who'd given him life—and then prevented him from living it. He *had* met Melissa at the center.

"There is no *her*."

His mother's lamb chops lay untouched on her plate. "What happened this time?"

Why, for once, couldn't she leave him to enjoy something? Even if it was still only a possibility at this point. The agent from Colter had called him that afternoon. She thought she had a son for him.

Or would have in about six months. As soon as he was born.

"Luke? What happened?"

Setting down his glass with more force than he should have, Luke picked up his knife and fork, attacking meat so tender he didn't need a knife to cut it. All he wanted was a few minutes to himself. "This conversation is going nowhere."

"I want you to be happy, Luke."

The soft words stopped him. They'd sounded so...rational. Sincere.

"I'm happy enough, Mom." It was true. For the most part he had a good life. A job that challenged him. One he was good at. He lived in a beautiful home. Had no financial worries. And a couple of relationships with people he trusted—which made him richer than most.

And now, perhaps, a son. He wouldn't hope yet.

It didn't pay to hope too much or too early. But there was satisfaction in knowing that the possibility was there. Beginning to exist.

"You need a family."

Could she read his mind?

"I have one."

"In addition to me. You're thirty-five years old. You need a woman."

Why tonight? His mother had had a good day. He'd planned to go home, lose himself in some good wine, and think about a future that would be different from anything that had come before.

"I'm serious, Luke."

He cut. Chewed. Swallowed. When she was well, his mother was an excellent cook. One of the best.

"I know, Mom."

"I ask a lot of you, Luke, but I'd rather die than be responsible for ruining your life."

*Ruin* was too strong a word. "You haven't ruined my life," he told her, his fork piercing a floret of broccoli to scrape against the Bavarian china that was their everyday dinner wear.

"So what happened?"

"To what?" The potato soufflé was perfect. The steamed vegetables more flavorful than he'd had in any restaurant.

"The woman."

For some reason, the words conjured up the woman he'd met—for the second time—the night before. Her quest intrigued him.

Not that his mother knew anything about that kind

of world, the world he and Francesca were investigating.

He looked up at her over the cherrywood table. Dressed in a canary-yellow pantsuit, her dyed brown hair expensively styled, she could've been any of the socially prominent women that quietly wielded their influence in this man's town. She wasn't eating. And was starting to curl the corner of her place mat. It was one of the lace ones that she washed, starched and ironed with such care every single time she used them.

"Nothing happened."

"So why aren't you with her tonight?"

*Tonight in particular because you didn't need me here, you mean?* He wanted to ask, but wouldn't. "I'm home on a lot of Saturday nights."

"Not when you get off work early, like you did today."

Not when she was well.

"Then who would've enjoyed this wonderful dinner?"

"I could have called the Allens," she said, her fingers moving more quickly. They'd always been frail-looking to him, but with age had become almost translucent. "And it would be fine for dinner tomorrow, too."

Luke's attention was on those fingers. "Okay, Mom, if I tell you something, will you promise me you won't make too much of it—and that you'll take a few bites of this incredible meal?"

The jerkiness of her nod caught at his heart even now. After all this time, he still couldn't stand to see her struggle. Dealing with her after she'd lost control, when she wasn't aware and wouldn't remember, was much easier.

"I've tried, honestly tried, to find a woman I want to spend the rest of my life with. It just doesn't happen." And that was all he'd ever tell her about that.

"You just haven't met the right one, then," she said shakily. "You have to keep looking, Luke. Your father was in his thirties when we met. You should be out tonight...." Her volume was growing with every word. He had to distract her fast.

"Mom, I said I had something to tell you. That wasn't it."

"What then?"

"I *am* interested in having a family."

"You have to have a wife for that, Luke." Her tone wasn't quite at the panic stage. Not yet.

"Mom." He patted her hand. "I'll do almost anything for you, you know that, but I can't get married to make you feel better."

"I understand, Luke. I would never expect that." The fingers were working so quickly the movement was almost inhuman. And mesmerizing in its dexterity and rhythm. "It's just that..."

Her gaze centered on the table, she appeared to be staring someplace far, far away. And while there was little he wouldn't do to avoid one of her anxiety attacks, he refused to lie to her, or tie himself up in a marriage he didn't want just to reassure her.

Even if it worked for a while, there was one thing he'd learned over the years. With Carol Everson, nothing worked for long.

"I'm adopting a son."

Fingers still frantically engaged, she looked over at him.

"I wasn't planning to tell you until I knew more, but you'll have to know soon enough, as you're going to be his grandmother and I'm going to need lots of help."

Most of which he planned to get from the full-time nanny he'd decided to hire. Something he'd always wished his father had done.

Carol had been adamantly opposed to it, of course, and Marshall hadn't been willing to take away her sense of self-worth, her value as a mother.

At least, that was what Luke had been told on the one occasion he'd asked his father why he'd spent so much time alone with her as a child.

She was staring at him now, expression blank.

Carol hadn't been as ill then. Medication had done a lot. She hadn't needed round-the-clock care. Those episodes had come later—when Luke had been older, going out into the world by himself, and she'd become obsessed with the fear that something would happen to him.

Marshall claimed that was when the episodes grew into full-blown panic states he could no longer handle with a phone call.

Luke knew she'd found her way back to the present, to their conversation, when her fingers slowed. "What did you just say?"

"I'm adopting a son."

"A boy from the center?" Her voice was shaky but rational.

"A baby. From an agency."

The corner of the place mat fell back to the table. "When?"

He nodded toward her plate. "You promised."

She took a bite. And then another, and the muscles in Luke's back relaxed.

A trip into hell avoided.

And all he'd had to do was adopt a son.

"So, where you from?"

It took Francesca a second to realize the girl was talking to her. For more than half an hour she'd been sitting there, in the midst of a growing crowd of young people—mostly women—and while she'd made eye contact a time or two, smiled, there'd been no move to include her in the group.

"Sacramento," she said now. She'd been wondering how she was going to make the margarita, ice mostly melted, last much longer.

"When did you get to Vegas?"

"A couple of weeks ago."

The girl, a blonde as most of them were, was wearing a pair of the shortest denim shorts Francesca had ever seen. There was barely enough fabric to hold the silver studs that decorated them. She stood, hands on the back of the empty chair at Francesca's table.

Should she ask her to sit? She didn't want to appear too eager.

"Mind if I borrow this chair?" the girl asked.

"No, go ahead." So how *was* she going to make her margarita last?

"You sure? You aren't waiting for anyone?"

"Nope." Francesca punched her straw in and out of the large round glass.

After an odd, almost searching look, the girl pulled the chair out from the table and turned away.

So much for that.

Carl delivered her pizza about an hour into the evening. Along with a full margarita glass.

"Anything else I can get for you?" he asked loudly enough for anyone around her who was listening to hear.

"No, thanks" were the words she said, but her eyes begged him for a diet cola. She was thirsty and if she ate, would soon be more so.

Leaning down, he picked a fallen napkin off the floor. "It's virgin."

She barely caught the words as he stood.

"What's with Dr. Bishop's new receptionist?"

Sipping her drink, waiting for the pizza to cool, Francesca had been catching snippets of many conversations.

"Is she a bitch or what?" It was the girl who'd borrowed her chair.

"I thought it was just me she hated," a third girl said. There were five of them sitting around the table directly in front of Francesca. They'd been pouring down beers so fast it was a wonder they weren't all plastered to the floor.

"Hey, Chancey, you met Dr. Bishop's new receptionist yet?" one of the girls asked a pinched-looking young woman at another table.

"Yeah," Chancey said. "Last week…my…"

*Dammit, people, be quiet! I can't hear.* It had sounded like this Chancey had said she'd had a D & C.

Francesca leaned her arms on the table, attempting to catch any word that might float in her direction, but whatever else Chancey had to say was lost to her.

The short redhead was cute, if a little thin. And young.

A tall, big-boned brunette at the same table leaned back in her chair just as Francesca started in on the pizza.

"You new here?"

"Yeah."

The other girls at her table were watching. Francesca wondered if they wanted her pizza.

"How'd you hear about Guido's?"

Visually perusing them all, assessing, Francesca debated telling them she'd just been in the area, seen the place, decided to drop in.

"I've seen you in here before," the girl continued. "At the bar." She sounded more curious than anything.

"I'm staying not too far from here."

"Oh, yeah? Where?"

"The Lucky Seven." What could it hurt for them to know?

The girl steadied herself with a hand on Francesca's table. "So no one told you about this place?"

Dropping her pizza back on the thin aluminum

serving pan, she looked at the other girls watching her. More than just the one tableful was paying attention.

"Actually I met a couple of girls on the street," she said clearly, relying completely on instincts that, in her previous life, had almost never steered her wrong. "They told me this was a safe place for a girl alone to hang out."

Conversation resumed around her.

"Cool." The athletic girl, chin slightly jutted, nodded and dropped her chair back to her table.

"You're welcome to join us." Her back was turned to Francesca as she issued the invitation.

Francesca accepted, anyway.

Over the next hour, the girls ordered pizza. And drank. They talked about movies. And boys. College-entrance exams. And cosmetology school. The crowd had been growing progressively louder in proportion to the amount of beer they were consuming.

"It looks like I'm going to be out of here for a while." Francesca stiffened at the odd tone of voice behind her. There'd been a definite teariness there.

Enough to distract her from the conversation at her own table.

"Are you sure?"

She didn't know how many people were sitting behind her, but couldn't miss how quiet they'd all grown.

"Yeah. I just need Dr. Bishop's clearance."

That name again.

"The jerk claimed Star had an STD."

Sexually transmitted disease. Fabulous news. And who was the jerk? Dr. Bishop? Or someone else?

"Did you?" The words were slurred and directly behind Francesca's head.

"Not unless yeast infections have suddenly been recategorized." The girl they were referring to as Star stumbled over the last word and they all laughed. And then spent the next five minutes mimicking her and laughing some more.

It was Sunday morning and he was going to relax. To put on comfortable shorts, a T-shirt, sandals, and just walk.

"But it's hot out," his mother had exclaimed when he'd mentioned his plans over the blueberry muffins she'd made for breakfast. She'd been on her way to church with the Allens.

She'd been right, too, he found as he pulled his shirt away from his sweat-soaked back for the third time in the ten minutes he'd been out. Of course, being on the street made it worse. Blacktop not only soaked up the heat, it seemed to send it outward in shimmering waves. He felt it through the bottoms of his feet.

People were on the Strip in droves, never mind that it was ten o'clock on a Sunday morning. Not that Luke was among them. No, the less-traveled side streets were fine for now. But he could see the crowds every time he came to a corner. Sometimes forty or fifty or more crossing the street. In all manner of dress. Ranging from absurdly dressy to ridiculously underdressed. There were tennis shoes and fanny packs—mostly on ladies over fifty. Knee-length sweat shorts and bottom-hugging cotton ones. Bellies out. And bellies in. Spaghetti-strap dresses with spike heels.

Great walking shoes.

There were men, too. He just didn't look at them much.

He used to walk the Strip on a regular basis, finding within the frenetic activity a kind of escape. The wall-to-wall traffic, cabs slipping in and out of spaces that weren't big enough for a car to fit, the endless noise, were great distractions.

This was the first day he'd taken off work in almost a month. He'd debated going in, anyway—as he had every other day he'd been scheduled off since this new string of wins had begun—and could still end up doing so. But first, he was walking.

Nowhere in particular. He'd told his mother that when she'd asked. And the Allens, too. He was fairly certain he'd convinced himself.

It wasn't like he had any real idea where he'd find her, anyway. There were hundreds of phone booths in Las Vegas. And what seemed like hundreds of side streets off the Boulevard.

He should have asked her.

Or stayed home.

Or gone to work.

# *11*

---

"Luke, what are you doing here?"

Francesca's head spun as she jumped up off the hard cement, McDonald's cup in hand. The day's lethargy had already begun.

His eyes were wide as he gave her a once over. "My God, you weren't kidding!"

"What?"

"The homeless bit. I would've walked right past."

"You seem to have a habit of doing that." After several hours in the hot sun, and on a street filled with busy and largely dissatisfied people, she was relieved to see a familiar face. Relieved and hopeful... "Did you find out something, after all? You could've called. I always have my cell." She pulled it out of one pocket of the torn and dirty denim bag she carried.

"I wouldn't let too many people see that," Luke said. "Kind of blows the image."

He stood there, hands in his pockets, a friend in a very troubled world.

"And no, I don't have any new information. I guess I was just curious."

"About how the homeless half live?" She held up her battered cup with fingerless gloves.

It was a good thing she wasn't trying to impress this man.

"No, although I guess I should be."

She couldn't really read his expression. Not only was he squinting against the sun's brightness, but he was wearing a pair of expensive-looking sunglasses.

Like the ones floating around somewhere in her duffel at the Lucky Seven. From what she'd observed, homeless people just squinted a lot.

"Curious about what then?"

"You."

Oh.

"Luke," she started, thinking quickly. She didn't want any emotional complications. But now was not the time to offend him. She needed his help.

And then there was Carl....

"I'm only in town long enough to find my sister and then I'll probably never come back here again," she said, watching as a young couple walked by so engrossed in each other it was as if they were on another planet. Who could stand to have their arms around each other and cuddle so close in this heat, she had no idea. "I have to admit I'm not particularly fond of your town."

"I'm not all that fond of it myself." If his grimace as he glanced toward the Strip was anything to go by, he wasn't just sparing her feelings. "And I also don't want you to get the wrong idea. I wasn't putting any moves on you."

"Oh." *Well, take that, Francesca.* "Okay. Good."

"Not that I wouldn't want to, mind you, but my

life is complicated right now. And so, as you've said, is yours."

"Yes, sir, it is."

"I'd like to help you, though, if I can," he said, glancing around her nesting place. "I've never met anyone like you, with no limit to what you'll ask of yourself for someone you love."

Or was her quest to find Autumn just a reason to survive?

If she'd been so selfless two years earlier, or even before that, could she have made a difference?

"You having any luck?"

She jiggled her cup. "A couple bucks." Which she'd pass on to the first homeless person she saw later that afternoon.

He grinned. "That's not what I meant."

The traffic on the corner was heavy today, with a backup of two to three cars at any given time. They were mostly older cars, typical of the neighborhood. So far this morning, the only happy people she'd noticed had been that young couple.

"Not here," she said, backing up to the wall where, days ago, she'd discovered an illusion of shade offered by a six-inch overhang of roof. "Last night I sat with a group of girls at the bar." She told him about the conversation she'd overheard.

"Sounds like Bishop's a gynecologist."

"Yeah." She'd wanted to be wrong. "The talk was all pretty generic once I joined the group, but I caught a few comments made quietly at the table, between two of the women when they thought no one else was listening."

The young couple was still there. Down the street. Sitting on a metal bench at the bus stop. The guy, wearing baggy jeans and a white muscle shirt, held the girl as though she were the most fragile thing on earth. Her hair, a mixture of blond-and-brown streaks, appeared to be hastily chopped; it almost matched the young man's deeply tanned skin as it rested against his shoulder.

"They were talking about some guy getting them jobs," she said, glancing back at Luke. "From what I could gather, the jobs take the girls away for a while and then they're back, waiting to be called again."

He acknowledged what she was saying with nothing more than a slight bending of his head. But it was enough.

"The guy's their pimp, isn't he?" She didn't really need his confirmation.

"Or he could be an agent looking for dancers or some other part in a show that's only running for a short time."

"Dancers who all use the same gynecologist?"

Sweat trickled down between her breasts. She ignored it.

"And what about the girl who had to be cleared because they thought she had a sexually transmitted disease?" Didn't seem much point in maintaining decorum in this conversation after the things she'd seen with him the other night.

"That's a little harder to explain."

"I think Autumn used to be one of them."

"Why?"

"She was there. Had a job. Left. Came back. And now she's gone again. It makes sense that she's... working." Her voice didn't quite break, but she couldn't stop the tears that rushed to her eyes.

She'd thought she'd cried them all last night. Alone in her bed at the Lucky Seven. Nothing she did could wipe away the images of her baby sister, naked with some man, allowing him to do any number of demeaning and damaging things.

"Hey." He tilted her chin with the side of his hand, rubbing lightly before letting her go. "No point in torturing yourself with what you don't know yet."

She nodded. Took a deep breath. He was right, of course.

A group of giggling college-age girls walked by, bumping into Luke. "Sorry," one said, and then looked up at him. "Really," she said, as her entire demeanor changed from self-absorption to interest.

"It's okay."

One more quick look and then she was past, her long exposed legs firm and young, saying something to her friends that had them all turning around.

"You get that reaction a lot?" Francesca asked.

"Some." He wasn't watching the girls depart; he was watching her. "So did you learn anything else last night?"

Yeah. She didn't want to do this anymore. "One of the girls looked barely old enough to drive, let alone drink beer," she said, remembering the girl they'd called Chancey. "I asked Carl about it later, after they'd all gone home, and he said they all have

IDs that say they're of legal age to drink. He always checks.''

''Which is all he's required to do.''

''There's no way she was eighteen, let alone twenty-one.''

''He could call the cops.''

Carl wouldn't do that. They'd all just go somewhere else. Someplace less safe. She understood that.

And was actually glad. Picturing Autumn at Guido's was a comfort compared to the rest of the images she'd encountered since arriving in this town.

''The same girl, she'd apparently just finished a job,'' Francesca said, wishing she could slide back down to the ground. She was tired. ''Somebody asked her something, I didn't quite get it, but I think it was about a recent job.''

''What did she say?''

''Nothing.'' Francesca pictured again the vision of little Chancey sitting there, looking so young and lost and alone. ''Her eyes filled up as if she was going to cry, but she didn't. No one said anything, but it seemed they were all watching out for her the rest of the night.''

Francesca had wanted to take the little redhead home with her. But then she'd need to ferret out every bit of information she could, call the girl's mom and deliver her safely home to bed.

Life didn't work that way.

And these days she could barely get herself home to bed.

''I think some guy abused her.'' She hadn't really

meant to say the words out loud. Didn't want any validation for them.

For once, Luke's silence wasn't reassuring.

She hadn't thought about suicide in a long time. Not since she was thirteen. She remembered because she'd just gotten her period for the first time and Cesca had been home and helped her get all the stuff she needed. She'd taught her how to use tampons.

And after Cesca had left that night, her father had found the box of them in her bathroom. She'd been in her bedroom when he'd come storming in, hollering horrible things about her and her morals, and her desire to stick things up there. Scared to death and grossed out, she'd made the mistake of telling him she hadn't bought them, Francesca had.

She couldn't even think about what he'd done then—except to thank God that his abuse had never involved him taking off his pants. All she remembered was that when he'd finally finished hitting her, she'd wanted to die. She'd spent hours considering options, might even have taken one of them if she hadn't been too beat up to move. But sometime during that night, something inside her had changed. She'd been thinking about her big sister. And the way Francesca could always make something horrible look better.

Though they never talked about it, probably because Cesca had some crazy idea of protecting her, Autumn knew that her father had beaten Cesca worse than he'd ever beaten her. She'd come home from next door one time when they'd thought she was at a party.

She'd seen them in the living room, the belt flying, Francesca bleeding.

Right after that, Cesca had left.

Autumn had known on her thirteenth birthday that she had to do the same thing. She'd started saving that very day. Every bit of her birthday money—which she'd been planning to use to buy herself the coolest clothes on the planet—had been carefully hidden. As had every other dime she could get her hands on.

She'd just never realized how much it cost to live. Everything cost money. Hell, even going to the toilet cost money 'cause you had to pay the water bill and buy toilet paper.

As Autumn lay in her bed that hot Wednesday night in July, it all seemed too much for her. She couldn't even go to the toilet for free. If she said that to Chancey, her friend would've had something smart to say—something that would've made them both laugh.

But Chancey was gone, the job cut prematurely short. Autumn hoped the other girl was okay. No one would tell her anything.

She'd seen blood, though. Lots of it. Coming from the other girl's shorts when they'd carried her out of the apartment. Any way you looked at it, that couldn't be good. And she couldn't even tell Matteo about it.

Rolling over, cradling her body against the mattress, Autumn thought about ways to die.

\* \* \*

That next week, life took an upward swing for Luke. Or at least, it didn't head down. His mother, busy looking through catalogs of nursery furniture, hadn't had a single episode. She'd even responded affirmatively to a frequently offered but never before accepted invitation to the clubhouse in their gated community for a monthly ladies' luncheon. Betty Allen hadn't gone. But one of the members of the homeowners' association had come to get her and she'd actually had a good time.

She'd been agitated later that night, but Luke had been home and able to get her medication in her before she'd had a breakdown.

There'd been no other big wins anywhere on the Strip. Arnold Jackson, who'd turned up nothing on the streets, was fairly certain that whoever had been behind the wins had decided to call it quits.

Amadeo wasn't going to be satisfied with that. But if Luke could at least have a break from further incidents, he was certain he'd get to the bottom of it. He always did.

He'd just prefer to do so before Amadeo returned from his summer travels.

He intended to get to the bottom of Autumn Stevens's disappearance, too. It had taken four days longer than he'd expected, four days in which he'd either seen or spoken to Francesca at least twice daily, but he finally had some information for her.

He'd asked her to meet him in the lobby of the Bonaparte on Thursday and was taking her to dinner before her nightly stint at Guido's. He was half an hour late, having been waylaid upstairs by a possible room theft that turned out to be a husband taking more than a thousand dollars from his wife's purse and heading downstairs to the tables.

What kind of woman left a thousand dollars lying around in a hotel room?

Francesca wasn't in the lobby. Which meant she'd wandered into the casino. In all the time he'd spent with Francesca Witting during the past week, the only thing he'd found out about her that he didn't understand was how attached she was to slot machines.

The Thursday-evening crowd was thin and it didn't take him long to find her. Completely engrossed in spending two dollars and twenty-five cents with every push of the button.

She'd said she was a photojournalist on leave. She must have been a reasonably successful one. Not that *that* surprised him.

She pushed again. The video reels turned. She'd won bonus play.

That didn't surprise him, either. There was something else he'd learned about Francesca this week. When she wanted something, she made it happen.

"You said you're on leave from your job," Luke said as they left the casino after she'd collected her hundred-dollar win. "Do you work for a Sacramento paper?"

Shoving the money inside her black leather bag, she shook her head. "I'm not working at all right now. But when I did, it was freelance."

His estimation of her rose another notch. And it

had already been pretty damn high. "That's not an easy thing to do."

"Not and make a living at it," she said. "I sacrificed a lot."

Like what?

"Was it worth it?" he asked.

They were heading out to his car and then to a quiet restaurant in Las Vegas proper. The city where the real people lived.

"Mostly, it was."

It wasn't like her to be hesitant. Was it because of those sacrifices she'd mentioned?

"What did you find out?"

She'd waited until they were in the Jag. Francesca had a way of gearing herself up to take bad news.

"I told you it wasn't much."

"I know."

"There's absolutely no record of anyone with your sister's social security number ever having worked at Biamonte. Nor is there an Autumn or a Joy listed in the employment databases."

He was only repeating what he'd already told her. To remind her of the limitations.

"And?"

"Remember I told you we have an imaging system at the Bonaparte that uses computer software to find likenesses in a database? In real time, the cameras can pick a face out of a crowd in a casino and match it to a known card-counter or other counterfeiter in a national database."

"She didn't come up on a national database."

He turned onto the freeway. "No. I just used the imaging equipment to run a match on her photo."

"And?"

Her entire body, from four-inch black sandals to black shorts and white blouse tied above her belly button, was absolutely still.

"I *might* have found a match."

"Where?"

"Biamonte's big on photos," he said. He'd debated even mentioning the day's findings. They were about as weak as they could be without being absolutely nonexistent. But Francesca wasn't a woman you sheltered. "They not only have photo images attached to all employment files, but to all tenant and most contact files, as well. My boss is of the belief that you can't be too careful in this city. He's Italian and figures that in this town, that makes him suspect. He covers every single base to be able to prove at any moment that he and his businesses are on the up-and-up."

Or at least that was what he said, and Luke had no cause to disbelieve him. And just in case he was wrong to trust the older man, Luke had certain key files on his home computer.

"You said you found a match."

"I said I *might* have." He'd had some images scanned—a common practice in his job. It was completely his call, something done when he deemed it appropriate. Possible assistance in locating a runaway, who might or might not have been in the company's employ, was a reason he deemed appropriate. Today they'd shown him a particular picture.

"Where?" She was looking at him, but otherwise still hadn't moved.

"In a file of old tenant photos marked for the shredder."

"How many apartment buildings does Biamonte own?"

"Quite a few. But I have a feeling she wasn't renting from Biamonte, anyway." He signaled, exited the highway. They were in one of the few parts of town he honestly appreciated. A quiet winding road through desert and palm trees eventually wound its way up to a hill-top restaurant.

"I *know* she wasn't renting under the name of Joy or Autumn. But—" she drew in a deep breath "—aside from the name match, which means nothing since we have no idea what she's really calling herself, why don't you think she's a tenant?"

"From what I could tell in the hour or so I had to poke around this afternoon," he continued, "sometime in the past year and a half, Biamonte bought a series of run-down complexes, evicted the current tenants and renovated the places. Now they're rented out for three times what they'd been making. I think these photos were of the old tenants."

"They took pictures of the people they kicked out?"

"Apparently. They were asked to sign a form releasing Biamonte of any future liability, which is all a new owner needs. So I'm not sure why pictures were ever taken. My guess is, someone did it simply because it's Biamonte policy to photograph the parties in any and all business dealings."

"Did you see the forms?"

He shook his head. "I haven't found them yet."

"She's here, you know."

"I—" Luke started to speak, hedging his words, and then realized he didn't have to protect her. Not from the world. And particularly not from herself.

"If I had to place money on it, I'd say you're right." Not that he was a betting man. "And she's been here a while. But that doesn't mean you're going to find her." He glanced over at her. Had to resist the natural inclination to take her hand. "Or that you're going to like what you find if you do."

"I know."

She was staring straight ahead again, her short black hair spiky and cute.

"Can I ask you something?"

She glanced his way and then back. "Of course."

"Do you, by any chance, have Italian ancestry?"

Her head turned and he was driving slowly enough to be able to catch her frown. "Yeah, why?"

"It's something I've wanted my whole life and this damned blond hair never even let me pretend."

She laughed. "Why on earth would you want Italian ancestry?"

At the top of the hill, he pulled into the parking lot. "It's a long story, but it has to do with wanting to be Amadeo Esposito's son."

"You said he's Italian?"

"One hundred percent."

"My father was, too." Her voice was softer than he'd ever heard it.

"Was?"

"He died when I was five."

Luke would have said more, probably crossing a line neither of them was willing to cross, but she saved him by asking, "So why didn't you want to be your own father's son?"

"I did," he said. "My dad was the best. He just had other…responsibilities…and Amadeo, his best friend, always seemed to have whatever time I needed."

Amadeo had been a good friend to Marshall Everson. Marshall had saved Amadeo's life in the Korean War and had a servant in him ever since.

"So what does Amadeo do for a living?"

"He owns Biamonte."

"He's your boss?"

He nodded.

*His boss. And although only the family knew it, his godfather.*

He opened his door, ready to go in, to finish this conversation.

"Luke?" She brushed his upper arm, the lightest of touches and not meant to raise any reaction at all. So he would make sure it didn't. "How much trouble are you going to be in if your boss finds out you're doing this?"

"None." It would just mean answering some questions he'd rather not answer. Another reason to be grateful that Amadeo couldn't tolerate the summer Vegas heat.

Amadeo would make far too much of his willingness to go to such lengths to help Francesca. The old man was almost as eager as Carol to get Luke married off.

And settled permanently in this town.

# 12

Another Friday night at Guido's. The place was beginning to seem like home. Good food. Friends. A sense of belonging.

Even if—except for the food—it was all make-believe.

"I miss having you near me." Carl brought her first margarita over as soon as she arrived—half an hour before the rest of the young people would start wandering in. Dinner with Luke had made her much later the night before.

"I miss it, too," she told him. There was truth in the statement. She wanted Carl's friendship.

But she didn't have room for the complications.

"Thanks for this." She held her glass, took a long drag on the straw. The first was always loaded. The rest would be virgin.

"No problem. You gonna hang around as usual tonight?" Just as she arrived before the rest of her new "friends," Francesca always stayed until after they'd all gone home. To talk to Carl.

"Sure."

He nodded, the crease in his brow fading.

"You think the others are getting curious about the personal service?" he asked, waving his drink tray.

She shrugged. "They don't say."

"Do you mind? Just seemed the easiest way to make sure no one knows there's nothing in them."

She smiled up at him. It felt comforting to be protected. "Mind?" she said. "On the contrary, I'm grateful. I don't know how I'm ever going to repay you for all of this."

"I think I'd be content if I've taught you that you don't have to repay friendship. It just is."

He left before she could respond. But his words rang in Francesca's heart long into the night.

Was that what she thought? That she had to pay for, earn, something as natural and vital as human companionship?

God, she hoped not.

"I'm leaving."

Everyone at the two tables quieted as Chancey made her announcement sometime around ten on Friday night. Francesca, sitting at the same table, had lost count of the number of beers the girl had consumed.

"So soon?" asked Lynn, the athletic girl who'd originally invited Francesca to join them.

"You've got another job already?"

"Are you sure?"

"I'd say no."

The responses came in quick succession. After almost a week with these girls, Francesca was used to the casual references that told her nothing. And growing more frustrated by the hour. When were they going to trust her enough to tell her something real?

Invite her to apply for a job herself?

And what about the few young men who came and went in this group? They seemed to be friends with many of the girls, but special to no one in particular. What part did they play?

"No," Chancey said, her words slurred and loud enough to be heard by anyone in the vicinity. "I mean I'm leaving for good. Leaving Vegas. Everything."

A heavy silence fell. Francesca could feel the tension building—around her and within herself. What was going on?

A couple of girls who'd gone over to shoot pool set down their cues, wandered over.

"I wouldn't do that." Lynn's words dropped into the middle of the suddenly worried-looking group.

"Why not? This is a free country."

"It's not that easy," Wanda said. She was the first girl who'd spoken to Francesca. Not as friendly as the rest, more selfish maybe, or just detached, Francesca wasn't sure which, but she liked her.

"So you're planning to be here forever?" Chancey challenged, her face red with anger where others were lined with concern.

"Don't talk like this, Chance." Leila, a tall skinny blonde who was there almost every night, seemed downright scared. Francesca generally found the girl's comments to be off the mark, as though the physical gifts Leila had been given had come at the cost of some intellectual capacity. Tonight her fear seemed to find its target among many of the other girls.

Of course, fear bred fear. It might be nothing more than that.

"I don't plan to be here forever," Lynn told the group. They'd all gathered around, pulling their chairs closer, each looking around the circle to assess the others' reactions.

Had she been at another table, Francesca would probably have been left out. Because she was sitting by Chancey, she was right in the middle.

She glanced around, from face to face, eye to eye, knowing that the key to finding Autumn was hidden there. She thought about her camera. It would capture those faces, those expressions. Allow her to view them, again and again, until she figured out what messages they were hiding.

"But we have to leave when it's mutually beneficial," Lynn continued. She was the leader of the group. They all listened to her.

And in the week Francesca had been among them, she'd never once seen Lynn misuse the power that gave her.

What kept these girls sitting, night after night, in an out-of-the-way Italian bar in Las Vegas, talking about dreams and aspirations and gynecologists? Not daring to leave this town?

"Look," Wanda said, scooting her chair closer, "we have to tell her."

"Tell me what?" Chancey asked, the muscles in her face going from tight to sunken.

"It has nothing to do with us." Lynn sat back, picked up her beer, drank as though she was in a guzzling contest.

"I know it doesn't." Wanda didn't so much as blink. "But she's relatively new to town. She doesn't know what it's like here."

"Oh, I gotta differ with you there," Chancey said with a bitter chuckle completely lacking in humor.

"No, you really *don't* know," Lynn agreed. The other six or seven girls nodded. Francesca knew a couple of them.

"A few years ago there was this girl," Wanda said. Everyone else sat forward, gazes on the self-contained young woman. Their faces reminded Francesca of a bunch of kids around a campfire, listening to a ghost story with a mixture of curiosity and horror. "She made the headlines all over the state."

"Why?"

"What was her name?" Francesca hadn't meant to speak and, when the girls all looked at her, wished she hadn't. She'd realized from the beginning that names weren't a big deal around here. But having this girl's name would sure make looking up the articles a bit easier.

"She was found out in the desert, and at first the paper said that she'd gone for a hike, gotten lost, died of dehydration...."

Lynn took over the story. "Then it comes out that she'd been dead about a day and there was no sign of dehydration. It looked like she might've been murdered. They said it was likely a drug deal gone bad."

"Yeah," Leila said, the story gaining momentum

with each teller. "And then you hear that there was no evidence of drug use in or on her body, or anywhere near her."

"Next thing they say is that she was hiking, and fell and hit her head on a rock and that's what killed her." This was Wanda again.

"Some papers said that there were traces of alcohol in her body," Leila said. "Others said there was none."

Francesca stared from one girl to the next as they unveiled fact after fact.

"So then it comes out—some hospital employee leaked it and then later lost her job—that she'd been raped," Lynn said.

"Yeah, but there was no semen."

"About a week after the girl turned up, every single one of the papers ran the same story," Wanda told them. "The girl's body had been covered with blood, but not her own as they originally thought. It was cow's blood. And there were traces of raw meat on and around what was left of her."

"What was left of her?" It was the first time Chancey had spoken.

"She'd been partially eaten by coyotes," Lynn explained. "They figure whoever did her put the blood and meat on her so she'd be consumed before she was ever found."

"Gone without a trace," Leila said in somber tones.

"So then what?" The question was from a black girl Francesca had never met.

"Nothing." Lynn's voice sounded hollow. "None

of the clues added up. There wasn't anything more about it in the papers or on the news. No one was ever charged. The whole thing disappeared just as quickly as she did.''

''Was she from around here?'' Francesca asked. She'd already done the math. There was no way this could be Autumn.

But could there be others like her?

Girls who hadn't been found before the desert animals carried them off?

''Not originally,'' Wanda said. ''But she'd been around for a while.'' She paused, stared vacantly at a spot in the middle of the table, seemingly oblivious to the sounds of the bar around them, the pool balls clacking, darts being thrown.

When Wanda looked up, Francesca was shocked by the tears in the girl's eyes. ''She was a friend of mine.''

Luke was waiting for Arnold to finish closing his table just after midnight on Friday night when he saw Francesca walking toward him. She seemed about twenty in her full Guido garb. Tight denim skirt, black spaghetti-strap top and her black ankle boots. It should be illegal to look that sexy.

''Oh, good.'' She was talking before he could even say hello. ''You said you and your friend Arnold meet for drinks after his shift sometimes and I was hoping tonight might be one of those nights. I wouldn't normally do this, but do you mind if I invite myself along? If you're going, that is. I could really use a drink. And some company.''

Her agitation woke his investigative instincts. Something had happened. Something that upset her. A lot.

"If that's okay," she said.

"Of course it's okay." He waited for her to say more.

"Good." She nodded, hugging her black leather bag to her side as though afraid for its safety.

"Are you going to tell me what's wrong?"

"Yeah." She didn't seem able to meet his eyes, or to focus on much of anything. "Nothing's wrong. It's just…been a long night."

"Liar."

Nodding again, she glanced his way and then around the tables. "Which one is Arnold?"

Luke pointed to the gray-haired man standing with the floor person across the aisle.

"He looks nice."

"Did you hear something about Autumn?" Something she couldn't bring herself to talk about?

"No."

"The bartender guy. Carl, wasn't it?"

He waited for her nod, mostly to keep her engaged in the conversation as she tapped her foot and continued to study the casino, her eyes darting quickly around.

"He didn't do anything out of line, did he?" Luke would deal with the guy himself if he had. Francesca was a decent woman and this town had damn well better treat her that way.

"What?" She glanced at him only briefly. "No,

of course not. Carl's a nice man. He's been a good friend.''

Oh. Great.

''Is he more than a good friend?'' He asked for informational purposes only.

''No.'' Her gaze slowed, settled on him. ''I told you, Luke, I'm only in town long enough to find Autumn. I'm not going to get involved with anyone.''

Luke nodded, strangely satisfied.

Although she'd said she was hungover that first night he had drinks with her, Luke had never seen Francesca drink much.

Sitting with her and Arnold in the mostly deserted casino lounge, he saw two things he hadn't noticed before. She ordered two screwdrivers in twenty minutes. And visibly charmed the pants off the older man, putting on a show that was smooth enough to be considered art.

He almost cheered when Arnold, who was drinking beers as fast as Francesca was downing vodka, excused himself to go to the men's room.

''What gives?'' He peered unrelentingly at her as she tried to elude him.

She shrugged. ''Nothing. Really.''

As she took another large sip from her glass, her hand movements so deliberate they were more jerky than natural, Luke watched through narrowed eyes. Something *was* wrong.

''You aren't ready to talk about it.''

She shook her head. As much of an admission as he needed.

Nursing his first beer, he decided to make it his last. Whatever was going on, he was glad she'd come to him.

"So, Arnold, what do you like to do in your spare time?"

The older man had been back for fifteen minutes and Francesca knew more about his life story than most of the people who'd been working with him for years. Luke had known of the older man's divorce, but not that his ex-wife had been the one to leave.

He watched his friend as Arnold considered the question. The older man was engaged in a way he'd never seen. More alive and relaxed.

"These days not as much as I'd like to." When Arnold finally replied he gave the kind of nonanswer Luke was used to hearing. "But when I get a chance I still go out for a jump now and then."

Luke started. "A jump?"

"Hey, man, I might be old, but I'm not dead and it doesn't take much to throw yourself out of a plane."

*Tell me about it.* "You never told me you jump!"

"You never asked."

Well, no, he hadn't, but… "Did you know I—"

"—hold every record in the state? Yeah, I knew."

Luke wasn't often nonplussed.

"You *both* jump from planes?" Francesca looked from one to the other, eyes troubled, though whether from the current conversation, too much drink or the thoughts she was keeping to herself, he didn't know. "Why would you want to do that? There are any number of perfectly reasonable things you can do right here on earth to get yourselves killed."

"You'd have to—"

"Little lady, until you've..."

He and Arnold spent the next ten minutes tripping over each other as they extolled the virtues of a passion Luke hadn't even known they shared. They might as well have kept still for all the effect on Francesca.

"So, why didn't you say something?" Luke asked his friend. "We can go up together sometime."

Arnold shrugged in that noncommittal way he had. "I'm nowhere near as good as you, for one thing. My longest free fall is probably about half of what you do on a bad day."

"And for another thing?"

"You're management, Luke. Having drinks now and then is one thing, but I wouldn't presume to impinge upon your life away from here."

"Crap. How's next Saturday sound?"

Arnold opened his mouth to reply, glancing over at Francesca. When no sound came out of the other man's mouth, Luke's gaze followed his.

Francesca had tears streaming slowly down her face.

"You ready to tell me what's wrong?" he asked, forgetting for that second that Arnold was sitting there.

He'd only ever seen her cry once. The night they'd checked out the escort Web sites. She'd made it through every single site, forcing herself to look at things that must have been ripping her up inside, and when they were done, when they turned off the computer having seen no sign of her sister, she'd cried just like that.

And refused the comfort he'd needed to offer.

Francesca Witting was one tough bird.

And a beautiful one.

"Nothing," she said again. And added, "I mean it," when his look obviously conveyed his disbelief. "I heard a story at the bar tonight and I can't seem to get it out of my head. I'm overreacting, and I hate that."

She didn't wipe away the tears as she had the other night. Because she'd had too much to drink and the alcohol had made her sloppy? Somehow Luke didn't think so.

"Tell us about it." Arnold leaned forward, his eyes filled with more emotion than Luke had ever seen before.

The glance she sent Luke seemed to be looking for something, although he wasn't sure what.

"What did you hear?" he asked.

Luke remembered every detail of the story that had been in all the Nevada papers a few years before as she related them.

"Your source was certainly accurate," he told her when her voice fell silent, leaving so much unspoken pain in their midst.

She nodded. "I met a friend of hers tonight."

Arnold coughed—and then started to choke. "Went... down...the...wrong...way," he muttered, pushing back from the table to go to the bar for some water.

Luke watched him go, sorrow in his heart for the older man. Not many people knew it, but Arnold had lost a daughter many years before. Back in Phoenix. Luke didn't know the details, but from what Arnold had told him one night after he and Luke had finished an entire bottle of whiskey between them, the girl had been killed in some kind of hit-and-run accident and left for dead.

That was the night Luke had confided in Arnold about his desire for a family—and the mother who had him chained to her side.

Neither man had mentioned the indiscretions since.

''I know that the girl's death has absolutely nothing to do with Autumn, but I just can't seem to get rid of the feeling that it could just as easily have been my little sister out there in the desert,'' Francesca told Luke later that night as he walked her home.

He would've taken her in the Jag, but she'd needed some air—even hot Vegas air—to clear her head.

''It's understandable,'' he told her, having to make a conscious effort to keep his hands in his pockets so that his arm didn't slide around her shoulders as he wanted it to. ''I can only imagine how terrifying it is having a young woman you love unprotected in this city.''

They'd left the Strip behind on the first side street they'd come to and were walking slowly among two-bit motels, brightly lit massage parlors, an off-the-beaten-track discount wedding chapel or two and restaurants offering lobster and steak dinners for $9.95.

Her arm brushed his as she looked up at him. "Why do you stay here if you hate this city so much?"

"I don't hate it."

"You sure don't like it."

The night was calm, few cars driving anywhere but on the Strip at that early hour, but if there were stars, they were lost among the glittering lights.

"There are things about it that I like."

"Such as?"

"I like the energy. No matter what time of day or night, you can always find life and excitement."

"You hate gambling and gambling's what generates the excitement."

Maybe. Probably.

"I like that all different kinds of people live together here, for the most part peaceably. There are very few other places in the world that can boast the same."

"Okay."

They crossed a street. He could see the Lucky Seven sign two blocks ahead.

"And I like the old people." He had no idea where that had come from.

"The tourists, you mean?"

He nodded. "They're by far my favorite guests."

"Why?"

He shrugged. Didn't answer. Didn't think he had an answer. He hadn't even realized he'd noticed the old people, so vulnerable in their hopefulness. And comforting in their acceptance.

"So why *do* you stay?" Her soft question caught him unawares. As did his sudden desire not to lie to her.

"I can't leave."

"Why not?"

They were a block away from her temporary home. A place that wasn't anywhere near worthy of this remarkable woman.

And somehow half an hour had passed, and they were standing at the steps that led to her motel door, his hands still in his pockets, and she knew about his mother. It hadn't been as hard telling her as it had been with Melissa. Because things got easier the more you did them?

Not something he was planning to find out.

"I'd like to meet her." Her bag on her shoulder, she had yet to reach for her key.

"Why?"

"I don't know," she said. "She sounds interesting. Or maybe just because she's your mother."

Luke hadn't taken a friend to his home since high school. But then, he'd never had a friend quite like her. Or one so temporary...

"You want to come to dinner on Sunday?" he heard himself ask. And then remembered. "Sorry, the phone booth. For a second there, I forgot."

She laughed softly, although there was no humor in the sound. "Yeah, believe it or not, so did I. But I think I'd like to come, anyway. Looks like I might be at this longer than I'd figured and a few hours away might give me the ability to sit there an extra week or two.''

Always practical. Always focused on her goal. It impressed him—and made the woman safe.

''Can I pick you up at one?''

She nodded. Said she'd like that.

And Luke left her there. Wondering why the hell he'd just done that.

She needed a friend. His mother needed a friend. He wanted to be a friend. But there was no future in it. For any of them.

And maybe that was his answer right there.

# 13

Ever since she was a little girl, Sheila Miller had loved the smell of freshly brewed coffee. Every night for the past thirty years, since her first day in her first apartment off the Las Vegas Strip, she'd brushed her hair before bed, cleaned her teeth, smeared antiaging cream on her face, and filled the coffeepot. She used to plug it in first thing in the morning—even before visiting the bathroom. These days she didn't have to do anything. Coffeepots had automatic timers now. The smell permeated her home even before she opened her eyes in the morning.

And still, she loved it. It hung around while she showered, dressed, made her bed. While she planned. Worried. And fed the cat. It was a comfort. Something that stayed exactly the same in a world where nothing else did.

On the first Sunday morning in August, in the small kitchen in her twenty-year-old condo, that smell gave her the reassurance it always had. And more. It contributed to an overall sense of peace that had slowly crept upon her. Descended without her knowing.

Sheila didn't trust peace. Not that she was too familiar with the concept.

Toast in the toaster, bacon in the microwave and eggs frying in the pan. Breakfast was well under way—and timed perfectly. As perfect as the flow of her new silk negligee robe against her skin, the cool tile beneath her bare feet, the smell of coffee in the air.

"Mmm, smells good." She jerked back as Arnold came up behind her, nuzzling his face in her neck. And then she melted into the solid body behind her.

"It'll be ready soon," she said, although what she wanted to do was moan. In pleasure. And eagerness. The things this man did to her.

"I was talking about you." His voice was husky with passion, a sound she'd come to crave in just a few short hours. His hands came around her belly and moved up, cupping breasts that were aching and yearning.

She dropped the spatula, probably spraying butter and egg on her pristine if twenty-year-old tile floor, and didn't care.

Turning her head, she glanced up at him. "Again?"

"Hmm-mmm. You?" His lips moved along her neck, his tongue dipping into her ear.

"Yes. I'm sorry, but yes." The whimper that accompanied her words embarrassed her. And still her hunger drove everything.

"Don't be sorry, my love." Arnold's reply fueled the desire raging through her. "Don't ever be sorry."

She probably should be. Probably would be. At the moment, Sheila didn't care.

It had taken fifty-five years but she'd finally had an orgasm. This man was magic.

"The eggs burned." Standing with her in the kitchen, dressed only in the slacks he'd had on when he'd picked her up for dinner the night before, Arnold pointed to the congealed brown substance at the bottom of her frying pan.

"The bacon's cold." She'd pulled it out of the microwave and stood staring down at it.

"I'll bet the toast is hard, too," he said, his dear face solemn.

"Yes." She was sorry about that. Had wanted to fill him with a wonderful breakfast before he went home to get showered and ready for work.

And now it all looked so pathetic that...

Sheila felt laughter bubble up inside her—and discovered that he was laughing, too. And that was when she fell in love.

"You got any cereal?" Arnold asked a full half hour later. They were trying the kitchen a third time. Both fully dressed.

"I do." She pulled out two bowls, some bran flakes with raisins, skim milk.

"No sugar?"

Putting the box of cereal on the light cherrywood table she'd dreamed about for years before she'd finally been able to bring it home to her small condominium, she shook her head. "Not for me. But I do have some, if you really need it."

He grabbed the canister she'd indicated and brought it over with him as he sat down.

He was the first male guest in her little breakfast nook with its bay window that overlooked the tenth of an acre that made up the back of her property. The tiny fountain that held a place of honor on the patio outside that window would be lost in the backyard of her new home. Still, she loved the little boy sitting on a fish whose mouth spit water into the basin beneath them.

"I've never met anyone who didn't eat sugar on bran flakes," he said. "It's the only way to get them down."

"You don't like bran?" Neither did she if the truth be told.

"Nope. I'm an Apple Jacks guy."

"Froot Loops for me." It was probably the most closely guarded secret of her adult life.

He poured cereal into her bowl and then his own. She followed with the milk. He added sugar. But only to his own.

"Each box has about nine cups of sugar." He spoke, and then filled his mouth with cereal.

He meant her Fruit Loops. "I know."

"So why don't you put sugar on your bran?"

"Because it's fattening."

"So?"

"So I don't want to be fat."

With a full spoon on the way to his mouth he stopped, looked over at her. "You aren't fat," he said. "And, in fact, you could stand to put a little meat on those beautiful bones. You need something to fight back with if you get sick.''

Sheila reached for the sugar.

They talked about the heat. How nice it would be when September came and there'd be some relief from the unrelenting rays. They talked about a show they both wanted to see, which was coming to town. About a nonunion hotel whose staff was picketing, and new shows going in where a famous tiger show had come to an abrupt end after a run of more than ten years. One of the animals had turned on his trainer during a performance. And two hundred or so employees had found themselves unexpectedly out of work.

''There's so much unrest on the Boulevard these days,'' Sheila said as they lingered over a second cup of coffee. The grass in her tiny walled-in backyard was green and beautiful, offering a constant invitation to lie down in its cool depths and take a nice long nap.

''More than at any other time?''

Arnold sipped his coffee slowly. She watched his long, elegant fingers as he held the mug she'd found for him. At home she only drank coffee from china cups. She was quite proud of the collection she'd gathered over the years.

''Much more,'' she said. ''Sometimes I think I'm just getting older and less flexible, but things are changing. There's always been an edge to life in this city, and yet there used to be a culture you could count on, as well. If there was danger or illegal activity, you knew where it was and how to avoid it.

There were rules of conduct that were followed, whether you were a crook or some poor guy trying to eke out a living in the midst of it all.''

God, one night of love and she was turning into a softie. If Angie ever heard her talk like this she'd die laughing.

''How's it different now?'' He didn't seem in any hurry to leave. And although she hadn't had a man in her home for almost thirty years, she didn't want him to go.

''I don't know,'' she told him. ''There seems to be an each-man-for-himself attitude now. The sense of family is gone.''

''Or maybe you've just grown up.''

Holding his gaze for long seconds, Sheila recognized in his eyes some of the lessons she'd learned during her own life. She wanted to know how *he'd* learned them. Tell him some of the ways she had.

And that was when she knew for sure that she was losing it.

''Have you heard anything else about the big wins this summer?'' She was on the verge of the first experience of heaven she'd ever had in her life. With a loan shark and a builder's demands looming before her, over her. Threatening to take everything she'd worked for.

If Arnold found out, that admiration shining from his eyes would fade.

God, she couldn't believe she'd been so stupid.

''Actually,'' he said, glancing at her from beneath lowered lids, ''I did hear something.''

"What?" She leaned forward. "Who's doing it? Have they called it quits?"

*Slow down, old broad. Don't be so damned eager that you blow this.*

"I don't know much yet." His answer was disappointing. "Just that it's definitely an inside job."

"Have you said anything to anyone else?"

"No, and I'd appreciate it if you wouldn't, either. Not until I know more."

"But you told me." Even now, that was what mattered.

"I did."

"Thank you."

"You're welcome."

She loved him. And she was going to have to find out how to get the information from him, figure out how to use it to save her home and her life—without jeopardizing that love.

A tall order.

And this time she couldn't afford to fail.

Francesca had no idea why she'd accepted the invitation. She'd picked up her cell phone twice that morning while she hung out at her corner, intending to call and cancel. But there'd been some real truth in what she'd told Luke the night before. Finding Autumn could take weeks. Or longer.

She had to have some diversion or she'd lose whatever sanity she'd managed to hold on to.

"You sure your mother's okay with this?" Francesca asked Luke as he drove the Jaguar through the front entrance of his gated community. The night before, when she'd come in from Guido's, she'd rummaged in the bottom of her duffel for a pair of linen slacks and a short-sleeved matching blouse, ironed them and hung them for this afternoon. It felt good to dress like herself for once.

She'd called her mother this morning, too. Just to reassure her that they would find Autumn.

"You kidding? She was thrilled," Luke said, with a hint of derision coloring his tone. "She's been up since dawn getting ready."

"Well, I feel bad about that. I certainly don't want to be the cause of more work for her."

In truth, she didn't know what she wanted. Just to be a friend for a friend, she guessed. To connect to another human being, be in someone's home for an hour or two. Touch a bit of real life.

"Don't worry about it." He turned onto a long winding street with big beautiful homes set so far from the street they were barely visible. The smallest lot had to be more than an acre. "It's good for her. It's just that…" He paused, looking a bit uneasy.

"What?"

"She's going to make more of this than there is."

Oh. "Because you're bringing a woman home."

"Yeah."

"Don't worry, Everson, I'm not going to start hearing wedding bells or anything."

He stopped the car in the middle of the street. Glanced over at her. "I never for one second thought you were." That look in his eyes said he wasn't kidding. "I was thinking about you. She'll probably make things awkward."

"No problem," Francesca told him. "In the past ten years, delving into the intimacies of people's lives, I've been in just about every awkward situation known to man. I'll be fine."

"You mean that."

"Of course."

Her comment pleased him. Francesca was glad.

"Listen, Luke, we're both adults here. And friends, I hope. But I know you have no interest in me other than that, and obviously my life is far too complicated at the moment to even think about anything more. As long as we have this understanding, I don't care what anyone else thinks."

His smile was full and genuine and beautiful to her. "You are an amazing woman."

It was one of the few wrong things she'd ever heard him say.

"May I speak frankly with you?"

Alone with Carol Everson in her living room after dinner, having a cup of coffee before Luke took her back to town, Francesca nodded. "Of course."

The older woman sat rigidly on one end of the pale green silk brocade sofa, a lovely complement to the off-white pantsuit she wore. Her impeccable hair and makeup gave her an image of refined elegance—if only her right hand hadn't been continually tapping either the sofa or the top of her other hand.

Sipping from a bone-china cup, Francesca smiled at her. "You know something?" The words came from nowhere. "You remind me of my paternal grandmother. Her name's Sancia Witting. She lives in a little village in Italy, near Naples. I only just met her this past year and already I miss her so much.''

It was true. She hadn't even known it.

''You're Italian,'' Luke's mother said, smiling, too, although her lips were trembling.

''Half.'' Francesca couldn't tell if that was good or bad. ''My father died when I was five, but I adored him.''

''The feeling was mutual, I'm sure.'' Carol's face was pinched one second, as though she was trying not to cry, then smiling the next, and the rhythm her hand was tapping grew more intricate. She was nothing like Kay, who could affect a distant and coolly pleasant demeanor in almost any social situation, yet Francesca was drawn to her.

She'd been agitated when they arrived, rushing through the house trying to perfect what already seemed perfect—her beautifully set table, her exquisite meal. One would think she'd been entertaining royalty. At least twenty of them, given all the food she'd made.

But it was when Luke had left to take a long-distance call from his boss that she'd really begun to show signs of strain.

''Does it bother you, me being Italian?''

''Oh, my goodness, no!'' Carol's head jerked with the force of her words. She was staring at her fingers. Francesca wondered if she was even aware of their movement. ''My late husband's best friend is Italian. I'm sure Luke's mentioned him. Amadeo is also his boss. I used to think, when Luke was a boy, that he wished he was Italian, too.''

Her eyes filled with tears. She reached in the pocket of her slacks. Looking for a tissue?

"Can I get you something?" Francesca asked, sliding a little closer.

"What?" Carol glanced at her. "Oh, no. Did I ask you if I could speak frankly?"

"Yes."

"Did you say I could?"

"Yes."

"It's just that I have problems, you see." Francesca could sense the effort it took the older woman to push the words past whatever barriers her mind and body had erected.

"No one's ever been able to figure me out." She tried to chuckle. She looked over at Francesca, holding her gaze, but her eyes were moist—her chin shaking. "My dear, sweet Marshall made it his mission to seek out every doctor who'd made a name for himself in dealing with emotional issues. He'd come home all excited by this or that new idea or method, and off we'd go to see some new guru. He even took me to a medical intuitive once."

She stopped, out of breath. Without her usual detachment, Francesca waited.

"I tried holistic programs, spiritual programs and, at some point, have probably been on every medication known to psychiatric science. And still, I have problems."

"It's okay." Francesca didn't know what else to say. Moving closer, she took one of the older woman's hands, hoping that her closeness wouldn't upset Carol further. "Really, it's okay."

Carol shook her head. "No, it's not." She started to cry. Shook her head again. "I don't want Luke to walk in and find me like this."

"It's okay," Francesca repeated. "Luke loves you, he understands." Maybe it was because she'd just met Carol, maybe because her presence in Francesca's life was only temporary, but the heart that had been in deep freeze for two long months was reaching out to this woman. It was as though she could *feel* Carol's struggles to cope—or perhaps she was feeling her own.

"Tell me about your husband," Francesca said. She'd get Carol's mind on something that made her feel good. That suggestion had been made to *her* by a doctor in Italy while he was writing out a prescription for sleeping pills. "Think about the things that have made you happy," he'd said. She wasn't sure how well it worked, but it gave her something to do when the despair was so strong she didn't feel she could take another step.

"I'd love to," Carol said. "Sometime. But right now, this is important."

Acting purely on instinct, Francesca nodded, squeezed Carol's hand, and hoped that Luke's call lasted a bit longer.

"When it was just Marshall and I dealing with all of this, it was okay. We loved each other. We'd made a vow to take each other for better or worse, and while I hated how much my illness bothered Marshall, I also made sure that every single dream he'd ever talked about when we were young and foolish remained the focus of his heart and life."

"I have a feeling every one of them came true."

She smiled, and her expression was momentarily calm. Serene. "Every single one of them. We believed, you see. And that's all it takes."

Believing. It was a concept she'd forgotten along the way. Perhaps when she'd lost everything she'd believed in...

"But now that Marshall's gone, the burden of my illness has fallen to Luke, and it breaks my heart to see what this is doing to his life. He's become a virtual prisoner, never going far, never getting too involved, never bringing anybody home."

Francesca was beginning to understand.

"You don't want anything you might do or say to affect my coming back to your home," she said, listening with a heart that hadn't been able to listen to very much lately.

"There are times when my perceptions get skewed and I panic irrationally."

"That won't scare me off."

Carol shook her head, more hopelessly than before. "You don't know."

"It doesn't matter," Francesca said. "It really doesn't. Another day, when we have more time, we'll talk," she told Carol. "I might be young, but I've seen a lot of things and I can tell you that the love you describe between you and your husband, the way you care about your son—that's what matters."

Carol nodded, although she was clearly still disturbed. "I love my son more than life."

"He's a good man."

"He's a lonely man," Carol amended. "And..." She took a deep, shaky breath. "I'm afraid he's a stupid one."

"What?" Francesca frowned. "Why?"

"He's rigidly attached to a promise he made his father and won't put me in a home where I belong."

"You do not belong in a home." Luke's voice boomed in the quiet room as he came in behind them. She hadn't heard his footsteps on the densely piled wool carpet. "You belong right here, in your own home, and I don't want to hear another word about it."

His words were firm but loving.

"Ready?" He glanced over at Francesca, his eyes shadowed. Where was the man who'd invited her to dinner, the man who'd sounded as though he'd really wanted her there?

She stood. "I guess I should be getting back." She didn't want to leave, though. She wanted to talk to Carol about Autumn. She had a feeling the older woman might have some insights that could help her cope.

"Please come again soon," Carol said, squeezing Francesca's hand as she passed by. She didn't get up.

"I'd love to, if you're sure it's okay."

Carol smiled, and there was no missing the gratitude in her eyes. "It's more than okay...."

Francesca wasn't sure what had just happened. She'd been away for an hour and a half. Had dinner.

And life had changed.

# 14

Wednesday afternoon Luke strode into a viewing room in back of the offices at the Bonaparte, asked the two young men who were working on the equipment to leave, locked the door and sat down. Pulling a beer out of the six-pack concealed by a brown paper bag, he unscrewed the top, took a long swig, then unzipped the compact disk case in his hand. After a second gulp from his bottle he slid the first recording into a machine. Another drink, another disk in another machine, a third drink and yet a third machine. Finally, he'd activated a total of eight DVD players.

This particular room—the backup equipment room—had enough portable disk players to play every single DVD he had with him. They were all digital recordings of every suspect win that had taken place on the Strip in the past four months.

An hour later, four empty bottles around him, he was still sitting there, his tie slightly askew, his jacket hanging open, but still sitting there. Staring at screens. From one to the next to the next and then back again. He watched and watched some more.

He had nowhere else to be. Nothing else pressing on his time. Francesca was at his house having dinner with his mother before her nightly sojourn at Guido's.

He'd been planning to join them but had called at the last minute, claiming work that needed his attention.

What needed his attention was the disappointment burning through him. The woman from Colter had called just as he was leaving the hotel that afternoon.

He wasn't going to get his son. The thought required another sip from the fifth bottle, which was no longer cold at all.

She hadn't said he wouldn't eventually get a son. But something had happened with the one he'd been promised, and all of their other babies were currently spoken for.

Images flickered across the monitors. Dealers, patrons, bets laid, cards pulled from shoes, cheques passed across the table. Again and again. Once or twice he caught some possible card-counting, but it always amounted to nothing more than amateur attempts. No wins resulted.

He'd asked the woman from Colter what had happened to his son. She wouldn't say. Said she couldn't.

Had the child died? Or the birth mother changed her mind? Had someone objected to the boy going to a single father?

Luke cued the DVD players for another run, starting this time just before the start of the winning deal.

Amadeo was due to call again by the weekend. Luke had to have something to tell him. Maybe he'd tell him about his mother and Francesca. Luke talking about his mother at all would throw him.

But not for long.

One of the dealers smiled at a player, glanced up briefly with his left hand hovering just above the shoe, prepared to deal. He scratched his shoulder with his free hand, pushed down on the top card in the shoe with the middle finger of his left hand, slid it toward the table, grasped it between index finger and thumb. He flicked his wrist so the card was faceup then grasped it with his right index finger and thumb and laid it on the table in front of the first player. Absolutely nothing.

On the next screen, the dealer was smiling. And the next.

So many smiles when he couldn't feel less like smiling. How was it that all around him were images of happy people while that particular state of mind remained forever elusive to him?

He'd point-blank asked the woman at Colter if *he* was the problem. If someone had objected to him. Had there been some red flag in his file?

He'd received the same evasive response. She'd told him all she could and she wasn't saying he wouldn't eventually get his son.

Another smile on the screen. To taunt him?

He finished off the last of the beer in his bottle just to show them he wouldn't be taunted. And pushed the replay button on a screen he'd missed this go-round.

The dealer smiled. Rubbed his chin. Pressed down on the top card in the shoe with the middle finger of his left hand. Slid it down toward the table…

Nothing. Nothing. Nothing.

He'd lost his son. The dealer smiled. He pulled

out the last beer. He wasn't going to get his baby. The dealer smiled.

Everywhere he looked the dealer smiled.

And touched himself with his right hand.

And slid the card down with his middle finger.

The beer was really warm. But who cared? It didn't taste bad.

The dealer slid the card down with his middle finger.

His middle finger.

Wait.

Setting the beer down on a little table to his right, he leaned forward. Punched every single machine until they were cued in exactly the same spot. And one by one, hit Play.

He wasn't looking at the winning deals now. He'd gone back before that point, to view nonwinning deals. Many of them. From each dealer.

Heart pounding he watched, certain he'd found something. It made no sense. It seemed ridiculous— even in his own more than half-drunk mind. But he knew he'd found *something*.

Three of the eight dealers in front of him regularly slid the card out of the shoe with the index fingers of their left hands. Perfectly acceptable choreography. And on the big wins, every single one of the dealers used the middle finger of his left hand to slide out the card.

He'd noticed because Jackson used his index finger, too. Waiting for a meal or drinks, Luke had watched him often enough to know that. The middle-finger draw, while not wrong, was not what he was used to.

And something else was different, too. It took him a while to find it. Sitting back, knowing he was going to have to sober up and think hard about all of this, Luke watched the tapes again. What was missing? If he'd had a few less beers he'd probably know.

He nursed the sixth bottle. Enjoying the liquid as it slid down his throat. He probably wasn't getting his son. At least not soon.

*Yeah, go ahead, grin at that,* he challenged the dealer on the screen. The man didn't crack a smile. Not once. Not in all the deals Luke watched. He turned to the next screen and the next, until he'd viewed all eight of them. Four of the dealers never cracked a smile.

Until just before the winning deal.

He had no idea how he was going to prove anything. Or how the wins were even happening. But of one thing he was certain.

This was an inside job.

"Can I walk you home?"

Looking into Carl's kind, dark eyes, Francesca couldn't do anything but nod. Guido's was closing at midnight on Wednesday to have the wood floors treated, and she'd already told him that she'd walked over after dinner with Carol Everson. It was only a fifteen-minute trip from the motel and she'd wanted to be outside, among the people, living with them.

She'd wanted to feel a part of the life around her.

Instead of shut away in her own world, her room, her roles by day and night, her car.

"We met three weeks ago tonight," Carl announced. They were walking slowly, close but not touching, approaching the Strip.

"We did?" Had it only been that long? Sometimes it felt as though she'd been living this vagabond life forever. Thoughts of Italy, of another life, weren't as consuming.

But every bit as agonizing when they crept up on her.

"You planning on staying awhile longer?"

Why did she weigh everything he said to her now?

"You trying to get rid of me?"

"No." Hands in the pockets of his jeans, Carl wasn't as open as usual. "The opposite, in fact."

"Oh."

"What does that mean?"

"I don't know." *I don't want to hurt you.* "You tell me." *I don't want to lose your friendship.*

A light-skinned black man wearing beige shorts and a red short-sleeved polo shirt was walking down the street, in a lane of traffic, as though he were a car. When he passed and caught Francesca's gaze, the lost look in his eyes took her breath.

"It looks as though you aren't going to meet up with your friend, but you don't appear in any hurry to go anywhere," Carl was saying.

"I haven't given up hope of running into her."

"She must be something special."

"I just owe her, that's all," Francesca told him. There was no reason not to tell Carl about Autumn.

He wasn't going to expose her. Still, she didn't come clean. Possibly because the truth—that she'd been lying—would hurt him. And to what end?

The fewer complications, the fewer people who knew her well enough to really share her life, the better.

Francesca stumbled as Carol Everson came to mind. She'd told the other woman at dinner that she had no interest in her son. But she wasn't sure Carol had believed her. She couldn't see her again, spend any more time at Carol's home, until Carol accepted that fact. She wasn't going to be responsible for adding to the emotional difficulties that already consumed the older woman.

But she hadn't been able to refuse when Luke's mom had begged her to come to dinner again on Friday. She could only hope that Luke would be working late so Carol didn't see the two of them together and build up hope where there was none.

They passed a brand-new drugstore whose architecture was stunning. And right next to it, a billboard for beer. And then another wedding chapel. All she could see of the half-lit sign was Heavens.

*God, I hope heaven doesn't look like that.*

Heaven. Did it really exist? And was her little Gian safe and happy there?

"I'd like to take you out for dinner. Someplace nice—just the two of us."

*Oh, Carl. Don't.*

"You work every night."

"My brother agreed to come in and tend bar any night this next week."

"I—"

"It's dinner, Francesca, not a marriage proposal."

He was right. And he'd been so good to her. "Okay," she said. And hated herself for agreeing.

Carl kissed her good-night at her door. Nothing deep or passionate. A closed-mouth kiss. And yet, one that had lingered. Inside her room, Francesca leaned back against the door, wishing she hadn't agreed to go out with him Monday night. She resented the time away from Guido's.

She was frightened by how much she wanted his friendship. And Luke's. And Carol's. Francesca Witting didn't need people. Other than Antonio once upon a time.

And maybe Autumn.

"I don't know, Luke," Arnold Jackson said the next morning. He sat forward, placing his cup of coffee on the second shelf of a rolling television rack. "Play that back one more time," he said, studying the monitors in front of him.

Luke pushed the buttons that would reset all eight machines. He was showing the dealer exactly what he'd seen himself the night before. Sober, he still saw the smiles. The middle-finger choreography. The right-hand touches of various places on the dealers' bodies.

He knew he was on to something. But before he moved ahead, he'd wanted Arnold to see the tapes. There wouldn't be a more expert opinion.

"A lot of schools teach middle-finger dealing,"

Jackson said, and Luke stopped the machines, rewinding a couple.

"Yes, but in every other instance on these tapes—" he pushed Play "—the dealer uses his index finger to pull the cards."

Frowning, Jackson watched the scenes before them, saying nothing.

"What do you think?"

He shook his head. "I'm sorry, Luke, but I don't see it. The rhythm and movement is exactly the same. If they were switching cards, there'd be a change in wrist posture at least."

Biting back the colorful words that came to mind, Luke slowly nodded.

"But how do you explain the finger switch?"

Arnold shrugged, the broadness of his shoulders more prominent in the cotton polo shirt he had on that morning than in the tux jacket Luke was used to seeing him wear. "Cramp. Fatigue." He picked up his coffee. "You pull thousands of cards a night. It happens. You're only looking at the dealers who had big losses here, but if you viewed other tapes, even mine, you'd probably see the same thing occasionally."

"Well, look here." Luke rewound a couple of machines.

"See those smiles?" he said. "They happen immediately before every win."

"So you think someone in the casino is tipping him off and he smiles to acknowledge the mark?"

Elbows on his knees, suit jacket hanging open over his thighs, Luke looked over at his friend. "Don't you?'' While the evidence was still there before him, Luke was becoming a little less confident this morning that he'd stumbled on something valid.

Jackson shook his head again. ''Too obvious.''

''Then why didn't anyone pick up on it before?''

Jackson raised his cup. Sipped. Took one of the doughnuts Luke had brought up with him from the kitchen. ''No one noticed that they're all wearing tuxes and ties, either.'' Arnold's teeth cut into the glazed pastry. ''It's nothing.''

Luke sat back. He wasn't even going to mention the right-hand touching. It had been the least convincing of his observations, anyway. Making a mental note to remind himself why he didn't drink on the job, Luke turned off the machines.

''We still on to jump this Saturday?''

''Oh, shoot, Luke, I completely forgot. I took an extra shift, filling in for Phil Gordon. His wife's scheduled for a C-section.''

Phil Gordon. Luke had only met the guy once. And felt envious as hell.

He told his friend that he wasn't going to be getting a son after all.

Arnold frowned, jeans-clad leg across the opposite knee. ''Tough break.''

''Yeah.'' Luke ejected all the tapes, put them back in their cases very deliberately. ''I know better than to count on things happening as planned.''

''Sure makes living each day for itself seem like the best option.''

Luke glanced over. ''That something you learned before or after you lost your daughter?''

"After." Jackson didn't hesitate.

Luke stood. Making the most of the moment was great advice. Unless you had a mother who couldn't handle disappointment—and relied on unchanging routine to provide what little stability she had.

Francesca's cell phone rang before she was even awake Friday morning.

*God, don't let it be Mom,* she groaned silently as she rolled over. Talking to each other with nothing new to report was hard on both of them.

"I'm five minutes from your place. Can I come over?"

It was Luke. She scrambled to a sitting position. "Of course. What's up?"

"I just got some news. I'll be there in five minutes." He clicked off before she could ask any more.

Brushing her teeth and running her fingers through the cropped dark strands of her hair at the same time, Francesca listened for Luke's step on the stairs. She put on jeans and a T-shirt, and still he wasn't there. His idea of five minutes wasn't hers. Picking up a tube of mascara, she pulled out the wand, blinked at it a couple of times.

And heard his knock.

"It's about time, buster. If you're going to get a girl out of bed—" Francesca's voice broke when the odd look on his face registered.

"What? What's happened?"

It wasn't horrible. His eyes weren't filled with

dread. Or sympathy. Or grief. But she read concern there. Along with something else.

"Tell me."

"I've found Autumn."

Her stomach jumped, heart pumping rapidly. And then everything slowed. Her breath. Her thoughts. The world. Just spinning in slow motion.

"Alive?"

"Yes." He grinned then, but that look of concern was still there. "She's alive and only a few miles from here."

"Oh, God." Mouth hanging open, she stared at him. *Oh, God.* "I can't think. Is she okay? What's she doing? Have you seen her?" She was crying and smiling and needing to do everything at once. Get to her sister. Talk to Luke. Find her shoes. And her keys.

Luke's hand against the hot skin of her face was a relief.

"I don't know much," he told her, standing in the open door. "A few of the tenants who were living in the apartments Biamonte recently bought were apparently placed in other Biamonte properties instead of evicted. I don't know why some were given the opportunity and others weren't. I'm not even sure this particular property is a rental. It appears to be owned by the company and used for company business, but I haven't even verified that. Since the pictures didn't turn up anything positive, I had some people discreetly checking around Biamonte's interests for information on the tenants who were evicted. When I got to work twenty minutes ago, there was a message saying that a maintenance man had identified Autumn as a sixth-floor tenant in his building.''

Francesca loved that maintenance man. Hoped she'd get to meet him some day.

*Oh, my God.* She'd been waiting. Hoping. Praying. Determined. Doubting. She wiped her eyes. They filled right back up again.

''Do you think she'll be there now?'' she asked, sniffling. She needed a tissue. And her shoes.

''It's early enough. Most people are still home at seven in the morning.''

Right. Okay.

''Your sandals are at the end of your bed.'' Luke's voice had never been so kind or understanding. On some level she recognized that she must be in a worse state than she'd thought to warrant that tone.

''Yeah, and I need my keys,'' she said, remembering exactly where they were.

She was going to see Autumn now. She could deal with the ramifications, whatever they were, later.

''I can't believe I'm really going to see her.''

Francesca stared out the window of the Jag, seeing the older couple on the street corner, both plump, wearing tennis shoes and fanny packs and shorts that had obviously been purchased before their most recent weight gains. And seeing nothing. ''I can't believe she's really alive.''

Glancing over at her, Luke said nothing.

He'd warned her twice already. He knew nothing about Autumn's condition. If she was working. If she was healthy. He only knew that she was alive.

And where she was living.

Her baby sister. After more than two years, she was going to be in the same room with Autumn again. Able to hug her.

To hear how she'd been. What she'd been doing.

"She's really alive," Luke said. He turned a corner.

Maybe someday she'd tell Autumn about Gian.

And she had to tell her about her father's death. And to call her mom. The girl would probably need some things. Maybe new clothes. A good meal. A visit to a doctor. And perhaps a counselor.

Would Autumn be happy to see her? Should she hug her? Or play it cool? Be firm? Or just loving?

What if the girl slammed the door in her face?

"Hey." Luke reached for her hand, squeezed it gently. "It's going to be okay."

"I know."

But she didn't. She didn't know that at all.

They had to climb six flights of stairs. And knock twice.

"Maybe she's not here, after all." Francesca tried to detach. To shut down the panic that was so close to the surface. She wanted to take Luke's hand again.

She squeezed her own instead.

He knocked a third time.

She should've taken time to shower. "I think I hear something." Or was she just imagining movement on the other side of the door?

"Sorry, I was puk—"

The girl who pulled open the door stopped when she saw her visitors. Her jaw dropped.

"I thought you were Ant—"

She looked so old. All grown up. She'd dyed her hair. There was a tattoo of a butterfly on her right collarbone and three earrings running up each ear. But no lip piercing, thank God. Her T-shirt had the neck cut out but didn't seem all that worn, and her shorts were clean and not too short.

Her eyes were all Autumn. She'd promised herself she wouldn't cry.

"Cesca?"

As soon as she heard that voice, saying the name that only her sister called her, Francesca pulled the girl into her arms and held on. And on. Her cheeks were wet, and still she held on, breathing in the sweet scent of her sister, feeling Autumn's warm body, her heart beating so close to her own.

"Oh, God, Autumn, I can't believe it's really you." She heard herself saying the words over and over. Told herself to stop. But she didn't.

Her sister had gone rigid in her arms, and it was only then that Francesca realized her own feelings were irrelevant at the moment. She was the strong and responsible one. The comforter.

The one who had to take charge and make everything okay for both of them.

When things obviously weren't okay at all.

"Come on," she said, releasing her hold, "let's pack your things and get you back to my place and then we can talk."

Autumn turned away. "I can't."

"What do you mean you can't? Of course you can. You're seventeen years old. A minor. And a runaway. I'm your sister. Here to take you home. Of course you can come with me."

Autumn wouldn't look at her.

When she thought back on this, relived the memory, it was going to hurt. For now, the moment was frozen. No relief. No shock. No pain.

"You can't make me go," the girl finally said. Her voice had a hardness Francesca didn't recognize.

Why did everything have to be so much of a struggle?

"Of course I can!" she shouted, like some square old parent trying to lord it over a recalcitrant child.

"No. You can't."

Luke came into the little apartment from the doorway. "Maybe we should all sit down for a minute." He settled on the arm of the sofa—the only furniture in the room.

Francesca had forgotten he was there. His presence made everything real. Horribly real. As quickly as it had descended, the numbness encasing her was gone.

Autumn sat.

Fighting off a conflicting array of reactions, Francesca did, too. Beside her sister. She had no idea what to say. There were a million things she wanted to know. And just as many decisions to make. But nowhere to begin.

# 15

"How did you find me?" Autumn sat, stiff and unnatural, in a corner of the sofa.

"Luke is a friend of mine." With her gaze steady on her sister, hands clasped tightly in her lap, Francesca tilted her head toward the man perched next to her. "He works for the company that owns this building."

"Works for?" The look Autumn shot between Luke and Francesca appeared almost...hunted. "Where do you work?" She frowned, her expression confused. "Obviously not in maintenance or anything."

"I'm director of security at the Bonaparte."

"Oh." Autumn clearly didn't know what to make of that. "The casino? I didn't realize they had anything to do with...this place." The lines of strain on Autumn's pretty face as she glanced toward the front door aged her.

Was it possible that the manager of the property didn't know Autumn was staying there?

"Luke's employer doesn't have any part in finding you," Francesca added. "He just used his contacts to help me."

"O-ohh." Autumn drew the word out.

"Do you live here alone?"

"Yes."

She scanned the apartment—sparse furnishings, clean walls, newish-looking carpet. The fully furnished kitchenette. "It's nice."

And how did Autumn afford it?

"Thanks."

Francesca reached over, grabbed Autumn's fingers to keep her from picking at the nails of her opposite hand. "I can't stand this!" She squeezed. "I've missed you so much! Talk to me, tell me what's going on. How you've been. What you're doing here."

Close enough to catch the fruity scent of Autumn's shampoo, a familiar scent, Francesca just wanted to close her eyes and go back. Two years. Three. Fifteen. No matter how bad it had been—it'd been better than what ultimately came after.

"Talk to you?" Autumn jerked her hand away, clenched it in her lap. "Why would I talk to you now? I *tried* to talk to you."

Trying not to reel from the rejection, Francesca stared at her. "You did?" She was cold, filled with fear. "When?"

How had she missed something this critical?

"All the time," Autumn said. "I'd tell you I couldn't stand Mom and Dad. I couldn't stand being at home. I told you how much of a prisoner they were making me."

Yes, she had. And the complaints had sounded so normal compared to the abuse Francesca had suffered, unbeknown to Autumn, at her stepfather's hands, that she'd been too relieved to hear anything else. Certainly not anything that would've led her to suspect Autumn was being driven to the point of running away. The real abuse in their home had been because of *her*. Her stepfather had made that abundantly clear on so many occasions. She was her father's child. A constant reminder to him that he was second best in his wife's heart.

"I just thought it was normal teenage stuff...." She'd left to take the abuse out of Autumn's home, out of her life. Jack Stevens had adored his own daughter. Every single time Francesca had seen them together, she'd seen the love and gentleness in his eyes, his touch....

"It doesn't matter." Autumn jumped up, took a step back. "I just don't think you have any right to come here," she cried. "Asking questions that are none of your business." With each staccato sentence she took another step farther away. "Acting like you're going to be around. That you care at all."

"Autumn!" Francesca was having a hard time breathing. "Of course I care. I've always cared."

"Mmm-hmm. Have you?" The girl looked toward the door. It was the third time she'd done that.

"Of course I have! Every second since the moment you were born."

Her expression hard, empty, Autumn ignored her, glancing out the window in the front of the apartment.

"Are you expecting someone?"

"What if I am?"

"Nothing. Except if it's a friend of yours, I'd like to meet her. Or him."

"Well, you can't."

Autumn's eyes, narrowed and bitter, met Francesca's—almost as if by accident—and the girl's shoulders dropped. "At least not today," she finished.

"Okay. Another day, then?"

Autumn shrugged, her slim body bowed in a gesture of defeat as she stood there defending her turf—or her right to have it; Francesca couldn't be sure. One thing was certain. This reunion was not happening the way she'd hoped it would.

"I guess you've called Mom, told her where I am?" The tone was belligerent.

"No."

"Why not? Or are you lying so I won't take off again?"

"Are you going to take off again?"

"Maybe."

Francesca hadn't even thought of that. Not that morning. Not since finding out her sister was alive. And close. She'd been so grateful. So overwhelmed by the idea of actually seeing her.

With a glance at Luke, who was still sitting quietly on the edge of the couch, Francesca understood what he'd been trying to tell her earlier.

She hadn't been prepared at all.

And she hurt. The inside of her chest tightened, emotion squeezing the back of her throat. The pain reached an intensity that she couldn't sustain. Not on top of everything else. Not sustain it and continue to stand there.

Instinctively, she stepped outside herself. It was

either that or collapse. As if from a distance, she saw the morning play back from another point of view. Saw it as Luke must have done. The detachment that followed was the blessing that saved her.

She recognized it. Welcomed it. Clung to it.

And she knew she had a job to do. The most important job of her life.

"Okay," she said, suddenly calm as rational thought took over where emotion had been. "Let's make a deal. I don't call Mom and you don't run."

Glaring through angry eyes, Autumn said, "How do you know I won't run, anyway?"

"Because I know you." She was taking a chance, but she had to believe in something. "You've never lied to me. If you give me your word, you'll keep it."

Autumn stared at her another full minute. And then she nodded.

"You need us to go right now because you have someone coming over."

"Yes."

"Then we'll go. But only if you'll tell me when I can see you again." She didn't move closer or try to reconnect in any way.

"This afternoon?"

From her distant vantage point, Francesca noted the almost eager response. Filed it away as a good sign. "You got it. Can I pick you up?"

"No. I'll meet you outside the Riviera."

A hotel-casino on the less-refurbished end of the Strip.

Without so much as a touch to her sister's shoulder, Francesca nodded and followed Luke out the door.

Not much more came of the second meeting with Autumn. There were so many things they had to talk about, so many things Francesca wanted to know— and had to say. Not the least of which was telling the girl that while she'd been gone, her father had died....

She'd never had the chance. While Autumn wasn't as openly tense and defensive, she'd had to run inside the casino and throw up before Francesca had even gotten around to suggesting that they take a drive out in the desert and find some nice out-of-the-way place for dinner.

Autumn had had some bad pork for lunch. A fast-food variety that hadn't sat well, she'd explained. And because she so adamantly refused to let Francesca take her home, because Francesca didn't want to push the girl into running again, she had to stand there on the walk and watch her sick little sister walk away alone.

And on Friday night, Francesca became a Guido dropout—just another in the crowd of girls who disappeared with no warning. Carl called her cell phone but she didn't hear it ring in the casino at the Bonaparte. She got the message he left later that night but didn't return his call. Instead she made her way back to the Lucky Seven. Sober. Alone. Fifty dollars richer. Less frantic than she'd been in months. And sad beyond compare.

\* \* \*

There were two things Autumn Stevens loved about Las Vegas. The sunshine that touched her skin with such intensity it warmed her all the way inside. And Matteo. Italian like Beniamino Witting—Francesca's father, the father she would've had if he hadn't gone and died before their mother got pregnant with Autumn. Matteo was not only the best-looking guy she'd ever known, he also had such a strong sense of honor that a girl knew she could trust him to love her and keep her safe. Unlike her own jerk of a father.

"What's up, Golden Girl?" he asked when they met for their usual Sunday-morning date. Matteo's mother didn't work on Sundays and could be home with the little kids. He worked at the garage, like he did every other day of the week, but not until the afternoon.

Scuffing her feet on the sidewalk as they headed toward a park by his house, she wished she dared reach over and take his hand. "Nothing."

He wouldn't mind if she held his hand. She knew that. It was just that if she did, she might not be able to let go.

Grabbing her arm, he pulled her to a stop, gazing deeply into her eyes in that way he had that made her stomach go all soft and gooey, right there on the street. "We've been together ten minutes and other than a quick kiss hello you haven't touched me. Or looked at me. Or laughed at any of my jokes."

His grin was kind. So full of love she thought she might die. "You haven't told any jokes."

He grabbed both of her hands in his. "But if I had, you wouldn't have laughed."

Probably not. She didn't feel much like laughing. Maybe not ever again. "Can we just walk for a bit?"

He glanced up as a car drove past. "Only until I can get you someplace more private. Unfortunately my place is filled with kids. Anyone home at yours?"

"You know we can't go there."

"Yeah." He dropped her hands, sliding his own into the pockets of his jeans—ones that fit, not the stupid kind that guys her age wore, so big they hung down off their butts—and started walking again. "But I don't happen to think you're right about that," he said. "I'm in college, I work hard, I have one small tattoo, no piercings and a mother who'll vouch for me," he said, enumerating some of the things that made her love him so much. "I think if you just give us a chance, your guardians will accept me."

"No, they won't." That wasn't negotiable.

"How do you know if you won't at least try?"

It was the third time he'd brought up the subject. Each time he got more and more frustrated with her.

His insistence was one of the reasons she had to talk to him today, although she hadn't decided what she was going to say. What she *should* say. What she could say.

She had no idea how she was going to look into those gorgeous brown eyes and say anything at all.

"Tell me what's wrong." They were at the University of Las Vegas—where he was studying business—in the almost deserted Moyer student union. An hour later and he still hadn't given up.

He'd taken her to a corner of the reception area where there was an arrangement of modern red sectional couches. So far, in the ten minutes they'd been there, only one other person had walked through.

With an arm on the back of the couch, he was turned toward her. Any closer, and he'd have that arm around her shoulders.

Right where she wanted it.

"I can't see you anymore." There. She'd said it. She was safe. Her insides tightened into knots.

"What?" He hadn't moved. She didn't know what kind of expression he wore. She couldn't look.

Gaze focused on the grain in the rough-feeling fabric, Autumn picked at the cuticle on her right index finger. "You heard me," she mumbled. She couldn't say it again; she wasn't that strong.

"I heard you, I just don't understand." She wished he'd move. Get angry. Stand up. Stomp off. Leave her there to fall apart in peace.

Was a little peace too much for a girl to ask?

"Joy…" He sighed, a short, impatient sigh, like he was getting mad. Or giving up. "Joy—what's going on?"

*My name isn't Joy.*

"I can't see you anymore, that's all."

She finally heard him move, and out of the corner of her eye saw his forearms come down on his thighs.

"Because of your guardian?"

It would be easiest to say yes. Unless he followed

her home in an attempt to take matters into his own hands where her ''guardian'' was concerned—and then found out she didn't have one.

She shook her head.

''Is it me? Something I've done?''

She had to say yes. It was the only way. There was a small dark stain on the sofa, and she centered it evenly between her knees. ''I...I'm leaving.''

She wished. Leaving wasn't an option. Not yet, anyway.

''Leaving?'' He sounded so shocked. ''Where are you going?''

Nowhere. ''Home.''

''To Sacramento?''

She nodded.

''Are your guardians moving?''

God, why did life have to be so complicated?

Still not daring to look into his sweet face, Autumn stared at the tile floor, back at the couch, at the bruise just above her right knee where she'd walked into the edge of a chair in the doctor's waiting room the day before. She'd just had some upsetting news and hadn't seen the damn thing.

''My sister came.'' Her life was so much about keeping secrets, she hadn't even thought of the excuse before.

''Here, to Las Vegas?''

''Yeah.''

''And talked you into going home to the bastard who beat you?''

The words were harsh, horrible, bringing vividly to mind a life she couldn't bear.

''No,'' she told him, wondering where the closest bathroom was. ''He's dead, anyway. She's taking me to live with her.''

As if. Francesca couldn't be hauling her sister along on her travels all over the world. First, she'd insist Autumn stay home and finish school.

But it was easier to tell Matteo about her sister's exciting job, about how Cesca had been gone for a long time—out of the country—and then she invented the part where her older sister had missed her so much she'd given it all up to come back and make a home for the two of them.

In truth, her sister had told her when they'd met for a fast-food dinner—at Autumn's insistence—the night before, that it was Autumn's phone call home that had brought her to Vegas. She'd heard all about Guido's. And the phone booth. That had been hard to take. Knowing that her sister had been posing as some homeless deadbeat all these weeks, in the middle of the summer's worst heat, just to find her.

She couldn't hate her after that. And then Cesca had told her, very gently, that her father had died of a heart attack a year and a half ago. Cesca had been all set to be sympathetic, and there was no way Autumn could handle that. She was through with keeping up appearances about that twisted jerk. She'd faked an appointment and left the burger joint instead. Another reprieve.

Something told her she wasn't going to be so lucky when she and Cesca met again later that afternoon.

"I'm finished school at the end of this year," Matteo said. "I don't mind relocating to Sacramento."

She raised her head then. She couldn't help it. "But your family," she reminded him. "All those kids. Your mother needs you." Matteo's father, a policeman, had been shot to death during a routine traffic stop a few years before.

"You need me." His look was earnest. And open. Far more open than she'd ever been with him. Except when she'd told him how much she loved him. "And I need you just as much." He stayed there, looking at her with those compelling brown eyes that were glistening with the intensity of what he was telling her.

How the hell could she ever be expected to walk away from that? Hands on her stomach, Autumn wished the ground would just open up and suck her in.

"One of the hardest things to do in life is to put yourself in someone else's shoes because then you risk having your mind changed."

Luke stopped mid-chew, staring at his mother. Where had that comment come from? Her hand drumming a rhythm with a knife turned sideways, she hadn't eaten more than two bites of the eggs Benedict and fruit she'd prepared for Sunday brunch.

Francesca's fork hung suspended above her half-empty plate. In her tight black lace, short-sleeved shirt and jeans, she was breathtakingly beautiful—in a sassy sort of way. "I hadn't thought of it like that," she said.

Carol's nod might have been a normal part of the conversation if not for the nervous jerks that accompanied the movement. "It's why so many people resist, even when they think they're being open-minded," she said. "Giving up control of anything is frightening, but that kind of empathy is like handing over control of your mind, which is more than a lot of people can accept."

"So you're saying I need to trust Autumn enough to become her." Francesca, the most independent and private woman Luke had ever met, had told his mother about finding her runaway sister. And the painful reunion that followed.

"If you want to reach her, I think so."

Luke took a long sip of the mimosa his mother had poured from the iced pitcher in the middle of the table. He could do with a little more champagne and a little less orange juice.

His mother was giving advice. Sound advice. He'd forgotten how often he'd heard her doing that with his father while he was growing up. Probably because those conversations were overshadowed by her frequent loss of emotional control.

"I can do that." Francesca pierced a chunk of melon. "It's sort of what I do when I work. You have to become people, in a sense—feel their emotions and experiences accurately, in order to portray them truthfully."

Francesca didn't seem to remember Luke was there, so focused was she on her conversation with his mother.

He wished he could be as unselfconscious. She fit

into his home so naturally. God knew, it was a pleasant novelty having a beautiful woman sitting there,
charming the air around her. He rubbed the ache at
the back of his neck, pulling at the collar of his short-
sleeved white cotton shirt. There just wasn't a wardrobe suitable for the Las Vegas summer heat.

He'd gone out alone for the jump he'd scheduled
with Jackson the day before. Floating in the sky, in
control, yet not in control, he'd reveled in a few brief
moments of peace.

Thank God for those.

"You don't become her to the point of losing
yourself," his mother was saying. Luke had to re-
strain the impulse to reach over and take the drumming knife out of her hand before she put a dent in
the table. "Just long enough to go where she is so
you can try to bring her to where you are."

Was she talking to him? Looking up, Luke saw
that her focus was on Francesca.

He poured another mimosa. Had he ever done
that—attempted to really put himself in his mother's
shoes, to live, even for the space of one minute, in
the hell she had to cope with every day of her life?

Would he even want to?

He understood her plight. He always had. It was
why he was still there.

"And what if she doesn't want to come to where
I am?" Francesca put down her fork, her dark eyes
shadowed. The room buzzed with the energy that
seemed to surround her.

And to draw him in.

Soon, the claustrophobia would follow.

"In that case, you have to meet her halfway," Carol said.

And then, for no apparent reason, she started to cry.

The pill he'd given her an hour before had obviously not worked.

Luke was in for a long afternoon.

# 16

Although it was only a couple of blocks from her motel, Francesca drove to the Burger King on Las Vegas Boulevard, Sunday afternoon's meeting place with Autumn. There was no way she could get *inside* her little sister—as Carol had described it—to have a chance at reaching in and pulling her out, if she didn't spend some time with her.

"Come on," she said, when she pulled up beside the waiting girl. She hoped her surprise didn't show when Autumn unhesitatingly complied. Her sister was dressed as conservatively today as she'd been the other three times she'd seen her. The colors of the tops and shorts had changed, but little else. Almost as though her clothes had been bought in bulk.

Or donated that way?

She liked the short spiky curls Autumn was wearing these days, but didn't see the point of the dark blond streaks in the younger girl's naturally blond hair.

"I thought we'd go back to my place," she said. "It isn't much, but it has a bathroom and it's private."

"Whatever."

Was the sullenness a result of the circumstances

of her current life, or the age? Autumn had always been such an enthusiastic kid. Spunky. Determined. And filled with zest. Francesca could remember her at two—as fine-boned as she was now—and determined to have chocolate for breakfast.

After a couple of turns, which took almost ten minutes on the busy Sunday-afternoon Strip, Francesca pulled up outside her door.

"You're staying *here?*"

"Yes."

"Shit, you hit hard times, or what?"

Francesca had to bite back the plea for Autumn to watch her language.

"No." Not in the way Autumn meant.

Inside, Autumn gave a lot of attention to the two double beds with their cheap flowered spreads, and the one chair under a window with bars on it. She even went in to inspect the bathroom with its missing piece of tile, the rusty drained tub and freestanding sink.

"I always pictured you in high-class places," she said, coming out of the bathroom to plop down on the edge of the one chair.

Grabbing a couple of pillows, Francesca propped them against the headboard. "You're welcome to the other bed," she told Autumn. "That chair has some suspicious stains."

Her sister didn't even acknowledge the offer.

*Okay, why?* Francesca asked herself. *Why is Autumn acting this way? What's she feeling? And how do I find out?*

How in the hell, when facing a sister you'd give your life for, did you detach yourself and go to work?

"Why are you so angry with me?" she asked.

"I'm not."

"Well, I just want you to know that I've kept my word. I've talked to Mom—mostly because she goes crazy if I don't call every few days—but I haven't said anything about finding you."

It had been harder than she'd expected—not being honest about this. Their mother hadn't been the greatest protector, but she was still their mother. And still hurting.

"If you had, I'd just leave again."

"She loves you, you know."

"Who needs it?"

"You?"

"Uh-uh." Autumn shook her head, stood up, wandered around the room, opening drawers, reading the television guide. "Not that kind of love."

"What kind of love?"

At the door to the bathroom Autumn turned, blue eyes narrowed. "The cheap, cowardly kind."

To Francesca's knowledge, Kay Stevens had never been cowardly in her love for her youngest daughter. She'd had no need to be. She was a strong, competent woman; the only person who'd ever cowed her was her equally strong and much larger, much more powerful second husband.

Who'd adored his only daughter as much as she had.

*Get inside her head,* she reminded herself. And

again she wondered how on earth she could do that when her heart was so deeply involved.

"So, for the time being, we're agreed that I don't tell Mom about finding you and you stay put, right?"

Autumn slid open the closet door. The only thing in it was Francesca's duffel.

Peering around the corner, she pinned Francesca with an uncompromising stare. "Depends."

"On what?" Legs left mostly bare by the shorts she was wearing, Francesca crossed one over the other, and almost immediately felt sweat gathering. The air conditioner at the Lucky Seven wasn't all that effective.

"You give me my space."

She grabbed one of the pillows from behind her and clutched it tight in the effort to hold herself back. What she wanted to do was haul the kid out of there, put her in the car and drive. For as far and as long as it took to find the little sister she'd lost. "What exactly does that mean?"

Autumn went back to her inspection of a space that was virtually empty. "When I say no, it means no."

"Obviously."

"And you stay away from my apartment. Period. Don't ever come back."

Love and compassion didn't seem to be working.

"Only if you give me a phone number where I can reach you."

"I don't have one."

"I saw a phone on the wall by your refrigerator."

"I didn't pay the bill."

"I'll pay it."

The closet door shut with enough force to knock it off its track. "Forget it."

Forget what? The deal? Or Francesca paying the bill?

"I have to have a way to contact you, Autumn."

"My name's Joy." The girl opened the pressed-wood armoire, revealing a television that got three channels. Sometimes.

"No, it isn't."

"As far as anyone here knows, it is. So it is."

"Then, when I meet your friends, I won't call you Autumn. But when we're together that's who you are."

The girl reached up to straighten a poster of the Las Vegas Strip in a cracked wooden frame.

And Francesca froze, her stomach turning over.

"What?" Autumn had turned around. Was staring at her.

Slowly Francesca's eyes rose from the small strip of skin she'd seen at her sister's back to the belligerent—and vulnerable?—blue eyes.

"He hit you. With the buckle end of the belt."

"Yeah, so? He hit you, too."

Skin burning, Francesca sat there, arms limp on her pillow as wave after wave of remorse and fury spread through her. Over her.

"Mom said he didn't. Ever. I asked her many times. Even after you ran away. She said it all stopped when I left. He never hit her again."

Autumn's expression was somewhere between a

sigh and a snarl. "Since when did she ever tell the truth about him?"

Tired beyond measure, Francesca studied the girl. *Oh, baby girl, I had no idea. I'd have taken you with me if I'd known.*

And then the two of them might have been living in this city together, both of them living the life that seemed to have changed Autumn so irrevocably.

"It was all because of me," she said, half talking to herself. There was no reason for Autumn to believe her. "Mom even said so. I was my father's daughter and he hated the constant reminder that to Mom, he was second best. All I had to do was walk in a room and he'd become furiously jealous. I had to leave so the anger would stop. So the hitting would stop. That last day, as I walked out, they promised that you'd never know...." She shook her head in hopelessness and confusion.

"He didn't want you to know," she went on. "You were always his precious little angel who adored him. Which is why he never touched me—or her—when you were around."

"Yes, he did."

*No.* "You were only three the last time he beat me."

"I saw you."

"What?"

"One time. I saw you." Autumn was sitting on the edge of the opposite bed, her legs out in front of her, hands in her lap. "I was supposed to be next door at a birthday party, but this kid told me I was ugly so I ran home. My father had you in a corner and he was kicking you. When you turned around, he hauled off his belt and started whipping your back.''

Francesca's lips started to tremble. It had been the last time. She'd been eighteen.

''You were barely out of diapers.''

''I don't remember that,'' Autumn said. ''But I know I was little.''

''What did you do?'' The tears filled her eyes but didn't fall.

''Ran back to the party.''

''You didn't say anything to anybody?''

''Who would I have told? Mom was right there in the room, watching him do it.''

Kay had tried to intervene. Until he'd slapped her across the mouth. If she'd said any more, she would've been as bruised and bleeding as Francesca. And then who would have cared for Autumn?

Francesca didn't say anything for a while. She couldn't. Horrified images of that day, of a three-year-old child witnessing her father's brutality, burned themselves on her heart.

Other than crossing her feet, Autumn didn't move.

''When did he start in on you?''

''Not until I was thirteen.''

''What happened?''

''I had my first period.''

Francesca stared at her little sister. ''I was home that weekend! I took you to the store for the stuff you needed. Everything was fine.''

''Until you left and my father found the tampons you'd bought me.''

"He beat you because of a box of tampons?"

Autumn muttered something she didn't catch. Francesca's heart began to pound. Dropping her pillow, she walked over to the other bed. "What did you say?"

"Nothing." Autumn shrugged, moved a few inches farther away. "I didn't say anything. Yeah, he beat me because of the tampons."

*Step into her shoes,* Francesca told herself. Well, maybe she had because she was fairly certain there was something Autumn wasn't telling her. "What did you just say a minute ago?" she asked again.

"What does it matter?" The eyes turned on her reminded her of the homeless old woman she'd seen on the street that night during her first week in town. Hopeless. More dead than alive.

"It matters because you do," Francesca said softly. "It took me years to figure that out for myself," she added. "To find anything about me that was worthy of life. Or love. Or success."

"But you were always the best at everything you did! Mom told me about you all the time. You went to college on a full scholarship. And got a job taking pictures with a local paper. And then, after only a year, you were good enough to freelance—"

Francesca stopped the girl by touching the clasped hands she held in her lap. "I was doing great on the outside," she said. "And so alone inside I couldn't bear it. I just worked more. Harder. Faster. To cover up."

Autumn stared at her, wide-open eyes filled with

questions. And emotions Francesca was afraid to name.

"Tell me what you said before." Francesca's words were insistent.

"Whatever." The girl was adept at infusing one word with enough belligerence to discourage anyone who wasn't awfully determined.

"Tell me, honey."

Motivated partially by indecision and partially by a strange kind of instinct, Francesca simply waited. For several minutes. Just sitting there, available. There didn't seem to be anything else to do.

"I said that wasn't all he did." Autumn's shoulders were hunched, her chin dropping to her chest.

The change in the girl's demeanor was obvious, showing Francesca the fragility she'd somehow known was there.

Taking her sister's hand in hers, Francesca moved closer, until they were touching. "Tell me."

"He said I was just like you, that you'd corrupted me. That no daughter of his was going to be fixated with sticking things up…there."

Oh, God. Francesca had left that Sunday afternoon and blithely driven back to San Francisco, to her expensive apartment and comfortable life, while Autumn had had to face that bastard.

If he weren't already dead, she'd kill him. With her bare hands. She'd drive to Sacramento, put her fingers around his prominent political throat and squeeze until there was no air left.

"And then he hit you."

"Not…quite." The girl's voice was barely audible. Francesca suspected that she was crying, though there was no sound, no sobs.

"What did he do?"

"He...it doesn't matter."

"Yes, honey, it does. No matter what it is, you have no reason to keep it hidden inside, torturing you. No reason to feel guilt or remorse or self-disgust. I promise you that. The shame is all his."

Autumn sat silently, and the fact that her hand remained in Francesca's was all the testimony her older sister needed. "Tell me. You need to talk about this. And I guarantee you'll feel better after you do."

"Did you ever?" Autumn's chin remained at her chest, her words mumbled. "Talk, I mean."

"Once."

"To who? Mom?"

"No." She thought of that night in Milan. The dams that had burst, one after another.

"Who, then?"

Only for the child sitting next to her could she make herself go to a place in her mind she'd refused to visit since that last day in Italy. "Antonio."

"Oh."

She'd expected Autumn to ask what had happened. Why they weren't married. To at least want to know if Francesca was still seeing him. When the girl ran away, Francesca and Antonio were still dating. She'd brought him home a few times and had suspected that the then-fourteen-year-old Autumn had a crush on him.

"It helped," she said now. So much that—in Milan—when she'd finally laid her heart completely open, she'd been unable to resist when the need to make love with him had overwhelmed her. It was the first and only time, and she'd also known that, because of his commitment to a disabled wife, she ultimately had to send him away.

He had no way of finding out that she was back in the States. And she'd spent every moment in Sacramento looking over her shoulder, avoiding any of the places he frequented, so she wouldn't have to see him again.

She couldn't even imagine how much that would hurt.

"So tell me."

Autumn's hand was soft beneath her own—and suddenly holding on tight.

"He made me go in the bathroom and take out the tampon I was wearing."

It was horrible. And yet not as bad as she'd feared.

"Before or after he hit you?"

"Before."

She could do this. Detachment was the key. Her task wasn't to imagine what it had been like for the sweet little girl she'd taken to the store that day to have her father humiliate her at such a tender, vulnerable time. She was there to provide the safe environment Autumn needed to speak of the trauma, get it behind her.

"He was waiting for you when you came out of the bathroom?"

Silence followed the request. Francesca's stomach filled with dread.

"Autumn?"

"Nooo…" The word became a wail and Francesca suddenly realized why her sister hadn't spoken. She hadn't been able to because of the emotion she was attempting to keep inside.

"Tell me," she said again. Pulling the girl against her, she cradled Autumn's head beneath her chin. "Come on, baby, I'm right here. Just tell me. It'll be okay. I'm right here."

Again and again she repeated the words, just as she'd done so many times in the past when Autumn had been hurt or upset by the loss of a pet, the disloyalty of a girlfriend, a boy who'd kissed her and told the whole school he'd hated it.

"He…" She took a wobbly breath. "He pushed me…"

Francesca's nerves started to buzz with agitation. With panic. Maybe she wasn't ready for this.

"…inside the bathroom…"

Autumn took another breath. And shuddered. Francesca held on.

"…he told me to take it out…"

Oh, God. No. She knew what was coming.

"…I told him I would—but he wouldn't believe me. He said you'd corrupted me and I wasn't to be any more trusted than you were."

She brushed the girl's hair back from her forehead, touching her lightly, careful not to give Autumn any sense of being trapped or held in a way that took away her freedom.

"He wouldn't leave." One sob escaped, and Francesca could only guess how much more the child was holding inside.

"You could've shown it to him afterward."

"I s-s-said so." Another break in Autumn's composure and then she was still again. "He s-s-said I'd fake it...."

She didn't need to hear any more, could easily follow the story through to the bitter end. But this wasn't about her. It was for Autumn.

"So what happened?"

"He made me pull down my pants in front of him. And take it out."

"While he watched." They were in this together. Francesca could take part of the telling upon herself.

"Yes."

Neither of them said anything for the next minute. Just sat there, safe in each other's embrace, thinking about a man they both hated, the man who'd given life to one of them and stolen life from them both.

When Autumn's tears started to fall, Francesca held on, willing her sister to let herself cry. To heal. And to find in herself the strength that had seen her through the worst abuse life could bring her.

She had no idea how much time passed. Summer days were long in Las Vegas, the sun continuing to shine well past the dinner hour. There was no sense of time in that dingy motel room, just anguish.

Eventually spent, they lay down, Francesca cradling her sister against her as she had so many nights in the past. She didn't move as Autumn's breathing took on the deep evenness of sleep. And lay there awake, listening to the occasional hiccups that interrupted her sister's rest. She'd done that on those long-ago nights, feeling each little sob deep inside herself, filled with a need to make this precious child's life so much better than her own. To protect Autumn from all the harsh realities that had come so early to her own life.

Darkness had fallen by the time Autumn woke.

"What time is it?" She sounded alarmed as she shot up, looking around for a clock.

"Just after nine."

"I have to go." Autumn was off the bed and at the door before Francesca had even sat up.

"I thought we'd have some dinner," she said, searching for the sandals she'd kicked aside earlier. "We can stop for a hamburger and then I'll take you wherever you want to go."

Which she hoped was home. Surely, after all this, Autumn wouldn't continue to ban her from the apartment.

"I can't," the girl said, her voice sharp with tension. She stood stiffly at the door, hand tapping against her leg as she waited.

"Can you tell me why?"

"No."

She tried not to let herself be disappointed. "Okay." Grabbing her keys and bag, she opened the door. "Where would you like me to drop you?"

Autumn named a corner a couple of blocks from her apartment.

"I don't want you walking alone in the dark."

"I have to." They were at the car.

"Who says?"

"Cesca?" The girl glanced over as she started the ignition, her voice soft, tentative.

"Yeah?"

"No more questions tonight, okay?"

It was the look in Autumn's eyes that prevented Francesca from pressing any further. Whatever was happening in her little sister's life had her teetering on the edge. Francesca was there to pull her back, not push her over.

"Okay."

So she hadn't come as far as she'd hoped.

They weren't on their way home.

But something had changed that night, bringing them so tightly together that nothing would ever separate them again. Not time or space, not any person, dead or alive. Not even death itself.

With that, Francesca would have to be satisfied.

# 17

She'd known it couldn't last. Nothing good ever seemed to last in Sheila Miller's life. One minute she was in the bedroom in which she'd spent her loneliest hours, filling the space with sex and excitement and cries of love, finding a fulfillment beyond anything she'd ever imagined possible. And the next, she was walking out to her kitchen to discover the man she'd just done wild and crazy things with standing there, holding a letter in his hand that would ruin it all. She'd forgotten she'd left it lying there. Forgotten because she hadn't thought she'd be seeing him tonight. They'd both been on the late shift, had decided earlier that they'd have to wait until the next day to be together again.

And then he'd surprised her, showing up at her table just as she was closing, insisting that while he didn't know about her, he couldn't wait another six hours to see her again.

They'd had a couple of drinks, talked about ordering breakfast, but had been too eager to get back to her house, her bed, to bother with anything as mundane as food.

And this from the woman who used to think eating was the only reason to get up in the morning.

"You make a habit of reading other people's mail?"

"I came out to get us each a bottle of water. It was on the counter. And kind of hard to ignore. Who is this guy?"

He flung out the letter with the big bold damning words typed across the top. *Final Notice*. How fitting.

"Somebody I met a while back. He used to be a regular at my table."

"And you borrowed money from him."

"Mmm-hmm." Kind of odd, having this conversation with them both stark naked. She wished she'd grabbed her robe.

So why not? What did it matter now? Turning, Sheila went back to her room, not looking for the negligee she usually wore when he was around, but for the worn cotton robe she'd had since her thirtieth birthday. It had been a present to herself. A homecoming of sorts. To know that she was thirty and alone and okay all by herself. To know she'd always be there for herself. That she didn't need anyone else to feel happy or complete.

A bunch of hogwash if she'd ever heard it.

"He's suing you for misrepresentation." Arnold had followed her and was sitting on the edge of her rumpled bed, the letter still in his hand.

"Yep." Picking his pants up off the floor, she tossed them in his direction.

"Why?"

"What can I say? I was stupid." It was far too late to pull this together. *I'm losing my home, my life and now him.* There was no way a man as virtuous and honorable as Arnold Jackson would see any value in the likes of her. Her supposed values, contrary to those of most of their peers, was what had attracted him in the first place.

''How stupid?''

When it became clear that he wasn't going to put his pants on until she told him the whole damn story, she did so. The building contract that had taken all her life savings and then escalated in price every time she needed a window or floor tile, light fixture or faucet. The second mortgage on her condo. And when that hadn't been enough, she'd taken out a loan at nineteen percent interest, using the already fully mortgaged condo as collateral. She'd thought the house would be done by the time payment was due. That she could sell the condo, get out from under the double mortgages, and take out a second mortgage on the house. She'd had it all planned.

But costs continued to escalate and her builder continued to stall. She had to live in the condo, so she couldn't sell it. There was no house to mortgage.

Arnold sat there a long time. Probably wondering how to extricate himself from her house. Sheila didn't have a lot of experience with this type of situation. In fact, she had none. So she sat beside him. And waited. He'd figure out how to do this, and she'd graciously accept whatever excuse he came up with. He'd go. And then she could hit the cupboard above her stove, take the cap off the new bottle of Scotch she kept there for emergencies and finish the thing off before morning.

It might not solve her problems, but it would alleviate the immediate one. The sense of hopelessness that was stripping her of every shred of the dignity she'd fought so hard to win.

"I think I can help."

Lost in her visions of Scotch and oblivion, she almost missed his words. He had to be kidding.

"You do?"

He nodded, his eyes serious but not grave.

"I heard who's scamming the Bonaparte."

"You know who's behind the wins?"

He nodded.

And when he'd elaborated, telling her exactly what he, a man with values and an inspired sense of what mattered most, could do, Sheila dared to hope that her ship really had come in.

All the gold she'd ever wanted rested within this man's heart.

Carl was a good friend—if only Francesca could feel sure he'd be satisfied with that. At dinner Monday night, Francesca came clean with him, telling him that her "friend" was her runaway little sister. He wasn't noticeably hurt by her deception. If anything, his admiration of her seemed to grow. Which allowed her to open up and tell him about many of the things scrambling around inside her—mostly to do with Autumn.

Even though finding her sister meant she wouldn't be in his town much longer—destroying any hopes he might've had that they'd explore a more intimate relationship—he ordered champagne to celebrate.

And listened, attentive as always, as she answered all his questions.

"So you've seen her every day since you found her?" he asked as they enjoyed fresh-baked bread, warm from the oven, with their champagne while waiting for the pasta they'd ordered at a little out-of-the-way Italian diner not far from his home.

"Not usually for very long, but yes." She'd worn her only dress—a spaghetti-strap black shift that had enough cotton to make it thin and cool and enough Lycra to make it comfortable. At the appreciation in Carl's eyes, she wished she'd worn jeans.

"So you've seen where Autumn lives? Where she works?" Carl asked as she enjoyed the melt-in-her-mouth ravioli she'd just been served.

"I've seen where she lives once, and she won't tell me where she works." That conversation had left Francesca very unsettled. "As a matter of fact," she said, looking at him over the candlelit table for two, "when I pushed her this afternoon, she said she wasn't working at all at the moment."

"But she lives alone?"

"Apparently."

"So who's paying her bills?" He frowned, his forearms on the table giving her a sense of his quiet strength.

"That's what I'd like to know."

Carl poured more champagne for each of them. Asked how she was enjoying her meal so far. Talked about the dishes yet to come, describing the chicken marsala and the tiramisu. She was never going to be able to eat it all. She hadn't eaten more than one meal a day in months, had lost more than twenty pounds in that period, and the thought of so much food at one time made her stomach roil.

Their plates were cleared away, the table between them empty except for the champagne while they awaited their next course. "So what explanation do you have for all of Autumn's secrecy?" Carl asked. "Her struggle for independence?"

She shook her head. "She's hiding something." There was absolutely no doubt about that. "I'm just not sure what."

"Maybe she's living with someone."

"Maybe." The thought had certainly occurred to her. "But I don't think so. I didn't see much of her apartment, but it was small. She wasn't expecting us and there was absolutely no sign of a man's presence there."

"So what do you think it is?"

She had no idea. Or perhaps she didn't want to have one. She'd just found her little sister, was still in the process of reconnecting. "I don't know, but whatever it is, it's making her sick."

His brows drew together, concern shining from those compassionate brown eyes. "What do you mean, sick?"

"She's thrown up twice in the four times I've seen her. And now that I think about it, that first day, when she answered the door, she cut herself off mid-sentence, but I'm pretty sure she was saying she'd just puked."

Certainly not dinnertime conversation. Carl didn't seem to mind.

"She's nervous, tense, high-strung in a completely negative way," she continued. "And scared to the point of nausea." She was going to have to face this. Much sooner than she wanted to.

"She's always had a weak stomach when it comes to emotional stress," she told him. "For a while there, she'd throw up on the walk to school every morning."

That crease was still marking his forehead.

"What?" she asked, when he remained silent.

"Nothing." He wouldn't meet her eyes.

"Tell me."

He did look up then, his expression flat—and completely sober. "Are you sure you're ready to hear it?"

"No." She took another sip of champagne, appreciating the warmth of the liquid as it slid down her throat. "But tell me, anyway."

"She's a runaway."

"Yeah."

"In Las Vegas."

"Uh-huh." She took another sip. As though the warmth would spread from her stomach to her heart where she was suddenly very cold.

"The pressure she's feeling..."

"Yeah?" She didn't want to hear this. Didn't want to be in Autumn's shoes and know he was right.

"Is probably from a pimp."

While Luke was waiting for Francesca on Wednesday, the phone in his office rang. Expecting to hear from his employer, a follow-up to the unsatisfactory call over the weekend, he considered ignoring it. The thought was tempting. But of course Amadeo had the numbers for Luke's cell and home phones, and he had the determination to keep trying until he reached his godson. He also had the orneriness to speak with Luke's mother and get her to come nagging to his aid if all else failed. Luke had spoken to Amadeo on Sunday. Listened to his tirade of dissatisfaction and orders regarding the unsolved thefts, his demands that Luke resolve the damn thing and before they suffered another hit. As if Luke wasn't already doing everything humanly possible, contacting every expert, reading every report, studying every tape, speaking to every possibly involved party.

Worse, though, had been the string of expletives he'd had to suffer through after the old man heard about the loss of Luke's potential son. It was hard enough to live with his own disappointment, let alone deal with someone else's. This was one of the reasons he hadn't told his mother the bad news yet. She wasn't expecting anything to happen for another six months. By then Francesca would be long gone and he'd be the only one around to cope with the episodes that were sure to follow his announcement.

On the fourth ring, he glanced at the caller ID. A local number. Not one he recognized.

Francesca had said she'd meet him at his office as soon as she dropped off her sister. They were going out to dinner and then to a show. Francesca had never seen any of the Cirque du Soleil performances and he'd felt it his duty to ensure she didn't leave town without the experience.

A fifth ring. It was after five. He'd expected her before now.

On the sixth ring he picked up.

He didn't recognize the female voice, nor did he appreciate the bored tone of his caller as she asked to speak with him and proceeded to verify his identity when he told her she was.

A reaction that changed completely when she stated the reason for her call.

She was from the Colter Adoption Agency. They had a son for Luke. He would be born exactly six months from that date and at seven o'clock on the evening of his birth, Luke could come to the hospital to take him home.

Six rings. One phone call. And just like that, Luke had a son.

''Carl thinks Autumn's prostituting to support herself.'' They were walking along the Strip, something Francesca liked to do at night. She liked feeling the energy of newly arriving vacationers as they approached the slots, liked seeing the lights and watching the free outdoor shows many of the upscale resorts had spent millions to produce for viewers' hourly pleasure.

Hands in the pockets of his dress slacks, Luke didn't say anything for a few minutes. He'd shed his jacket, rolled up his sleeves, but said he hadn't wanted to take time to go home and change.

His arm brushed hers, and as her stomach reacted

to his warmth she moved farther away. What was it with her all of a sudden? Carl the other night, Luke today. She'd never had a thing about forearms.

"What do you think?" She was still wearing what she'd put on to have lunch with her sister that afternoon. A short denim skirt, white T-shirt and white sandals, her black leather bag over her shoulder. She'd retired the homeless-person denim version.

"I've suspected as much."

Francesca crossed her arms, warding off a chill that couldn't be coming from the early-August temperatures. "But you've met her. What do you think *now?*"

"I think she's in some kind of trouble." The crowds weren't too thick that night. They had to slow for a group in front of them, but were soon able to pass and continue on their own.

"Drugs?"

"Maybe. But I doubt it. The signs aren't there."

She didn't think so, either. Autumn's color was good. Her eyes weren't bloodshot. There was no bruising or other evidence of shooting up on her arms. Her behavior, while stilted and tense, wasn't erratic.

"What, then?"

"Sounds like your friend Carl could be right."

Waiting at one of the Strip's many streetlights, Francesca wondered if Autumn had ever done any of the kid things in town—like go to the M&M's store across the street. Or ride the New York New York roller coaster a block or two down. Had she ever played in any of the casinos' circus-game rooms?

Won a stuffed toy? Or had someone win a toy for her?

As they crossed, she glanced down a side street and saw several people walking alone, walking as though they had somewhere to be. Almost as though they were immune to the frenetic world of chance just a few yards away—where the illusion of opulence and success and luxury enveloped the lucky and eluded everyone else. Looking around her at the glittering lights that made the Strip appear as bright as midday, at the wedding chapels and tourist shops, the slot machines ringing through open casino doors, the liquor stores and signs offering everything from hot dogs to prime rib for almost the same price, she knew that the people who lived in this town, who were residents, didn't live like this. They had lives completely apart from all of it. Normal lives.

So why couldn't Autumn?

"This Carl guy, you like him a lot?"

The question gave her pause. Because she was feeling so guilty about her lack of interest, considering Carl's obvious attraction? Or because Luke was the one asking? "He's a very nice man."

"Has he become more than a friend?"

"Of course not."

He waved aside a man trying to hand him a baseball-card-size pornographic photo. The man and woman beside them each took one.

An older couple, in their seventies at least, walked slowly in front of them, hand in hand. She was laughing at something the man was saying.

"You're the first woman I've known who actually

enjoyed walking the Strip,'' Luke said half an hour later. The Bonaparte's sign many blocks behind them looked like a prop from a miniature car track.

''As crazy as it is, there's something mesmerizing about it, too.''

''If nothing else, there's enough to look at that you can't possibly get bored.''

She nodded. They'd slowed their pace again. ''I think that's what I like about it. There's so much stimulation it distracts my brain for a while.''

''When I was a kid, I used to come out here sometimes when my dad was working late and just walk. Ironic as it might sound, those were some of the most peaceful times.''

''You said I'm the first woman who enjoyed being out here with you. Have there been a lot of them? Women, I mean?''

''Some.''

''Care to elaborate?'' They'd reached a less expensive area, the signs now more about massages and adult bookstores than prime rib dinners. Someone was giving away free chips and salsa with every drink. A red-and-white blinking sign proclaimed yet another wedding chapel. And there was a billboard advertising sightseeing tours to the Grand Canyon.

And somehow, she and Luke were talking about things neither of them normally spoke about—even to themselves. He told her about his resentments of his mother, about the shame. About his quest in his younger years to escape himself and that life by finding a woman with whom he could start a family of his own.

"You thought that would free you from the family you already had? Like you'd just trade them in for a new model?"

He chuckled. "I think it's pretty obvious I *wasn't* thinking," he said. "In any case, it didn't work."

"You got married and it didn't work?"

"No." He shook his head, met her gaze for a sideways smile that held more nostalgic sadness for the young man he'd been than it did humor. "As soon as I acknowledged to myself that I might be close— to love, to marriage—I'd suddenly feel trapped by the relationship."

"Leaving lots of broken hearts behind, huh?" she asked, feeling a moment's empathy with the nameless women. Had she been in a position to allow herself a romantic relationship, she'd probably have been one of them herself. For all his standoffishness, Luke Everson was a compelling man.

"It's the major reason I gave up the search," he told her. "I couldn't stand to look into one more set of beautiful eyes and see the pain I'd inflicted there."

Francesca understood as though she were walking in his shoes.

# 18

"Carl wanted there to be something more between us than friendship."

Luke wasn't surprised to hear that. Nor particularly pleased, either. Not that her love life mattered to him; it didn't. But *she* mattered. And she wasn't ready to have some bartender getting intimate. She had things to do, issues to resolve.

"And?" he asked, not sure he wanted to know. He might not be able to keep his mouth shut if she told him she was going to give it a try. As one of her only friends in town, he'd have to tell her what he thought about that.

"I set him straight. Gently, I hope. I told him I'd keep in touch."

"How'd he take it?"

"Good." The admiration in her tone rankled a bit. "I told you, he's a nice man."

His instant response—wondering if perhaps the man wasn't a little *too* nice—he put down to base maleness and kept to himself.

"What about you?" he asked. "You're young, beautiful, successful. There must've been men who wanted a part of that."

He'd completely messed up that remark—he'd made her sound like property.

"I guess," she said, her arm touching his as they moved slowly into the night. This end of the Strip wasn't as brightly lit, yet still had a sense of escape. "Mostly I was too busy with my life to have time for anything to develop."

"Why so driven?"

Her lack of immediate answer was telling. Francesca Witting had more secrets than he did. Perhaps that was why he found himself thinking about her so often.

"My talents were in a very competitive field where for every hundred who wanted in, only two or three made it."

A surface truth, maybe, but he'd bet his month's salary that it wasn't the real reason she'd left no time in her life for love.

Her feet looked so small compared to his—especially in those thin strappy sandals. And they'd walked for miles. Small but mighty. Just like her.

"Can I ask you something?"

"Of course."

"Why'd Autumn leave home?"

She stumbled. For the first time in all those blocks. "Aside from the usual reasons," he added.

They walked another block. Past a sign for a strip club. Then another one, with the words Strippers and Dates splashed across the front of the building. Followed by a place where one could go for marriage licenses. Only in Las Vegas.

"Her father beat her."

Luke walked on beside her, mulling over the quiet words. "Her father would have been your stepfather?" he finally said.

"Yes." Before, her gaze had been all over the Strip, taking in the sights, but now she was staring at the ground.

"Did he hit you, too?" The question wasn't his to ask. And yet, it felt as if it was. They'd been through a lot together, he and this woman who'd be in and out of his life as quickly as a daydream.

She nodded. A gesture he almost missed. The way her hands were tucked beneath her arms on either side caught at him. A protective, subservient gesture from one of the strongest women he'd ever known.

Without further thought, Luke reached over and took the hand closest to him.

Nothing was said, no acknowledgement, one way or the other, of what they were or weren't doing. They talked about other things. She told him about a man named Antonio. Not much. Just enough for him to know that the man was the only one she'd ever loved. That he'd been married, so the relationship had gone nowhere. Enough for him to know she'd been badly hurt by the experience.

He told her about his decision to adopt a son, and was a bit relieved by her lack of shock at his plan for single fatherhood. So much for his concern that people were immediately going to challenge him about the boy's right to a mother.

"I got the call just before you came in this evening," he heard himself saying—probably because he was still reeling from the news. "I pick him up six months from today at seven in the evening."

"She must be having him by Caesarean section to have the time locked down like that."

He nodded, picturing himself walking out those doors with his newborn son in his arms.

Glancing down at Francesca, he was struck by the blankness of her expression. She couldn't have been less interested. The reaction surprised him. She'd been so nurturing with her sister, he'd expected her to be one of those women who warmed up to talk of babies and children.

He'd known a lot of women like that.

"Have you ever considered having children?" he asked now.

"That is one thing I will *never* consider doing," Francesca said with such certainty he wouldn't have dared argue. "Not ever."

The first hands-off sign she'd ever sent him. As she'd obviously intended, it stopped him from asking any further questions—but not from thinking them. Had the abuse she'd suffered prevented her from having children?

Or maybe she felt so strongly because Antonio couldn't father her children. It could also be the heartache she'd gone through with Autumn.

He really wanted to ask, but didn't. He asked about her photography instead. Told her about his lack of progress uncovering any explanation for the barrage of big wins that had hit the Strip—and most damagingly, the Bonaparte. She asked about his mother. He told her about his suspicion that Arnold had a new woman friend.

And when, a long time later, they arrived back at the Bonaparte for their cars, they were still holding hands.

She'd wanted him to kiss her good-night.

As she drove the few miles between her apartment and the corner near her sister's where Autumn would be waiting, Francesca finally admitted what she'd refused to acknowledge the night before, when she'd made her way back to the Lucky Seven and the sleeping pill awaiting her.

It had to be hormones. They were still out of whack from her having given birth and then breast-feeding. And then stopping so abruptly.

Her breasts tightened and she pulled her mind back. She wasn't going to think about those things. No exceptions. She'd done well these past few weeks. She could continue doing well. Luke's talk of a son didn't *have* to raise dead issues. Nor did the mention of Antonio. They just didn't. People could choose what they thought about.

Autumn was waiting, as usual, jumping into the car before Francesca had come to a complete stop.

"What's the hurry?"

"Nothing!" She glanced around. "Let's go, I'm starved."

Because she was relieved to see the girl with an appetite and no longer sick to her stomach, Francesca let the moment go.

But she didn't forget.

She'd give Autumn a few more days and then, if the girl wasn't more forthcoming, she'd have to start probing. If some pimp believed he owned Autumn, he was going to learn differently.

Beyond that, any thoughts of what her sister might actually be doing while Francesca lay in her bed in the Lucky Seven or walked the Strip, played slots and had dinner with friends, were just going to have to wait. Francesca couldn't do everything at once.

"Where are your cameras?" Autumn asked on Sunday afternoon when she met her sister at the UNLV campus. "My whole life, I can never remember you being ten feet from a lens, but in all this time I haven't seen you take a single picture."

"They're in my room." She'd had dinner with Luke and his mother the night before. Carol Everson, too, had been surprised to learn that Francesca hadn't taken a single picture since she'd been in Las Vegas. And later Luke had asked why—since she specialized in pictorial studies of the human condition—she hadn't chronicled any of the people who visited the town or lived there. He hadn't been satisfied with any of her explanations. He was getting to know her too well.

It felt like they were all ganging up on her.

"So when you're not with me, you're out taking pictures?" Autumn asked, turning sideways to watch Francesca as she drove.

"Not really." The truth wasn't up for discussion. But she couldn't lie. "Until last week, I was looking for you every waking moment," she reminded her.

"And speaking of which, I need to talk to you about something."

Two things, actually, but she'd deal with them one at a time.

"What?" It still didn't take much to bring the defensiveness back to Autumn's posture and tone.

"How about if we drive through and bring lunch back to my place?" They'd reached her car and McDonald's was on the way. Francesca hadn't eaten there in years, but since being in Las Vegas, it had become one of the restaurants she frequented most.

"Uh-oh, this is going to be bad." The girl stared out the window. At least she wasn't jumping out. Running off.

"No, I just hate how you're always looking nervously around when we're out anywhere around here. Like you're afraid you're going to see someone you know."

"It'd be pretty weird for a young kid like me to be seen hanging out with an older woman like you," the girl said dryly.

The reply was total bullshit. Francesca let it go, anyway.

"So? Let's have it."

They were back in Francesca's room, on the bed that generally served as table, laundry basket and storage shelf. The hamburgers and French fries were spread out between them. Autumn had ordered a couple of burgers and the largest order of fries they had.

"You sure you're going to be able to eat all that?"

"Yeah, like I said, I'm starved," the girl said, dig-

ging in unselfconsciously. Francesca couldn't remember ever taking a bite of food at that age without
being concerned about her weight. But as sick as
Autumn had been, she had some eating to make up
for.

Was the fact that she was able to eat a sign that
whatever had been troubling her was dealt with and
gone? Had whoever was harassing her, bringing fear
to her every movement, agreed to leave her alone?

Francesca wasn't beyond hoping.

"I want to tell Mom I've found you."

"No way." The girl spoke with her mouth full,
not missing a bite.

"Hear me out, Autumn, okay?"

"Whatever."

As always, Autumn was wearing half-length shorts
and a pullover shirt of the same style as all the others.
One of their next outings was going to be the fashion
mall just down the street from the Treasure Island
hotel. The girl could do with some choices when she
got up in the morning, minor though such choices
were.

"I know she let you down," Francesca said, trying
to eat and have this conversation at the same time.
"She let me down, too."

Autumn glanced up then, shared a look with Francesca that almost made Francesca cry. It hurt so
badly to think of all the years Autumn had suffered
alone. It should never have been that way. She'd
promised herself she wouldn't let it be that way
again.

"But the thing is, Autumn, by blaming her, holding a grudge against her, we only hurt ourselves. I found that out the hard way.''

''So what.'' Autumn yanked a fry out of the paper carton. ''We're just supposed to say, *It's okay, Mom, don't worry about the fact that you let that man beat the crap out of me?* It's okay that even while she was cleaning the blood off my back she was telling me to keep things quiet because she married a prominent politician who'd only make things worse for us if I went to the cops?''

She couldn't eat. And she couldn't interrupt, either. She had to help her sister through this. To set her free.

''Well, sorry, it's not okay. And I don't care what she said, things *couldn't* get any worse for me. I didn't care about financial security nearly as much as she did.''

''I know.'' Autumn's words expressed exactly the thoughts she'd had herself. So many times. ''But the thing is, hon, Mom wasn't just worried about financial security. He had her beaten down, too. Worse, I think, because she shared such an intimate relationship with him.''

*Come on, Autumn, the compassion's inside you. It's safe to feel it. I'm here.*

''Yeah, well, bully for her, but she could've stopped that, too, anytime she chose. It makes me sick, you know? To think of her in bed with him, doing *that,* after everything he did to us.''

''She was scared. More for us than for herself. Afraid of what he'd do to us if she left him.''

''Being dead would've been better.''

"At the time, it sure felt that way," Francesca agreed. "But once you get through it, once you heal, you're glad your life was spared. There's so much good out there, Autumn, so much love and laughter and hope and just plain joy. If he'd killed us, we wouldn't have had the chance to know any of that."

The girl finished off one burger. Started on the second.

"So how much love and hope and laughter you having these days?" she asked.

"More and more since I found you again." It was a truth she could speak with her whole heart.

"Yeah." Autumn looked up at her for a long moment, and then her gaze dropped. "Well, sorry, I still can't pretend what she did is okay."

Autumn didn't have any chance of getting on with her life if she couldn't let go of this.

"I'm not asking you to. Only asking you to let me call her and tell her you're okay. I've already gotten her word that she'll leave you in my care, so you don't have to worry about going back or seeing her, at least not yet. But she's human, too, Autumn. She went through a lot for both of us. She's alone. And she's hurting every bit as badly as you are."

"Doubtful."

*What's hurting you so badly, child?* Francesca's eyes asked the question she knew her half sister wouldn't answer.

"If you hate her this badly, why'd you call her?"

Autumn's head sank lower. "It was stupid," she muttered. "A moment of weakness. I was scared."

"Of what?"

She glanced up, with nothing but an unreadable glint in her eyes. "What do you think? I'm a seventeen-year-old runaway."

*God, how do I get through to her? Get her to talk to me? Tell me what she does all day? And all night?*

"She's had a hard life, Autumn. Her future isn't stretching before her like yours and mine. The only thing she still cares anything about is the two of us. Just let me tell her you're okay so she can at least start eating and sleeping again."

Autumn chewed. Swallowed. Took another bite. And another. She finished the second burger. And all the fries. Sucked at her drink until she was sucking air from the bottom of her cup. And then she methodically packed up all the trash and shoved it back in the bag.

"Whatever," she said, getting up to toss the bag. "Just keep her away from me."

"You got it," Francesca said, grinning inside for the first time in a long while. Whether she knew it or not, Autumn had just taken the first step toward freedom.

"I gotta get going," Autumn said Tuesday afternoon. The two of them had made a habit of having lunch together in Francesca's room. It seemed to be the only place Autumn ever relaxed. At least with Francesca.

Francesca, lounging against the headboard on a bed of pillows, didn't move. "Of course I'll take you back, but I wish you didn't have to go."

"Yeah, well, I do." Autumn stood, grabbed her purse.

Francesca wondered how long this could continue. Seeing Autumn for lunch was great, but at some point she had to get on with her life. Sleep somewhere other than the Lucky Seven. Do something besides eat with her sister, worry and try not to read too much into whatever time she spent with Luke Everson. "I think tomorrow we should go shopping. Buy you some new clothes."

"No!" Autumn spun around, the fear back in her eyes. "I mean, why? What's wrong with my clothes?" Her belligerence was a second too late.

"Nothing. What's wrong with buying new ones?"

"I…can't afford it and I…don't want you spending your money on me. I can take care of myself." The words gained momentum as though Autumn was starting to believe an excuse she was creating as she spoke.

Francesca straightened. Much as she wanted to, she couldn't put this off any longer.

"Sit down."

"I gotta go."

"In a minute."

Looking past her sister, Autumn sat. "All right, but make it quick. I really have to go."

"One question, one answer and we're out of here," Francesca said, hating the wild, wide-eyed look in her little sister's eyes.

"What?"

Francesca opened her mouth but couldn't make the horrible words come out. "You've left me no choice here, Autumn.'' She wanted to take the girl's hand, tell her it was okay, to remove that haunted look from her eyes. Take her home. Do whatever Autumn wanted that would make her happy. Give her all the space she needed. Stay away from her home, her life. . Allow the girl her secrets.

''You won't tell me what you do when you're away from here. Won't tell me where you work. I've met none of your friends, or anyone you know in this town, and I'm not allowed in your apartment. You give me nothing.''

''I'm here. Every day.''

''Yes, I know, but—''

''I've told you things no one else knows....''

She swallowed, tried not to cry. She'd made it through most of her adult life, not to mention some pretty brutal beatings during her teenage years, without tears. And now, with this child/woman, she was crying all the time.

''I know, honey, I understand. But you're in trouble. I think you need my help. I know I need to help you. But I'm in the dark here. How can I do anything if I don't know what you're hiding from? Or hiding from me? What has you so frightened?''

Autumn's gaze darted to the door, her eyes alight with pain. ''You said one question,'' she said in a clipped voice. ''Which one?''

The girl wasn't giving her any other choice. If she only got one...

''Are you a prostitute?'' Her eyes flooded with tears as she asked. It felt wrong, sordid, a sacrilege to all she knew Autumn to be, and to the unconditional love she had for her sister. The girl was only seventeen years old. Still a child in so many ways.

Autumn's face slowly rose, her eyes, which met Francesca's, clear and strong. "No."

No? *No?* "Did you say no?"

"Yes."

Was Autumn's calm response a front for unspeakable things? Or the truth it seemed? She wished she had some of Carol Everson's assurance that stepping into others' shoes was possible. How did she know if she was there, inside that other person's life? Or merely standing in a version of her own?

"You're sure?"

"Cesca." Autumn actually smiled. "I think I'd know if I was doing something like that."

"But…"

"I promise you." The girl leaned forward, grabbed Francesca's hand in both of hers and reached up to dry the tears that had fallen to her cheeks. "On this one issue, I can tell you everything because there's absolutely nothing to tell." She moved to Francesca's bed, slid an arm around her back.

That young arm felt fabulous.

Autumn turned, her eyes wide open as they gazed into Francesca's. Francesca couldn't have looked away if the whole place had been burning down around them.

"I am not making money, nor have I ever made money, sleeping with a man. Or a woman. Or an animal or any other sick thing you hear about here in Vegas. I'm a virgin, Cesca! Hard to believe, I know, considering that I'm seventeen and have been on my own for two years. I guess you can put it down to what Daddy did to me, but I just couldn't let that happen. Sex, I mean. Not at any cost.''

Francesca didn't even try to stop the tears that poured from her eyes. She couldn't seem to speak, to form a coherent thought. She could only feel relief. So much love. And gratitude greater than she'd known herself capable of feeling.

''So we have something to thank him for, after all, don't we, Cesca?'' The girl's soft words touched her deeply.

''I guess so, honey.'' Francesca pulled the girl into her arms while they both cried away more stored-up pain and shame and loneliness.

# 19

_____

"Hello?" Francesca's voice sounded hoarse with sleep when she picked up after the third ring.

Luke hadn't intended to wake her. He'd been hard at work in his office on the top floor of the Bonaparte for a couple of hours already that Friday morning. Amadeo was due back the following week.

"Hi, it's Luke."

"I know. Your number came up on caller ID. What time is it?"

"Seven-thirty."

"Oh." He heard rustling. Her covers? He pictured her in an oversize T-shirt. He didn't figure her for a gown type of girl. "What's up?" She sounded more fully awake.

"Just wanted to know if I could see you tonight. If you aren't busy with Autumn, that is."

"Since when am I ever busy with her in the evening?"

It bothered Francesca a lot, the fact that her sister still refused to tell her what she did every night. And most days, too, except at lunchtime. Luke didn't blame her for feeling that way. He'd only met the young girl once, but something about the whole Biamonte apartment setup bothered him, too.

"Is that a yes?"

"I suppose."

Good thing he wasn't a man who suffered from ego problems. Her lack of eagerness would've done him in. "We don't have to if you'd rather not."

"No! I mean, yes, I want to, it's just…"

"What?" He glanced at the report in front of him. A daily log he'd been getting since the day following his drunken videotape venture more than two weeks before. He'd called up a friend of his from Marine Corps days—a guy who now ran a private investigation company—and on his own dollar was paying his team of plainclothes officers—ex-MPs trained in the art of surveillance. Amadeo would have foot the bill, but Luke felt better keeping the job quiet. If no one knew, there'd be no conversations to overhear, no leaks to tip off a perpetrator. He could get Esposito to reimburse him later.

For two weeks his buddy, Don Brown, and his crew had been walking the casinos on the Strip, watching for any card-counting, dealer liaisons, possible security breaches, anything at all that might explain the unusual happenings these past months.

One thing was certain: whatever insiders were behind those wins were fully aware of normal security measures because they'd been so successful in sidestepping them.

"It's just that…I don't know, aren't you worried about how much time we're spending together? This week it's been every night except for one."

And that had been because his mother had had an episode and he'd had to cancel. A couple of times they'd met at the Bonaparte for drinks. Two other nights he'd taken her home with him and the three of them had dinner and visited until Carol went to bed. Luke had actually enjoyed several of those conversations, seeing past his mother's illness long enough to get a glimpse of the person inside.

Or perhaps Francesca brought out a side of her that was previously hidden....

"Why should I be worried?" he asked, giving the report a preliminary read.

"Because neither of us wants to start anything."

A Bonaparte guest had been counting cards the day before. One of his plainclothes men was planning to follow the guy around that day to see if anything came of it. It was a long shot. Card-counting wasn't all that unusual. But he might as well be paying the guys to do something more than drink Cokes and stare.

"Your time in town is limited," Luke said now, wondering if he could catch Arnold before he left home. He could ask the older man to join him and Francesca after his shift. He'd been so busy with her, he'd neglected his friend lately, had been the one to cancel out on their skydiving plans this past week. They hadn't talked, other than briefly, in several days, and he wanted to check in.

And to meet Arnold's new lady love.

Not that Arnold had told him about it. No, he'd had to find out from his undercover surveillance team that his friend was sleeping with a thirty-year veteran dealer who had a reputation as sterling as his.

"So, we don't have the opportunity to pursue anything lasting, which makes things pretty much perfect as far as I'm concerned. You getting tired of my company?''

"On the contrary," Francesca chuckled, sending spirals of tension straight to his groin. "Enjoying it too much, I'm afraid."

Yeah, he could say the same about her. Not that he would. But he could. "So I can pick you up tonight? Say around six?"

"How about if I meet you there?" she said instead. "I'll hang out downstairs until you're done."

Playing the slots. He made a mental note to go down early and watch her for a bit. As much as he detested gambling on principle, he had to admit that watching the peaceful anticipation on Francesca's face as she pushed those buttons, the innocent excitement when she hit a win, big or small, was something he didn't want to miss.

Yeah. It was a damn good thing she was only in town temporarily.

Opening a file, he studied the newest win-ratio analysis he'd sent for. Someplace in all this mess was the clue he was waiting for.

And come hell or high water, he was going to find it.

Autumn threw up again on Friday. Francesca had had the brilliant idea of taking her little sister to a nearby suburb to shop for new clothes so Autumn wouldn't have to worry about being seen. Her sister hadn't seemed nearly as pleased about the prospect as Francesca had expected. They'd been discussing the idea when Autumn suddenly yelled at her to pull over and barely made it to the side of the road before she lost the contents of her stomach.

"Okay, young lady, we're going to talk," Francesca told her after she pulled a premoistened antibacterial wipe from her glove compartment and handed it to her. "I don't care where we go, but when we get there, you'd better tell me what's wrong."

Autumn mumbled directions to a park a couple of miles from her apartment. "We'll have to sit in the car, 'cause it's too hot to get out," she warned.

"Fine."

"Why are you mad at me? I can't help it that I was sick. I didn't get any on the car or anything."

Sending her sister an exasperated smile, Francesca said, "I don't care about the car, you dolt, I care about you. And I'm not mad. I'm determined. There's a difference."

Autumn mumbled something unintelligible and Francesca, picking her battles, let it go.

She drove to the park, stopped the car and unfastened her seat belt, then turned to face Autumn. "Now, let's have it. What's all this about? Why are you so upset that you throw up all the time? Did you think I'd forgotten that's always been a sure sign of emotional distress with you?"

Autumn looked younger than her years at that moment, her hair unspiked and lying against her head, her eyes wide and lost.

"Talk to me, sweetie."

"I..." The girl's eyes dropped.

"Autumn, enough is enough. If you don't tell me what's going on, I'm following you home. And attaching myself to your side until I find out."

"I'll run away again."

She wondered if Autumn knew how empty that threat sounded. Two weeks before, it hadn't. Even a week before...

"I'll risk it."

"I—" Autumn glanced over. The look in her eyes had changed. She'd made a decision. "There's this guy."

Francesca's heart dropped. But she kept herself from jumping to conclusions. Or tried to.

"I really love him."

"Are you sure?"

Autumn stared. "Absolutely!"

"Okay, so what's the problem? Does he hit you? Is that it?" The pattern was common—an abused girl getting involved with a man who had the same tendencies as her abuser. There was no more stepping carefully. They were going to meet this one head-on.

"No! Of course not."

Oh. Well, good. Thank God.

"Then what?"

"I'm just having problems with him. And I love him so much and I can't imagine life without him, but I don't see how things will ever work out between us."

Could that be all? A seventeen-year-old's case of puppy love? Or even real love? Growing up, Autumn had made herself ill over less.

"What kind of issues are you dealing with?"

Francesca asked, relaxing against the seat. Romantic troubles she could handle. "What makes you think you won't ever be together?"

As she considered various possibilities, she sat straight up. "He isn't married, is he?"

"No, Cesca, he's only twenty-one. He's a senior business major at UNLV, works seven days a week in a garage near his house and spends most of his free time helping his widowed mother care for his five younger siblings."

"Wow."

"Yeah, his dad was a cop, killed in the line of duty a few years back, and Matteo's been the man of the house ever since. His mom works at one of the five-star restaurants on the Strip, waiting tables, but he still has to help out with finances."

"Matteo? He's Italian?"

Autumn's saucy grin might have been sickening if it wasn't so cute. "Yeah, although I'm the only one who calls him that. To everyone else he's just plain Matt."

Her little sister in love with an Italian man...

"You said his dad died at work. Doesn't the city help her out?"

"Uh-huh, but with five kids to put through college, it's not enough."

There *were* scholarships and bursaries available. Still... "So that's the problem? His family? You don't like it that he has no time for you?"

"No..."

"Then what?"

"He doesn't know...things, and I can't tell him

and if I did, his whole opinion of me would change. I told him the Sunday before last that I couldn't see him anymore, but then I couldn't stay away. Now I'm just going to have to tell him all over again.''

''First, what *things* doesn't he know?''

''Like the fact that I'm a runaway. He thinks I live with a guardian.''

''Yes, well, we need to talk about your living arrangements, too, my dear,'' Francesca said. ''I'm curious to know how you can afford the rent on that place.''

Autumn glanced out the window at the mostly deserted park. ''I worked. Saved money.''

''Autumn?''

''It's true,'' she said, looking her straight in the eye. ''I swear, I earned the money myself. The place is really mine.''

''You signed a lease?''

''I have it for another six months.''

''You signed a lease?'' she repeated. Luke had found no record of one.

''Come on, Cesca, give me a break! I'm a runaway. Some stuff you just don't ask questions about when you're on the street. A guy offered me the chance to have a place of my own. I took it. I'm paying him rent, fair and square.''

Running the back of her hand down Autumn's face, Francesca smiled. ''You know I'm only asking because I care, don't you?''

''Yeah.''

''So this guy, this Matteo, is he the reason you don't want me around your apartment?''

"It would be a little hard to explain a big sister who's come to take me home. Or wherever."

"Okay, so we'll work on that."

"What do you mean?"

"If he loves you, he's going to understand the lies you had to tell to protect yourself, honey. And if he doesn't, you need to know that before you give him any more of your heart. We'll figure out how, but you have to be honest with him."

It took her several more minutes of convincing, but eventually Autumn accepted the inevitability of what Francesca told her. And then she spent the next half hour regaling her older sister with all the incredible virtues of the near-perfect young man she'd been lucky enough to find.

If Matteo had even half the character Autumn attributed to him, Francesca was ready to welcome him with open arms. And to spend the rest of her life grateful to him for being there for Autumn at a time when Francesca was not.

"I don't believe this boy is all that's bothering her." After a dinner of fajitas and margaritas, she and Luke were up in his office, sitting on the couch in the outer suite—a room that was more living room than anything else. If not for the telephones with their multiple lines, they could've been in his home.

He'd invited Arnold Jackson to join them for dinner, but the older man had already had other plans. Francesca wasn't really sorry about that.

Succumbing to the pleasure of his fingers drifting

lightly through her hair, she laid her head back against his shoulder.

"What else do you think it is?"

"I have no idea." She should have pushed further. She'd known it at the time. "She was just acting so much like a normal teenager, going on and on about him, that I didn't have the heart to stop her. And then, as always, she had to leave. There's never any compromise on that."

"If the kid works seven days a week, goes to school and helps with his siblings, chances are his opportunities to see her are pretty limited. Might not be much possibility of compromise there."

"Maybe."

His fingers moved down her neck, sending interesting chills in their wake. "I hear hesitation in your voice." Knowing that he'd still be wearing his suit from work, she'd dressed up a bit, choosing the same black dress she'd worn that night with Carl. As his fingers found the base of her collarbone and her belly responded with a surge of heat, she regretted the dress.

"She seems so scared whenever it gets late, you know? If this guy is so wonderful, he wouldn't scare her, would he?"

"You sure it's not just tension associated with the fact that she doesn't want to be late? To miss even a second of her time with him?"

She turned and looked at him. "Not miss a second of her time with him? For a guy you're pretty aware, you know that?"

He blinked, tilted his head as if to say something, and then pulled her against him.

"It's not tension I see," she told him. "It's fear."

"So you think this guy *is* hurting her?"

"No." She almost wished she did. It was something she knew she could handle. "Not once, in all the time she spoke of him, was there anything but complete adoration. And the things she says he does for her, says to her, they don't come from a guy who beats up on women."

"Then what do you think it is?"

"I have no idea," Francesca said. "But I intend to find out."

Luke gave a playful tug to her ear. "I have no doubt about that."

Turning her head, she grinned up at him. "You have a problem with my determination, Everson?"

"Not at all. In fact—" he paused, his gaze following his fingers as they traced her lips "—I find it a bit of a turn-on."

"Oh."

"How about you?" His face was so close, those blue eyes mesmerizing her.

"I find you a turn-on, too."

He grinned, though his eyes lost none of their intensity. "I was asking how you felt about being so determined all the time."

"Oh."

"But—" his mouth lowered "—I'm glad to know the other...."

She wasn't at all prepared when his lips touched hers. And yet she'd never been more prepared in her life. Maybe it was because they'd been together so much—and waited so long—but his touch was as much a homecoming as it was an adventure into unexplored terrain.

Francesca couldn't have resisted him even if she remembered that she wanted to. When his lips teased, she opened hers without hesitation, inviting him inside.

She'd only been with one man since the defiant college days when, for some reason still unclear to her, she'd been hell-bent on proving that she was exactly the whore her stepfather had so often accused her of being. And while that time with Antonio in Milan had been filled with desperate passion, those hours had also brought guilt that had taken away much of the joy.

With Luke, for the first time, she touched without that sense of guilt. And the experience was worth having lived through hell. She felt not one second of self-consciousness as he undressed her right there on the couch, with all the lights in his office blazing. Nor embarrassment when he just as quickly stripped down to nothing.

"Why does this feel so right?" she whispered as, with hands on either side of his waist, she held him standing before her and kissed her way down to his belly.

"I don't know, but I'm willing to spend whatever time you'll give me finding out."

Any time she'd give him. Not a lifetime. Not her heart. Just what time she had.

She could do that.

* * *

While sitting at the breakfast table finishing a much-needed cup of coffee early Saturday morning, Luke got a call from the head of his private team. "I wanted to catch you before I left to go out on the floor," Don Brown said.

"What's up?" Glancing at his mother, whose face had grown pinched at the tone of his voice, he quickly shook his head, letting her know the news wasn't anything that would concern her.

"Probably nothing," the man said. "But we weren't the only ones watching the card-counter yesterday."

Luke stood, moved into the other room—away from his mother's worried eyes—where he could find complete focus. "Who else?"

"We're not sure," Brown reported. "But the man followed him to the elevator. They had words and then parted."

"Hostile words?"

"Didn't appear to be."

Luke stared out the front window at the desert landscaping his mother had chosen so long ago, with the promise that it would bloom and be beautiful in the years to come. She'd been right. "Friendly, then?" he asked.

"Didn't appear to be that, either. More like business conversation."

"Could've been an acquaintance who wasn't sure he'd recognized him."

"Could have been. Except there was no greeting. No handshake. And no farewell. None of the signs of casual conversation between strangers."

"So it was someone who wanted to know how to count cards?"

"He'd have to know how to do that to realize the guy was doing it, wouldn't he?"

"Maybe. Maybe not."

"So, like I said, might be nothing."

"You've got a guy assigned to shadow him?"

"You need to ask?" Brown prided himself on his reliability, which served him well in the job he did.

"Keep me posted."

Luke hung up happier than he'd been pretty much ever. His son was on the way. They were closing in on whoever had been cheating the Bonaparte out of money at the tables. And he'd just returned from the most incredible night of sex....

"Luke? Is everything okay? That wasn't Francesca, was it?"

Carol Everson was worrying the hem of her short-sleeved silk jacket with the fingers of her right hand.

"Everything's fine, Mom," he said, giving her a smile. He squeezed her shoulder, meeting her eyes.

"I'd tell you if it was Francesca. You'd find out if there was trouble, anyway, because she'd tell you herself."

The fact that Francesca's needs, her hardships, her life, shouldn't mean so much to his mother didn't faze him that morning. It was true. Just a problem for another day. Or at least another hour.

"So who was it?"

"Work."

"Are you getting any closer to finding out what's going on?"

His head tilting in question, Luke was all set to ask her who'd told her about his troubles at work when his mother continued. "Francesca said something the last time she was here. You received a call then, too."

Ah, yes, Francesca. The woman had a lot to answer for. Some of it very very good...

# 20

On Sunday afternoon, Francesca and Autumn drove out for fast-food Mexican to take back to the Lucky Seven.

They talked while they ate, neither of them ever seeming to run out of things to say. And yet, there was so much unsaid.

Life was more than the two of them in this one room.

"We can't do this forever," Francesca told Autumn after the trash had been disposed of and she was, once again, lying back against her headboard. If nothing else, she was getting the rest everyone had been telling her she so desperately needed.

"Do what?"

"Just hang out here. In the first place, I have no desire to live in this room indefinitely."

"So get a place."

"I live in Sacramento."

Unfolding her thin legs, Autumn stood, looked out the window. The only view was of a gravel parking lot and the gray brick wall of the building next door. "Why? It's not like you have a place there. Or at least you didn't." She turned. "You said earlier that you put your things in storage when you went to Italy. Are they still there?''

Francesca nodded.

''So send for them.''

Watching her little sister as she moved restlessly around the room, Francesca wondered if Autumn's shortsightedness was a condition of youth or if the girl's refusal to face the future was based on something more. Something that prevented her from moving forward.

The same something that so often brought fear to her eyes?

''If I did, would you move in with me?''

Stopping in midpace, Autumn stared at the outer door. ''I can't. At least not for a while.''

Francesca sat forward, knees bent, hands resting helplessly on the bed between them. ''Why not? I don't get it, Autumn!''

''I'm obligated to pay rent for the next six months. I told you that.'' The girl had moved to the closet, was speaking to the few pieces of clothing hanging there. To the shoes on the closet floor. Since Autumn's advent into her life, Francesca had moved out of the duffel.

''I'll pay the rent.'' Francesca leaned forward, needing to see her sister's face. ''What's it to the guy if you don't actually live there?''

''I don't know.'' She caught the end of Autumn's shrug. ''He just doesn't want the place vacant.''

''So we'll sublet.''

''It's not allowed.''

Francesca raised a hand, let it drop. ''Autumn,

people move. You can be financially obligated to a place, but they can't keep you a prisoner there."

The girl bent, picking up something from the closet floor. The homeless-girl tennis shoes? She'd asked Francesca about them once and Francesca had promised to show them to her.

"Let's go out," Autumn said. "Take a walk in the desert."

"It's awfully hot."

Autumn stood, an object in her hand as she turned. "I know, but we could take some pictures. One of my best memories of us is the times you took me out to photograph stuff."

The girl approached the bed, and Francesca's gaze fell to her hands. And the camera resting there.

Her throat closed on the words she'd been about to say. She watched almost in slow motion, as Autumn's tutored fingers removed the lens cap, slipping it into the back pocket of her shorts, and raised the camera to her face. Finger on the shutter mechanism, she said, "Smile."

"No!" Francesca couldn't move. She just sat there, the blood draining from her face and neck, leaving her cold. "Don't! No pictures. Put it down. Put it away."

"Cesca?" Autumn moved the camera to one side as she looked over. "What's wrong?"

"Nothing. Just put it away."

The girl dropped her arm, lowering the camera to her side. "I won't hurt anything. You know that. You're the one who taught me—"

"Put it away. We can't take any chances."

She was light-headed. Dizzy. Couldn't think clearly. Just... "Put it away. It has to be put away. That's all."

"Okay..." She heard Autumn's voice, knew her sister was still talking, knew, in one part of her mind, that she wanted to respond, that she had to pull herself together. She was the strong one and she absolutely would not, could not, lose control in front of her sister.

In front of anyone.

She was okay. Fine. Life went on. As long as that camera was in her duffel bag with the others. Safe. Hidden away. Where she never had to look at it. Touch it. Think about what lay inside.

"Cesca?" The dipping of the bed was her first indication that Autumn had returned. Her thin fingers ran along Francesca's cheek and, in a distant way, felt comforting. "What is it?"

"Nothing," she said again. She blinked, then focused on her sister's sweet and concerned blue eyes. "Really." She looked away and quickly back, lifting a hand to smooth the bangs from the girl's forehead. "I'm fine. I'm just funny about my cameras. You know that."

"I know you always trusted *me* with them."

She had. From the very first. Because an expensive camera had been far less valuable than the building of Autumn's self-worth. Now Autumn's hands, in her line of vision as she gazed down at the bedspread, were empty. The camera was gone.

Back where it belonged. Put away in the past. She was safe. Could breathe. She'd survived. Again.

"Cesca? What happened?"

She grabbed the girl's hand, squeezed. "Nothing, honey. I'm just tired. Out of sorts from this weird lifestyle, you know? I'm used to being so busy, and lately all I do is lie around and wait for the hour or two every day when I can see you."

"It was more than that." The determination in Autumn's voice was reminiscent of old. "What is it? You don't trust me enough to tell me?"

It wasn't that. Oh, God, it wasn't her little sister she didn't trust.

"You wanted me spill my guts, and I did," the girl added. "I told you all about Matteo."

That was different. So very different. Autumn's problems could still be solved.

Autumn stood. "If you can't tell me, then you might as well take me home and just forget this whole thing. 'Cause if you don't trust me, I can't trust you."

For such a juvenile attempt at blackmail, it was powerful.

She glanced up at her sister, hearing far more than Autumn had said. Here she was, preaching to her sister about getting secrets out in the open, leaving the past behind, while she was burying herself in it.

That knowledge did nothing to ease the constriction in her chest. The panic running through her.

"What do you want to know?" she whispered.

Autumn sat close enough to touch her, although

she didn't. "Why did my having the camera upset you so much?"

An easy question. One she could answer. She was feeling stronger already.

"You didn't have anything to do with it. I'd have reacted that way no matter who brought it out."

"Why are they all packed away like that?"

"I'm on sabbatical."

"You're always taking pictures, Cesca, whether you're working or not."

Francesca could barely withstand the pressure of Autumn's earnest blue stare. It took most of her concentration not to look away.

"People get burned out."

"People, maybe, but not you." Autumn's words were soft. And sure.

"There's film in that camera."

There, the facts were out.

"I know you've got three pictures left."

"Yes." About that. She'd taken twenty-one. Over the space of two days. When she'd known she was leaving Italy. Before she'd packed...

Thoughts beyond that were blurred. Confusing.

"So? You generally have film in your cameras."

Autumn held her stomach. Was the girl going to be sick again? Over this?

"There are...pictures...there," she managed, squinting against the pain in her head.

Precious pictures. They were the only ones she had left.

Deeply wrenching pictures. Visions of smiles that could only bring more heartache and pain.

"I don't understand." Autumn frowned. "If they mean so much to you, why not finish off the roll and get them developed? Or just expose the rest of the roll? You've done that more times than I can count."

Autumn knew her so well. She'd forgotten how good that felt. To be known. Instead of alone.

"I...I, uh..." She couldn't look away from the concern in her sister's eyes. Yet seeing the love there, the innocence, was breaking her. With her lips clasped firmly together, holding back the emotion that was consuming her, she felt her eyes tearing up. Big drops welled—and spilled over, one after another, to trace a familiar path down her cheeks.

"Cesca?" Autumn moved closer. Francesca felt her there, taking her hands. She was so cold and the girl was so warm. "What is it? Tell me."

"I...Gian..." Sobs tore through her, exploding so fiercely she couldn't speak. *Gian.* Dear sweet baby boy. *Where are you, my love? Are you happy? Can you feel how much your mama loves you?*

"Shh." Autumn rocked her. Francesca had no idea how her head had come to be on her sister's shoulder. She just lay there, unable to move or even rouse herself, fading in and out of awareness. "It's okay, Cesca. Whatever it is."

A couple of times she drifted back enough to be conscious of Autumn and tried to speak. And each time, as she searched for words, she'd fade out again, into the pain that had consumed her in Italy. And in Sacramento. It had been two months and still the anguish was so intense she couldn't face it, couldn't breathe, didn't want to breathe.

Eventually, physically drained, she quieted. And recognized the moment. She'd experienced it a few times now. It always came after a particularly bad bout. She'd be okay for a moment. Peaceful from exhaustion and the sheer inability to feel, or to know. Or even care.

"Who's Gian?" Autumn's soft words broke through the moment.

Tears started to fall again, slowly, barely there. "My son."

Luke wasn't positive that she'd be home. But he thought she might be and was willing to risk it. He could call, of course. But if she was there, back from taking Autumn home by her three o'clock deadline, his first conversation with her after last night could be just the two of them together. Alone. In a bedroom.

Shedding the jacket of his suit as he turned the last corner and pulled into the lot, Luke thought briefly of what he had to tell her. The card-counter had met with the man at the elevator again an hour ago. It could mean nothing. But Luke knew better than that. The instincts that led him today had seen him achieve recognition time and again in the Marine Corps.

Francesca's Grand Cherokee was in her spot. He wasn't really surprised. It was that kind of day.

He had to knock twice. Kind of odd considering how small the room was. Unless she was on the phone. Or in the bathroom. Or asleep in the bed...

They'd had a very late night.

"Cesca's not—oh." Autumn stood at the door,

guarding the entrance, obviously not sure what to do with him.

He wasn't sure what to do with her, either.

"Is Francesca here?"

"Um, yeah, but…"

Girl talk. He understood. Half turning, he started to tell Autumn to have Francesca call him when she was free, but before he could say anything, a disturbing sound came from inside the room. And then came again.

"Is she crying?"

Autumn nodded. "She's really upset—"

Without another thought, Luke pushed by the girl and strode in to find Francesca huddled in a fetal position in the middle of her bed, crying softly.

"I didn't mean to upset her so much," Autumn said, looking down at her.

"How long has she been like this?"

"Not long. A few minutes, maybe. She keeps saying she's fine."

One look at the huddled mass told Luke that wasn't the case.

He tried to talk to her, asked a couple of easy questions. It was as though she didn't even hear him. When he sat beside her, she didn't seem to notice. Her eyes were open but unfocused.

Luke couldn't let her go through this—whatever it was—alone. This wasn't like the emotional distress endured by his mother, someone who suffered from a psychiatric condition, and would suffer until the day she died, no matter what anyone did. This was raw pain.

And, maybe because of his mother, Luke knew instinctively what to do.

Picking her up, he put her on her feet. "Let's go for a walk," he said. "Get her outside. She needs to see life around her. To reconnect."

If that didn't work, didn't bring her out of her stupor, she needed a doctor.

"I don't..." The protest was feeble.

"What happened?" Luke asked Autumn, keeping his voice even, calm, reassuring. Something at which he'd had years of practice. A lifetime of practice.

Glancing from Francesca, half-limp against him, up at Luke, Autumn shook her head, the worried frown still wrinkling her forehead.

"Maybe we shouldn't talk about it," she said.

"Oh, I think we should." He started to walk and relaxed just a little when Francesca's legs moved automatically in stride with his.

She was going to be fine. "Can you get the door?"

Autumn hurried in front of them, pulling open the door.

"You have a key?"

The girl nodded, walking stiffly beside them as they started down the walk. She looked scared to death.

"Why don't you take her hand?" he suggested. "I'll keep an arm around her and we'll leave her to do the rest."

He knew Francesca was listening and trusted her to rise to the occasion. His trust was not misplaced. Although her movements were detached, her expression empty, she walked.

"Okay, one of you tell me what's going on." He looked at Autumn.

"I got out her camera and she flipped."

"I…didn't." Francesca stumbled, but righted herself. "I'm fine…I really…am."

He believed her. She *was* fine. Just in need of some tender care and a bridge back from whatever hell she'd fallen into.

A memory of some abuse she'd suffered at the hands of her stepfather? He'd almost cried aloud when he'd first seen the scars last night. And had wanted to break every bone in the bastard's body.

What possessed a man to treat a young girl that way? What part of his humanness was missing that permitted such atrocity?

"She has a son!"

Autumn's words nearly stopped him in his tracks. She couldn't have a child. Autumn must have misunderstood.

Francesca didn't want children.

"No, she doesn't," he told the girl.

"Yes, she does!" Autumn's expression held a warning as her gaze moved meaningfully to the bent head of her older sister. "She said so, right before she got like this. I think something bad must have happened to him."

It was a lot for him to take in. Francesca a mother. Without her baby.

And then it hit him.

Maybe she'd been like many single women, finding herself in trouble. Alone. Had she given the child away? And was regretting that? Had Luke's recent confidence about his own son set off some emotional minefield?

"Where is he?"

"I don't know." Autumn shook her head again. "We didn't get that far."

He stopped a block short of the busy Strip. "Francesca?" He had to call her name three times.

"Yeah?"

"Look at me."

She turned her head, but it took a couple of seconds for her sight to focus on him. "Where is your son?"

"Dead."

Luke's heart dropped. Autumn started to cry. And Francesca just walked on. Alone. Suffering with an anguish he could sense was there but couldn't really even imagine.

"He was only two months old."

They were back in his office just before dusk on Sunday evening, after a long walk during which they'd spoken only of the sights, sounds and smells around them. At one point they'd stopped for something to eat. Not that any of them had much of an appetite. And then, after leaving Autumn close to her apartment, he'd brought Francesca back to the Bonaparte, to spend an hour or two at the nickel slots. She'd won thirty dollars.

"What happened?" It felt cruel, making her talk, but they both knew that she had to release the feelings inside her.

She shook her head, laid it against his shoulder.

Her short-sleeved blue shirt and denim shorts were in sharp contrast to the dress she'd had on the night before. They were a whole lot more real—indicative of her real life.

"I was right there in the room with him...."

Her voice was a thin rendition of its normal self, her exhaustion more emotional than physical.

"He was in the hospital?" Had the child taken ill suddenly or was it something he'd been born with? Either way would be hell.

"No." She wasn't really with him. He understood that. And had to rein in his impatience. There were so many questions he wanted to ask. Starting, for instance, with who—and where—the child's father was.

"I was in Italy—that's where he was born." Her voice sounded faraway. The heaviness of her head against his collarbone revealed how little of her own weight she was supporting.

"We were at my grandmother's—my father's mother...staying with her."

There was so much about her he didn't know. And wanted to know. Lacing his fingers through hers, he held their hands together against his thigh.

"I was in our room packing." Her mind was obviously traveling again as she fell silent for a bit. "We were coming home to the States.... I'd received a commission...."

Luke waited. Wished there was some way he could ease this for her.

"He was right there...in his b-bassinet..."

The skin on his face tightened.

"I didn't even know...."

Damn. This was worse than he'd expected. At least with illness there was warning.

"I was standing there...packing...while he was dying from sudden infant death syndro—" The end of the word was lost as her breath caught on a painful sob. "I...I..." She was gasping.

"Shh. Catch your breath. I'm right here."

Ten minutes passed. And then another five. He wasn't sure she was still awake. Hoped she'd found a respite in the peacefulness of sleep. But he didn't think so. Her breathing was too uneven.

"I zipped up the duffels, turned and slid my hands under his little body and he was limp...and...and...his color was...horrible...and he didn't move."

He couldn't even imagine it.

"Where was his father?" he finally asked.

"Nowhere. I never told him I was pregnant."

"The man doesn't know he had a son?"

She shook her head, every movement lethargic. "It was Antonio. And he's married to a disabled woman. We only slept together that one weekend."

As if that said it all. The man should've been there. Had the right to be there. Or to rot in hell for knowing and not being there.

"Was there an autopsy?" he asked quietly.

Her nod was a clumsy jerk of her head.

"How long ago did this happen?" How long had she been carrying that camera around with its pictures of her son?

"Two and a half months."

Two and a half months? He'd been thinking years. A couple of them, at least. Hell, it had taken him six months to even begin to get over the shock of his father's death.

Two and a half months and here she'd been, tackling the streets of Las Vegas all alone.

# 21

Luke was in his office Monday afternoon when his cell phone rang.

"Luke, you probably want to get down here."

Recognizing Brown's number on his caller ID he was already on his feet. "What's up?"

"I think we're about to witness the next big win at the Bonaparte."

He'd known, ever since his night of drunken video-watching, that he was after a dealer in his own casino. The moves were too intricate for anyone but a dealer to devise. And most of the wins were at Esposito's newest resort. But he'd never suspected—even once—who that dealer was.

All the way down in the elevator he'd run through a mental list, checking off each one of the many talented men and women in their employ. Arnold Jackson hadn't even been on the list.

Yet, when he found Brown lounging at the bar across from Jackson's table, he knew there was no mistake. The morning he and Jackson had viewed the tapes, the older man had been a little too certain as he'd explained away Luke's suspicions. If he'd shown even a small measure of doubt, given Luke's ideas any credibility at all...

His determined attempt to convince Luke that not a single one of the clues he'd noticed were significant had been his one mistake—a tip-off that he was purposely leading Luke astray.

He hadn't actually suspected Jackson—thinking, if anything, that Jackson was protecting someone else—but Luke's unease had been enough to keep quiet about hiring his plainclothes crew.

Still, as he slid onto a stool behind a support beam where he couldn't be seen and leaned over just enough to follow the detective's head gesture, he hoped that for once in his life Don Brown was wrong. He and Arnold had spent some pretty long nights together, talking about things guys didn't talk about—especially with each other. If he couldn't trust *him,* who could he trust?

Luke ordered a beer. Sipped. Watched and waited. And, when half an hour had passed, started to relax.

Jackson never missed a cue. He cut, shuffled, loaded the shoe, burned and dealt. Took cheques from the tray, over the tube with thumb and middle finger; he cut them, proved and handed off. Again and again. In perfect rhythm every time. The man made blackjack dealing into an art. And as with any great artist, what made his work stand out from all the rest was the integrity he brought to it.

Luke sipped. Arnold glanced up. Smiled. Luke smiled back. And then sat up straight. Jackson couldn't see him. Hadn't been smiling at him as he'd naturally assumed. There'd been no one to smile at. The older man had just grinned at the post behind which Luke sat.

A smile. Then a right-hand touch.

Jackson scratched his nose with the knuckles of his right hand—keeping his palm in clear view.

He wasn't palming cards.

And the player in spot one put out a maximum bet.

Left hand on the shoe, Jackson reached with his middle finger. Pulled. Transferred the card to his right hand. Placed the cards on the table in their appropriate places. And again.

Jackson called out totals, not that Luke could hear him from where he sat. Players gestured for hits. And it was time for taking and paying. He paid spot one. For the next half hour, he paid spot one again and again. Not always, but enough so that the player was racking up a sizable fortune.

"I'll be damned."

"You say something?" the bartender, a new kid Luke hadn't seen before, asked.

Luke shook his head, nodded at Brown to proceed and went up to his office. He'd wanted something to report to Amadeo upon his return later in the week. And now he had it.

He'd rather be out of a job.


Autumn, Luke and Francesca went together on Tuesday afternoon to get the roll of film developed. They dropped it off at a one-hour photo place, then had lunch at one of Luke's favorite sneak-away places on the Strip, a little-known brewery that he claimed had the best chicken wings in the city.

While he and Autumn filled up on chicken and

fries, Francesca munched on the celery and carrot sticks that came with their orders. She could hardly manage to do even that. The closer the minutes ticked to the hour, the tighter her stomach grew— and the more it filled with the uncomfortable flutters of panic she'd been trying to avoid. In just a few short moments, she was going to be seeing Baby Gian.

Autumn asked about the expensive-looking apparatus built around *them,* pipes and tubes for making beer. Luke told them about his first visit to the place. They were trying their best to help her pass the time. She barely registered a word they said.

"So how come these are the only pictures you have of Gian?" Autumn's voice was soft, tentative. She'd stopped looking everywhere but at Francesca and met her older sister's gaze.

"I was pretty crazy with grief." She tried to smile. Took a sip of Diet Coke, hoping to dispel the lump in her throat. "I already had that duffel packed with all his stuff so I put the photo albums in with them and left the whole thing at the cemetery, telling the undertaker to bury it with him."

It was the truth. And the end of lunch.

Francesca noticed Autumn holding her stomach again as they waited in line to pay for the photos. The envelope in her hand was hot. Burning her. And obviously upsetting her little sister.

"Where should we look at them?" Autumn asked, climbing into the back seat of Luke's Jag. "Here?"

"Let's wait until we get back to my place." That

way if she fell apart, her bed would be right there. For as long as it took.

Autumn had both arms wrapped around her stomach. Her lower stomach.

"Is something wrong?" Francesca asked, a little concerned by the paleness of her sister's skin.

"Nah." Autumn shook her head, but looked uneasy. "Just…cramps." She glanced at the back of Luke's head.

"I've got some ibuprofen back at the room."

Autumn nodded and Francesca turned around, the packet lying in her lap. Waiting for her.

*Baby Gian, are you there? Waiting for Mama to see your sweet smile?*

"Cesca?"

Francesca swung around at the panic in her sister's voice. "Take us to the nearest hospital," she cried immediately. There was a strange color staining her sister's shorts. This was no ordinary period.

Francesca sat there, frozen, staring at the doctor who'd come into the Emergency cubicle to tell them that Autumn was fine and could go home.

"Everything checks out fine, young lady, but you need to take better care of yourself if you want that little one to get here strong and healthy."

*Little one?* Little one!

Her gaze flew to Autumn's solemn face, expecting her sister to assure this woman that she'd made a mistake. Autumn couldn't possibly be pregnant. She was only seventeen. A child. And a virgin.

One glance at the twisted sorrow on the girl's face

was all it took for Francesca's world to fall apart for
the second time in as many months.

Not only was Autumn's young life being thrown
prematurely into adulthood, but she'd *lied* to her. It
all made a horrifying kind of sense. The nausea. The
fear Autumn exhibited around her sometimes.

Probably afraid Francesca would find out.

Her need to keep Francesca away from her apartment. Were there baby things? And perhaps a father
for the child?

And clothes-shopping. It would've been a little
difficult to hide that thickening waistline in a dressing room.

It was so devastatingly clear now.

Autumn had been lying to her all along.

For the first time since she'd met him that day last
spring when she'd hurried into his garage to get out
of the rain, Autumn missed a date with Matteo. She
had no idea what he'd make of that. He'd been a
little distant ever since that Sunday a couple of weeks
back when she'd told him she couldn't see him anymore. He'd talked her out of her craziness—as he'd
called it—and had been just as attentive. But he
didn't seem to be smiling as much when she was
around.

Standing at her living-room window, waiting for
the car to stop out front, she hardly noticed the palm
trees or the reddish rocks that she'd found so pretty
and unusual the first time she'd seen this place. She'd
thought the desert landscaping gave the area class,

considered herself lucky to be there. Now she just thought about the future. What it might bring.

Maybe Matteo would take this missed date as a chance to get rid of her. She couldn't have him calling her, since she wasn't allowed to have a boyfriend, so the only way they could make dates was to arrange them when they were together. And now they weren't together to set up the next meeting. Maybe he'd been waiting for a chance like this.

The thought caused a huge ache inside her. But it didn't bring her to her knees. The look of betrayal on Cesca's face had done that. She'd missed her big sister so much these past two years. And since Cesca had been here in town, Autumn wasn't so scared anymore. Being with Cesca had always given her a feeling that everything would be okay.

Even when she knew it wouldn't be.

A blue sedan slowed as it approached the building. Autumn's heart sped up. The car passed. It hadn't been *his* anyway. It was too small.

No matter how horrible this might be, she had to do it. She couldn't take any more. And she couldn't do it to Cesca, either. She'd wanted to die right on the spot that afternoon when Cesca had looked at her, so sure the doctor was wrong, and then, when Autumn hadn't been able to refute the doctor's words, as if Autumn had just ripped out her heart.

She hated that she'd done that. Especially since knowing about little Gian. Cesca had been hurt so much.

Thinking of the baby who'd died, Autumn started

to cry again. She'd been an aunt. And hadn't even known it. She'd never been able to hold him.

Of course, she'd been a mother, too, and never held her babies, either.

Turning from the window, Autumn wiped away her tears with an impatient hand, wandering through the apartment. If only she could fix it up the way she'd like it to be. Some plants. And posters. Color on the walls. But they weren't allowed to do that. As soon as she'd had the baby, they'd move another girl in and they couldn't be repainting and fixing holes in the walls every seven months or so.

Even though she'd waited more than an hour, the knock on her door came before she was ready. This might mean her death. Everyone had heard about that girl out in the desert a few years before. These guys, whoever they were, didn't mess around.

Death would be preferable to living like this. There were only two people in the world who'd ever really loved her. And she was hurting both of them.

"Hey, I got your call. And then one from the hospital right afterward. I came over as soon as I could. I'm really proud of you getting yourself there like you did."

When the nurse at the hospital had insisted she had to call the contact name on Autumn's chart, Autumn had begged the woman not to tell Antonio she hadn't been alone there.

"Whatever," she said now. "It's not far."

Antonio walked into her living room, running a hand down her arm as he passed. She used to like it when he touched her. But not anymore. After being with Matteo, she had a feeling that Antonio's touch wasn't as big-brotherly as she'd once thought. If she wasn't such a dolt, she'd have figured it out long before. Like about the first time his fingers had accidentally—or not—brushed her breast as he touched her arm.

She wanted to tell him he'd had a son. And that the baby had died. It would serve him right. But she was too much of a coward.

He sat on the couch, patting the spot next to him. More than once they'd sat there together, with him holding her, comforting her—or so she'd thought—as she cried out her heartache and fears, her worries about impending childbirth. More than once he'd rubbed her bulging stomach, talking to her about the happy family awaiting the baby she was giving them.

She used to think she was so lucky. She was the only girl Antonio actually looked after. As far as she could tell, his job was primarily one of making the initial contact. He found potential girls. And turned them over to the women who supervised them. With his real job—second-in-command at his father-in-law's retail company—he was too busy traveling all over the world to baby-sit them all himself.

These days she didn't feel lucky at all. And had begun to wonder if there *were* happy families. Or if maybe they—whoever the women worked for—did something else with all the babies.

He smiled, the smile that used to melt her heart, back when he'd been Francesca's boyfriend. He needed to shave. And comb his hair. As black as Matteo's, Antonio's hair wasn't nearly as thick.

She liked Matteo's.

"Come sit."

"I don't feel like it."

Unable to meet the warmth and kindness shining from those dark eyes of his—emotions she'd long ago begun to suspect were the practiced art of an actor—she turned her back.

"This isn't like you, *cara.* Something's wrong. Come tell me what it is."

She couldn't make herself move. Not back there. With him. She was never going back. And not forward, either. She didn't know the steps to take.

Seeing him, sitting on her sofa where Cesca had sat, remembering how helpless and panicky she'd felt on Sunday when her sister had been huddled on her bed in so much pain she couldn't get up, Autumn really hated him. Funny, when she'd first seen Cesca again, she'd had a crazy thought about her and Antonio getting together and somehow fixing her whole screwed-up world.

She'd known, even then, that the thought was foolish. She'd just been desperate enough, and stupid enough, to make-believe for a second.

Now she didn't even want the jerk to know her sister was in town. It would kill Cesca to see him again.

Besides, she had hopes for Cesca and Luke. He was a nice guy. And Cesca had melted right into him the other day when she'd been so upset and he'd come to rescue her. Like Autumn melted into Matteo…

"I want out."

"Of course you do. You always do about this time."

"No." She stood her ground, looking at the floor. And then, somehow, found herself turning to face him, a resolve inside her that she could only remember feeling once before. The night she'd first started her period. "I mean it. I'm not scared like I was before, Antonio. I'm leaving."

He stood, smiling in that way of his, meant to make her feel like an idiot kid. "Come on, *cara,* you know better than this."

"Because of that Mary girl, you mean? Too late, Antonio, I'd rather be her, dead in the desert with cow blood smeared all over my body than me here and now."

His expression changed so suddenly it shocked her. "No way, Autumn. You can't do this."

He'd never called her that here. "My name's Joy."

"Look, we had a deal, you and I. I got you out of Sacramento, didn't I? I've given you everything I promised. A chance to be on your own. To live in your own place. And never have to have sex for money."

"No, but I sure spread my legs for it, don't I?" She didn't know where the words came from. But they gave her the impetus to confront him, in spite of the six inches he had on her.

"You were coming to Vegas, anyway, kid. I never would've let you in on this deal if I hadn't already known that."

He was right about that. After Francesca had left

to go back to San Francisco the night of Autumn's fifteenth birthday, her father had come into her bedroom. If her mother hadn't shown up a few minutes later...

She couldn't even think about that. She had no way of knowing what would've happened. None.

But she'd known she had to leave. She'd run into Antonio one night while she was in Old Town, hanging out with her friends. He'd seen her crying. Asked what was wrong. Francesca had confided that she loved Antonio, said how honorable he was. So Autumn had trusted him. Told him she was leaving, that there was nothing he could do to stop her, that if he went to Francesca, she'd just run faster, and farther. She'd even told him how much money she'd saved.

He'd shown such concern. Telling her about the kinds of things that happened to pretty young runaways in Las Vegas. And showing her how very short a time her nest egg would last there.

And he'd made leaving so easy. Made settling into her new life easy, too. Although he never went to Guido's himself because he didn't have contact with the girls after he handed them over, he'd told her about the place. Giving her ready-made friends.

"I saved you from a life of prostitution."

At the time, at fifteen and with a father who might have been planning to molest her, that had sounded like heaven to Autumn.

She knew better now.

"I can't do it anymore," she said. "Do whatever you have to. Threaten me, sic your wolves on me, I just don't care anymore."

"You're talking crazy, *cara*. This afternoon scared you." He brushed her arm. And her breast.

"No!" She jerked away and stepped back, looking for her purse. She'd leave right now. Let him have his damned apartment. Or whoever's apartment it was. Damn sure Antonio wouldn't have put his name on any lease.

His rich wife might find out and cut him off. That was what his "honor," his loyalty to his wife was all about. She'd realized that a long time ago.

"You don't know what you're messing with, Autumn." She'd never heard that hard edge before and turned to look at him. His face was as hard as his voice, and his eyes scared her.

"If this was up to me, I'd let you go. You've just about served your time, anyway. Once you turn eighteen, everything gets a whole lot messier. But this one isn't up to me. Seems the boss has a godson who wants a boy. He'd been told he was getting one. And then Chancey miscarried. Heads were rolling. Some people just have so much money it deafens them to logic, you know? Like we were responsible for fate taking that kid."

This was a side of Antonio she'd never seen. And didn't want to see now.

"Luckily it was only a week or so later that we found out you were having a boy...."

That had been the day she'd opened her door, expecting Antonio, who was driving her to her ultrasound appointment, and found Cesca and Luke there instead.

Life was screwed up.

Her baby was promised to the boss's godson.

"The boss gets what he wants, if you know what I mean," Antonio said.

"He'll come find me, haul me back until I have the kid?"

"And then make you disappear."

Antonio might just be trying to scare her. Autumn knew that. But could she take the chance? This was Las Vegas. She'd lived here long enough to know that a lot of the stuff she'd seen in movies really did happen. People really did disappear. And other people, people trying to hide, were usually found....

If she ran, she'd have to leave Cesca. Or put her sister in danger when Cesca came after her.

If she stayed...

"Luke Everson is one lucky son of a bitch to have such a powerful godfather...."

Autumn gaped at him. Luke Everson? Cesca's Luke? Was getting *her* son?

"What did you say?"

"Luke Everson, he's the boss's godson. And this baby is his."

Autumn's cheeks felt numb. And cold. She had to get rid of Antonio. To think. To save Cesca from a horrible mistake.

Or find a way to disappear, leave her sister and Matteo, have this baby, and know that Luke—and Cesca?—would be loving him.

"Okay," she heard herself say through the buzzing in her ears. Anything to get rid of him. "You win."

"I knew you'd see it my way."

With one last brush down her arm, one that Autumn allowed to meet its target, he left.

She didn't want to die.

She just wanted out.

# 22

"**I** want to be there for her, I will be there for her, I just can't get past the fact that she's been lying to me." Francesca leaned forward, elbows on her knees as she faced Luke's mother. She was in Carol's kitchen Wednesday morning, watching as the older woman made strawberry scones for a women's luncheon Betty Allen was attending that day.

"Why do you think she lied to you?" Carol asked.

She'd spent most of the night asking herself that question. Alternating with indecisiveness about getting up and opening the envelope she'd tucked safely away in her duffel. It'd been much easier to avoid those pictures when they were still in the back of her camera.

"I don't know. Maybe she thought I wouldn't still love her if I knew the truth."

Carol measured, mixed, rolled, all without looking at a recipe. Only when she stopped to lift the back of her hand to her forehead did Francesca notice how badly she was shaking.

Was she nervous because Francesca had called unexpectedly and asked to come over for a chat? Or because her friend Betty was counting on her to turn out delicious pastries?

"You said she's been frightened," Carol said.

"Yeah. Probably that I'd find out."

"Maybe." Moving swiftly at the counter, Carol added, "But whatever prompted her fear is also the reason for her lies."

Okay. But it didn't change anything.

She felt a little better, anyway.

"Who your sister is—that's far more important than what she does," Carol Everson said, turning from the cupboard to put a pan of perfectly shaped pastries in the oven. "Listen to your heart, dear, and don't judge too harshly."

Spoken by someone who'd suffered from the harsh judgment of others? And who'd also known the love of a man who'd seen only who she was and not what she did?

"My Luke needs a bit of that same lesson," she added, turning back to the sink and the dishes she'd piled there. She never stopped. Not for a second. Doing everything with a frantic kind of energy. Almost as though she was afraid that if she did stop, she wouldn't be able to start again.

"Luke? Why? What's up?"

"His friend Arnold Jackson's in jail."

Francesca stood. "In jail?" She'd only met the older man once, but she'd really liked him. And couldn't imagine anyone less inclined to criminal activity. "Whatever for?"

She hadn't seen Luke since he'd left her at the hospital the day before. After dropping Autumn at her apartment shortly before five, at the hysterical insistence of the younger girl, she'd spent the evening driving out to Hoover Dam, hoping for a few hours' peace.

"Apparently he was the mastermind behind all the wins on the Strip these past months."

Francesca gasped; she couldn't help it. Luke's friend. A man he trusted. What the hell was wrong with the world?

"Luke told you that?"

"No." She shook her head, scrubbing at a bowl that, as far as Francesca could see, was already clean. "I overheard him on the phone this morning."

Francesca didn't know what to expect when she picked Autumn up for lunch. The girl had called that morning. Asked if they could meet at their usual time and place. There was no way Francesca could have refused. But she wasn't looking forward to the meeting, either.

She'd tried, twice, to call Luke, and gotten his answering service both times.

"Can we skip lunch and just go straight to your place?" Autumn asked as she climbed in. At least now Francesca understood the cotton shorts and comfortable shirt. Autumn must have found a bargain. And the wardrobe was only temporary.

"Not in your condition, young lady," Francesca said, not quite meeting her sister's eyes. "You're going to take care of yourself, starting with three square meals a day."

Autumn moved as though she was going to say something, but she didn't. Just buckled up and sat back, completely docile, while Francesca drove through and ordered them both grilled chicken sandwiches and salads.

Less than half an hour later, they'd finished their lunch, eating mostly in silence.

"Are you ever going to look at me again?" Autumn's question was issued so softly, practically hidden beneath the rustling of trash Francesca was gathering up from the spare bed in her room.

"Yes," she said, giving far more attention than necessary to completing her task. "Of course."

She heard Autumn get up, but was still surprised when the girl stuck her face directly in Francesca's line of vision. "Now?"

She looked. And felt her lips tremble just like she'd feared they would. "Oh, Autumn, why?"

"I...well, I...you know in this town..."

"I don't mean why are you pregnant," she said, tilting her head as she gazed into her sister's tear-filled eyes. "I mean, why did you lie to me?"

"I had to."

The earnest expression, the pleading tone, almost had her convinced. "Why?"

"Cesca, I'm going to tell you the truth, I promise, but first I need a promise from you."

"What?"

"That you won't do anything rash. You let me handle everything."

It was too tall an order. But what choice did she have if she wanted the truth?

"Okay. Fine."

About as fine as anything else in her life.

"And one more thing."

"What?"

"That you let me tell you everything before you say a word."

"Fine." That was an easier promise to make.

Autumn was pregnant. Having a son. The baby was right there, in the room with them, growing up big and strong.

He'd be beautiful for sure.

And...

"When I first came here, things didn't sound so bad to me," Autumn started. "I guess 'cause I didn't care all that much. And...and what I was doing meant I wouldn't be forced into prostitution to support myself like everyone kept telling me would happen." She was plucking at the bedspread, but her gaze didn't waver.

So her little sister had hooked up with a guy who'd promised to support her. Francesca had to resist the urge to hug her. To tell her how much she loved her. She'd promised to keep still.

"But since meeting Matteo and then finding you again..." Autumn's voice grew thick. She looked off toward the window. Took a deep breath. And then refocused on Francesca. Heaved another sigh.

When she spoke, words pouring out so quickly they were hardly discernible, Francesca felt as though *she'd* been pushed from the high dive.

"I knew I had to leave. And I'd kind of decided Vegas might be my only shot at not being found. I mean, my father had clout in California, but he couldn't hold a candle to the power that's thrown around in this town. But the real reason I came was

Antonio, Cesca. I know you already broke up with him and that it's over and all, but I'm so sorry. Especially now that I know about little... Anyway, he wasn't worth your heart, Cesca. He's selfish and weak and he lied to you.'' She barely stopped for breath. ''He brought me here, set me up with this agency that he scouts for. It's run by a guy his family knew in Italy. I guess he met them when he was in Milan on business one time.'' She paused for a moment. ''I trusted him.''

As she listened, growing more and more horrified, and angry, and sad, and horrified again, Francesca's stomach fluttered alarmingly. Her breath left her lungs. The world was spinning, filling her with a very real sense that if she made it through this, she'd never see things in exactly the same way again.

Antonio was here? He was involved in this?

She shivered with cold. And burned with fever. Was Autumn telling her that Antonio was the father of her own child?

The man she'd loved with all her heart had screwed her seventeen-year-old sister?

Life couldn't be so cruel.

She'd kill him.

''This isn't my first pregnancy, Cesca,'' Autumn was telling her. ''It's my third.''

Her third. Uh-huh. Her third. The words just wouldn't register.

Francesca counted backward—and wished she hadn't eaten lunch. Antonio had got Autumn pregnant at fifteen?

The betrayal was more than she could comprehend.

"I work for a private adoption agency, and although it's obviously not a completely legal operation, I've been to their offices and talked to some of my friends and it seems they must do some legal adoptions, too."

Francesca bit her tongue to stop the dozen or so questions triggered by that statement alone.

"Antonio..." Autumn looked away. Composed herself.

The bastard made Autumn give her babies away?

"He's just a contact guy. He finds pretty young women, runaways, who're usually desperate and on the verge of prostitution."

"At...Guido's?"

The frown Autumn gave her reminded her that she'd promised no questions.

"No, Guido's is where we go between jobs. Except for me, Antonio doesn't have contact with any of the girls after he sets them up with Dr. Bishop's head nurse. She takes it from there."

Guido's was where they went between jobs. Did that mean Carl knew? Was he involved in this, too? Misleading her, leading her on, when he *knew* how desperate she'd been to find Autumn.

And Antonio.

The father of her precious Gian was scum. She couldn't believe it.

"You know Antonio travels all over for his father-in-law, and I guess he just keeps an eye open for runaways. He tells them he has a way for them to support themselves, so they don't have to go home and face whatever bad stuff they left behind, and can still preserve their sense of decency. If they agree, he buys them a plane ticket and delivers them here.''

She swallowed. Francesca offered her what was left of her diet cola and waited while Autumn sipped. She tried not to think of the father of her child. And the fact that she'd taken him home. Introduced him to Autumn.

Given him her trust. Her heart.

She glanced at Autumn's stomach hidden by the baggy shirt. ''Who's the father?''

The girl shrugged. ''No one knows. We're artificially inseminated from a sperm bank. I've been told they pay medical students and others to donate sperm for research.''

It was a testimony to how far she'd been stretched that this came as a relief to Francesca. A huge relief.

''You really are a virgin.'' She got that look again. ''Sorry.''

''Hard to believe, I know,'' Autumn said with a bitter chuckle. ''But yes, I am. I've gone through childbirth twice, but never had sex.''

Okay, well, there was time for that. She was only seventeen.

''For the price of being pregnant and giving the baby up, we get enough money to live on, and, while we're actually pregnant, room and board, too. What they don't tell you is that each time you feel that baby leave your body and hear him cry and then hear them take him away without you ever even getting a glimpse…what they don't tell you is that you're going to feel like you're losing part of your life.''

Oh, God, why? What had they ever done, she and Autumn, to deserve such incredible heartache?

And how did they hope to get beyond it?

"I can't believe you agreed to this," she said, with sadness, not judgment.

Autumn stopped, her eyes pleading. "Don't you see, Cesca? The chance to escape the possibility of a strange man's hands on my body…"

"You could have done that by staying home."

She really did fight the loss of her lunch when Autumn shook her head. "I'm not sure, but I think, the night of my fifteenth birthday, my dad was going to do more than kiss me good-night when he came into my room. He told me I'd grown into a beautiful young woman. That he was so proud of me. That I'd always be his special little angel. His hand touched me." She covered her breast. "He didn't seem to notice, but could he really not have?"

Autumn started to cry then, and all deals were off. Francesca had no idea what they were going to do, how they'd get Autumn out of this mess, but one thing was for certain: the child was no longer alone.

And wouldn't ever be again. Not while her big sister was alive.

Pulling Autumn into her arms, she held on for a long, long time.


"So do you have any idea how this all works?" They'd ordered pizza for dinner, neither ready yet to leave the relative safety and privacy of Francesca's shoddy room. Neither of them were eating, either.

"A little," Autumn said. She was leaning against Francesca. Had been touching her in some fashion all afternoon. "It's a private adoption agency that specializes in problem adoptions. And legally, a girl can choose a family for her baby. Or somehow, if the girl makes a choice everything's much simpler. And there's no father to sign off, so that helps, too. Anyway, part of our agreement is that we sign the baby over to a family. Maybe they say it's a relative—to satisfy the government, I guess. I never paid much attention. I don't think I really wanted to know."

They looked at each other for a while, considering the ramifications of Autumn's desperate choices. In between bouts of sheer panic, Francesca had spent the last few hours trying to figure out their best course of action. And to push all thoughts of Antonio out of her mind.

While the sense of betrayal was deep, something she'd never, ever forget, her heart didn't hurt over him as she would've expected. She really had buried the memory of their love—or the love she'd thought it to be—in that cemetery in Italy.

Maybe it had taken losing Gian, and for a while, Autumn, for her to recognize what real love was.

Antonio Gillespie had lost more than he'd ever know.

"They always induce labor so there's less chance of a girl delivering unexpectedly and running with the baby," Autumn was saying. "And so they can give the adoptive family a definite date long in advance.''

Francesca listened, her heart aching for the girl in front of her. She couldn't believe any of this was happening.

''I also learned that the agency charges a lot of money for the adoptions, so they make a huge profit,'' Autumn went on. ''Antonio slipped up one time when he flew in to check on me. I think he'd had a couple of drinks on the plane.''

''My God, it's nothing more than a baby-selling ring. These people are producing babies with the sole purpose of selling them, and using innocent young girls to make their product.''

Autumn smiled, but there was absolutely no humor in the expression. ''Sounds pretty sick, huh?''

It did. Worse than that.

''That bartender at Guido's, Carl, did you meet him?''

''The Italian guy?'' Autumn asked with a frown. She nodded.

''I never talked to him. I didn't hang out there much. But I've heard some of the other girls mention him. They think he's hot.''

''Do you think he knew what was going on?''

''I never heard one way or the other, but it seems like I would've heard if he did.''

If Carl *was* involved, apparently his role was far enough removed that he'd never be named. Maybe he knew. And maybe, even knowing, he really did just want to provide a safe place for the girls to hang out.

Francesca intended to find out.

"Do you have any idea who's behind it all? Who the owners are?"

For the first time in hours, Autumn wouldn't meet her eyes.

"Autumn?"

She glanced over. And the fear was back in her eyes.

"What?"

"I don't know. I really don't."

"But?" Francesca grabbed her hand.

"I tried to quit last night."

"You did?"

Autumn nodded.

"What happened?"

"Antonio says if I do, I'm as good as dead."

Francesca paled as Autumn told her about the girl who'd been found in the desert. "She worked for this agency, too?"

"Yes…"

Okay. So they were dealing with big players. That meant she and Autumn had to be smart. It didn't mean they had to lose.

"Did Antonio actually threaten you?"

"No, it's not like he has anything official to do with things at this point, other than they let him be my contact person. Anyway, it's worse than that."

What could be worse?

"Tell me right now, young lady. I don't have the patience for any more secrets."

Autumn stared at the bed. "He told me why I'd be hunted down. I work for the Colter Adoption agency. Apparently my…baby…has been promised to the owner's godson.''

Colter? The place in the Biamonte building? Francesca felt chilled.

The girl looked up, her blue eyes filled with pain. And tears. ''His name is Luke Everson.''

Francesca ran for the bathroom. And as she lay against the cool tile after suffering through worse heaves than she'd had the entire time she was pregnant, all she could think about was that night on the Strip when Luke had told her he'd just learned he was having a son.

He'd known the date.

The day they were planning to take Autumn's baby away from her and give it to him.

It didn't seem to matter that he probably didn't know it was Autumn's baby he was getting.

She remembered the day she'd seen him at Biamonte. He'd been leaving the Colter agency. A place that specialized in using young girls to create babies for profit. A place owned by his godfather? She hadn't even known he *had* a godfather. Apparently there were many things he hadn't told her.

Did he know about the girls? The baby ring?

Could he possibly know that the baby he'd bought was Autumn's? Would he care?

This betrayal was far, far worse than Antonio's. Because unlike the other man, Luke had possession of her heart.

She dropped Autumn at home, hating to leave the girl there but knowing that Autumn was right—until they had a plan they had to pretend it was business as usual. After that, Francesca drove straight to Guido's.

Luke wasn't answering her calls. Smart man.

"Francesca!" Carl came out from behind the bar. "It's good to see you!"

This early, the bar had only a few early-dinner customers, judging by the half-eaten pizzas on a couple of occupied tables. She didn't sit down.

"I'm not here on a social call," she told him. "I need to talk to you, but not here—outside, where we won't be overheard." Only the fact that she'd spent every single emotion she had on her little sister that afternoon allowed her to speak so calmly.

In truth, she welcomed the calm. She didn't know how much more she could take.

And knew there was more coming than she'd ever faced before.

"What's up?" Wiping his hands on a towel he pulled from the waistband of his jeans, he walked with her to the parking lot.

"You knew what my sister was doing, didn't you?"

His narrowed eyes gave her all the answer she needed. "I told you, I have suspicions, I don't ask questions. I don't want answers. I give the girls a safe place to relax. The rest is out of my hands."

She didn't believe him. "That night we had dinner, you were asking me all kinds of questions about my sister. You were just checking up to see what I knew, weren't you?"

"I found you attractive."

"That isn't what I asked."

He didn't say anything and she opened the door of her Cherokee.

"How much do they pay you to watch out and report?"

"I think it's best if you go now, Francesca, and let us part as friends."

Her fight wasn't with him. She knew what she needed to know.

"You and I are not friends."

She had no friends. No one she could trust. Not again. Ever.

As she climbed into the car and drove away, a glance in her rearview mirror showed him still standing exactly where she'd left him.

The week was not going well. Only three days into it and already Luke was tired to the bone. He'd tried twice to see Jackson in jail. The older man wouldn't speak to him. Amadeo had come home a couple of days early and wanted to cut the dealer's balls off, no questions asked. He was preparing to press every charge he could. Then Luke's mother had had an episode the night before that had lasted a couple of hours.

And he hadn't been able to get Francesca on the phone or find her at home. Her number had come up as a missed call on his cell phone, so he knew she was trying to reach him, too. But she hadn't left a message. Which made him that much more uneasy; he needed to get in touch with her, assure himself that she was all right. Despite the chaos in his own life, his mind was always half on her and Autumn.

"Mr. Everson?" The receptionist buzzed him from the front office.

"Yes?"

"There's a Francesca Witting to see you."

"Send her back."

Francesca here? Luke stood, more glad than he should've been that she'd come, and at the same time wondering why she hadn't called.

She was already at his door when he reached it.

"Hey, stranger," he said, meaning to take her in his arms.

She walked right past him.

"I'm going to say what I've come to say and then I'm leaving."

Dressed in slacks and a blouse, with heels and matching purse, she was impressive. And someone he'd never seen before.

"What's going on?"

"If my little sister can face her boyfriend with the truth of her life, I can certainly face you."

She seemed to be talking more to herself than to him.

"I'm listening."

"Look, you can give up the pretense, though why you found it necessary in the first place I'll never know. Unless it was maybe to keep on top of what I knew." She paused. "But then you were the one who led me to her...."

"I'm sorry," he said, arms crossed over his chest as he leaned back against his desk. "You've lost me."

"I know everything."

"Then would you mind sharing it with me? Because I can tell you right now that I don't have a clue what's going on here and it's beginning to piss me off."

"Piss *you* off?" She wasn't quite yelling. But close enough.

"Yeah, piss me off. Now, what is it that I'm supposed to know?"

She frowned. "How can you just stand there and play dumb?" The question was asked so quietly, so sincerely, it stopped Luke in his tracks.

"I guess I am dumb," he said, just as softly. "Because I can't for the life of me figure out what I've done, or what I know, that could possibly make you this mad at me."

"You don't think buying my sister's baby is enough to make me mad?"

He stood, stared. "Buying your *what?*"

"You heard me."

Yeah. He had. And wondered if he'd misjudged her, too. Had the loss of her son done more than hurt her to the core? Had it damaged her, like his mother was damaged? Until she couldn't differentiate between reality and illusion?

Or delusion?

"Maybe if you explained why you think that…"

"Because my little sister's life has been threatened by the owner of the adoption agency to which she's promised her son. That's because the baby's been promised to the owner's godson."

He was trying to follow her. Was used to ferreting through emotional nonsense for the facts. "And how do you link me to that?"

"The agency is Colter."

He didn't move. Couldn't. Inside everything was blowing apart faster than he could hold it together. There had to be some explanation.

"Your godfather is running a baby-selling ring, Everson. As his head of security, I have to believe you know that. Anyway, I saw you leaving Biamonte that day, remember? You were on Colter's floor."

He wanted to stand. "In the first place—"

"No, don't bother," she said. "I got enough information from Autumn. All I ever need to know. Antonio's involved, too. I guess you knew that, too."

"The only time I've ever heard of Antonio Gillespie is when you mentioned him to me."

She stared at him, but whatever headway he might have made wasn't enough.

"He brought her to Las Vegas!" she said, throwing her hand in the air so hard he wouldn't have been surprised if she'd dislocated her shoulder. "Right under my nose! There I was in San Francisco, driving back and forth to Sacramento, desperately searching for her, and he knew all along where she was!"

He heard, along with the pain, the debilitating cut of betrayal. After the past two days with Jackson, it was a feeling he understood.

"He brings a lot of them here. From all over. And every single one of them's underage. Children!" Her hair flew out around her face as she approached his desk. And then turned her back on him. "They're artificially inseminated," she said, her voice softer but no less fierce.

Finally Luke found the wherewithal to stand. Nothing made sense. Not a word she'd said. Not Jackson. Or Autumn. Not his mother's illness or his father's early death. And still Luke stood, drawn to the woman in front of his desk, needing to touch her. Needing to feel the way she always made him feel.

"Francesca, I swear, I don't know about any of this."

She swung around and backed toward the door. "Just tell me one thing," she whispered.

"Anything."

"Is Amadeo Esposito your godfather?"

"Yes."

Head held high, shoulders straight and strong, she walked to the door, opened it and walked out, closing it behind her with a very conclusive click.

But not before Luke had seen the trembling of her chin. And the sheen of tears in her eyes.

Fifteen minutes later, Luke was pounding on the door to Amadeo's private suite.

Given immediate entrance, he strode up to the old man's desk. With one look at Luke's thunderous face, Amadeo motioned to his bodyguards to leave them alone.

"They'd better stay," he said. He didn't want to be responsible for what he might do. "I'm washing my hands of you, old man. I'm done. Finished. My father was wrong about you."

"Luke, son, you're distraught." It was the smile on Esposito's face—that condescending I-know-best grin—that sent him over the edge.

"Yes, probably," he admitted. "But I'm thinking clearly. I have enough on you to destroy you if you bother me or anyone I care about," he said. "And I'll do it in a heartbeat. I'll go to the cops, the D.A., the FBI with everything I know—and everything I make it my business to find out."

Amadeo's eyes narrowed, but he was still smiling as he stood. "What's this about, boy? Let's talk."

"I have nothing more to say to you," Luke said, heading for the door. He couldn't engage in conversation with Amadeo, couldn't trust himself to listen with any level of decency or control as the man tried to con him, charm him, spin him in twisted circles. He turned when he got to the door. "Except this. I quit."

It took him less time to clean out his office than it had to quit his job of three years. There was simply nothing that he wanted to take with him. All his most important files were at home. He made one call—to Don Brown—thanking him for his help and letting Don know he could reach him on his cell or at home. Then, grabbing his jacket and keys, he left the suite without looking back, took the elevator down to the first floor, and exited the building.

The Jag was a comfort. Familiar. His. Knowing he couldn't go home to his mother in this state, he called the Allens to alert them. And then drove. And drove. Hours passed, and he wasn't even sure where he'd been. He had to see Francesca. And Autumn. He had to find a way to help them.

And warn them about the enemy they faced—and that enemy's resources. He should know. He'd set up Amadeo's protection system—both human and electronic. Though the surveillance had been put in place to prove Esposito's innocence, if the old man wanted to do something illegal, he certainly had the network to get away with it. Like anything else in life, for every good there was a corresponding bad.

Francesca had been more right than she knew when she'd called him stupid. He'd not only trusted a crook, he'd helped protect him. Slamming his palm on the steering wheel, he asked himself for the hundredth time how he could have missed Amadeo's duplicity. How he could have been so naive, so gullible…

His father had believed in this man.

Which was maybe why Luke had been so easily fooled. He'd worshipped his father, followed in his footsteps, had faith in his instincts. Well, on this one, Marshall Everson's instincts had failed him—and his son.

When his cell phone rang, Luke snatched it up, hoping it was Francesca. There was no reason for that hope. The woman hated him. Still…

It was a number he didn't recognize.

Autumn's apartment?

"Everson."

He didn't recognize the voice on the other end of the line, either. But when the woman identified herself as Sheila Miller and told him she'd just heard he'd left the Bonaparte and had to speak with him, something to do with Jackson, he agreed to meet her.

With his imagination running a little wild, given the week's events, he briefly considered that this might be a setup. But he didn't really take himself seriously. Because Amadeo knew perfectly well that Luke's death would point straight to him.

# 23

Sheila Miller was an attractive woman in her mid-fifties. She'd taken good care of herself—something to be admired in someone who'd spent thirty years dealing cards on Las Vegas Boulevard.

"Can I get you anything?" she asked, showing him into the tastefully decorated kitchen of her condominium. "Coffee? Or something stronger?"

"Coffee would be great, if you've got any," he said, dropping into the chair she'd offered.

"It'll only take a second." She was obviously very comfortable in her kitchen and had coffee brewing in a matter of seconds.

"I'm sorry I called so late," she told him, sitting down while she waited for the coffee. "I was on until eleven."

"No problem," Luke said, glancing at his watch. "I was out, anyway." It was almost midnight. Another couple of minutes and Thursday would begin. Dared he hope it might be a better day than this one had been?

Francesca had completely rejected anything he had to say when she'd left him, not ready to believe that he'd known nothing about the shady side of the Colter Adoption Agency. But he was going to convince her. As soon as he figured out how to nail Amadeo's ass to a tree...

"When I heard tonight that you'd left the Bonaparte, I knew I had to call you. I've been sick for two days, ever since Arnold was taken to jail. That last win was my fault. He'd already decided to stop. He said things were getting risky and he'd gotten what he came for, but then he found out I was in debt up to my eyebrows and he offered to make one more play. Just enough so I wouldn't lose everything..."

He was tired. Really needed that coffee. He made an effort to understand. "This last win, at Arnold's table. You were somehow going to benefit?"

She nodded. "He was giving me his cut. The thing is, Mr. Everson, what he did was wrong. I know that. He knows that. They're trying to pin over a million dollars on him. They've already set bond at half that. If this sticks, he's looking at five to ten years in prison. And I don't think he even cares about that as long as the end result takes Esposito down, too."

Luke shook his head. He'd once been known for his mental sharpness. Had it deserted him without his knowing? "Why?"

"Do you remember a few years ago when the papers were filled with the death of that girl out in the desert?"

"Of course. No one who was around here at the time will ever forget. Or get over the unease of knowing her killer was never caught." He frowned. "But what on earth does this have to do with Arnold Jackson?"

"He was the girl's father."

*Holy shit.* The news cut through him. "Are you sure?"

Sheila nodded. Looked away as her eyes filled with tears.

Even disillusioned and angry with the man, Luke could feel for his friend. And as terrible as he felt, it couldn't be anything compared to what Jackson lived with himself. Probably every minute of every day.

That initial shock took a few minutes for him to cope with. Sheila got up. Poured the coffee.

And then his brain kicked into gear. A young girl. Connected to the girls at Guido's. Who, according to Francesca, were all "employees" of the Colter Adoption Agency. Practically indentured servants, who lived in fear.

*Victims.*

He sipped coffee. Needed alcohol.

"Esposito was behind it."

It didn't take Sheila's nod to kill the vulnerable child still inside Luke. The boy who'd trusted and loved his godfather...

The nod just clinched things. Beyond the shadow of a doubt.

She leaned forward. "Arnold has papers on Esposito, Mr. Everson. Enough to send *him* to prison forever if he can get anyone to look at them. And fill in the blanks..."

The only reason Francesca got up when there was a knock on her door at two o'clock Thursday morning was that she thought it might be Autumn. One look at Luke's weary face through the peephole and she cracked the door open, anyway.

She didn't like him. Didn't trust him. Didn't want to see him again. And didn't know how not to love him.

"I'm sorry it's so late, but this is something you're going to want to hear."

She pulled on some sweats, took off the chain lock and let him in.


"So the girl found dead in the desert was Arnold's daughter?" she asked half an hour later, still not sure she wasn't having the most fantastical nightmare.

Luke nodded. "He and his wife were divorced—mostly because of him—and his daughter, who'd pretty much hated him by then, had taken his ex-wife's maiden name. Seems Arnold was an investigator for the state of Arizona. He was trained as a cop, but worked in the state's district attorney's office investigating white-collar crime. There's not a whole lot of money in government work—at least at that level—so anyone who's in it is there because he believes pretty strongly in what he's doing."

It wasn't hard for Francesca to picture the dealer as a state investigator. That was much easier to imagine than the switch from dealer to crook.

She sat on the edge of her bed, her knees directly across from Luke's, his position mirroring hers on the opposite bed.

"According to his girlfriend, Arnold blames his divorce and his daughter's eventual running away on his own inflexibility. He saw so much crap in his job that he went overboard trying to keep it out of his home. His expectations were unrealistically high. He says, looking back, no one could have survived living that way.''

''You have to feel sorry for the guy.'' Life was a confusing array of mistakes. There were fathers who didn't love enough but never paid for that. And fathers who loved too much and paid all their lives.

''Anyway, after Mary's death, Arnold hired a detective, who unearthed enough information to prove that Biamonte was somehow involved. Sheila said that when Esposito got wind of what was happening, he offered to pay off Jackson's ex-wife, just to avoid the bad press. Or so he said. But what he offered was a pittance.''

''This was before you came back to town?''

Elbows on his knees, head lowered, Luke nodded.

''It was the suggestion of a payout that tipped Jackson off. He'd been dealing with white-collar crime for twenty years and knew a bad smell when he came across it. He did some investigating on his own, and together with his hired man, managed to piece together what was happening at Colter. The detective went to the police—and then suddenly everything disappeared.''

''Damn! He's one powerful bastard, isn't he?''

Luke's gaze was completely serious when it met hers. They were talking about the man who owned her little sister.

''Jackson had leaked information to the papers about the blood on his daughter's body, and the next thing you know, everyone's silent about the whole case. It just goes away. No one knew of Jackson's connection to Mary Samuels. Colter had signed statements from the girl, obviously coerced, about her baby's paternity—stating that she had no idea who the father was, that she hadn't even known his name—as well as papers stating her desire to give up her baby for adoption. So the way it looked was that Colter had been supporting a young girl in need, clothing her, housing her, keeping her healthy. They came out looking like God incarnate.''

''Except that she was a runaway minor and they didn't send her home.''

''She had ID saying she was twenty-one.''

Of course.

''So these hits were a way for Arnold to get back at Esposito?''

''In part, I'm sure. He'd spent a lifetime investigating money crimes. If anyone was going to know how to move money without its being noted, it would be him.''

''You mean he stashed the money? To use it afterward?''

''Exactly.''

''So he's got it all put away someplace?''

Luke shook his head. ''Revenge was only part of it. If at all. His real motivation was his ex-wife. When they finally heard what had happened to their daughter, after more than a year of searching for her, his wife had a mental breakdown. Because of the responsibility he felt about everything, he took her care upon himself. But her medical expenses were far more than he could afford. All her insurance would do was put her in a state-funded home and he couldn't bear to leave her there. So he spent his life savings getting her set up in an assisted facility and, in his free time, studied blackjack dealing. When he was ready, he hired on at the Bonaparte and slowly worked to gather his organization around him.''

She was so exhausted her eyes felt swollen. And her mind was spinning so fast she wasn't sure she'd ever sleep again.

''As a trained cop, he knew all about security measures, and after a lot of study, had a fair knowledge of how to get around them. He'd slowly built a network of dealers and scouts to find potential clients for them. All the client had to do was agree to split the win fifty-fifty. The wins never exceeded the amount of a casino check payout. The clients were always picked at random, visitors to town who had no reputation with the casinos. With his tutelage, the scouts—his accomplices—were able to find people who exhibited small signs of criminal tendencies, just enough to ensure the success of their plan.''

''Like counting cards.''

''For starters, although it would've had to be a novice, as known card-counters are all on a database and the cameras pick them out as soon as they're in the casino. I think it was more like a willingness to push the boundary without really stepping over it. They couldn't use anyone with a record, obviously, or they'd raise suspicions, but they also couldn't use anyone with too much of a conscience. Sheila didn't know all the details, only that the winners were chosen more or less scientifically, based on criminal abstracts—studies depicting personality traits necessary for certain actions—and always with extreme care.''

His knee brushed hers. Francesca moved, only slightly, but enough that they continued to touch.

''Once the table was set,'' Luke continued, ''the dealer would look off in the distance and smile, a move meant to distract anyone else watching—including those studying videotapes—while he looked at the cards coming up in the shoe. After that, it was just a matter of finger positioning to make sure he pulled in the right order. He didn't need any attention-getting cards. Just needed to be certain that the right player won. The player knew to start playing max bets when the dealer touched himself with his right hand.''

''It sounds so simple.''

Luke nodded. ''Simple enough to slide right by all the experts looking for something big.''

''It was genius, really,'' Francesca said with a wan smile.

''Right down to the fact that, until this last game, no one suspected him. He'd insinuated himself with me—having found out about my commitment to my mother, he apparently determined that I was sucker enough to fall for it. He used our friendship not only to keep abreast of any investigation, but also to waylay any suspicions I might have.''

Francesca's heart fell at the self-deprecation she heard in his voice. ''You're not as much of a sucker as he took you for.''

With his head still bowed toward the floor, he glanced up at her. ''What do you mean?''

"You hired a private team not even he knew about when he tried to work you on those videotapes."

Luke smiled, hooked his hand around her neck, pulling gently until they were forehead to forehead. "You're very good for me," he said softly.

"We're *too* good."

He nodded and she wasn't surprised he knew what she meant. They thought alike.

"It could become addictive."

She swallowed. His nearness was already addictive. "And then I'd want to stay."

"And I'd want you to."

"And it would all go to hell in a handbasket."

"Look at us," Luke said, his gaze intent as he peered into her eyes. "Deception's everywhere. It's all around us. Antonio. Esposito. Jackson. Even Autumn deceived you."

"Kind of hard to figure out who to trust," Francesca agreed. "Or even whether to trust."

"I'm not a man who can handle being tied down."

"And I'm a woman who needs my freedom."

He sighed, brushed her lips with his. "Can we forget all these difficult questions about trust and freedom, just for tonight?"

"So we can crawl into bed and get some sleep?"

"You read my mind."

Five minutes later, curled up to Luke Everson's chest, one leg thrown over his, Francesca fell asleep.

She woke abruptly to the insistent ringing of her cell phone. She wasn't sure how many times the caller had dialed, but suspected it had been more than once.

"Hello?"

"Francesca? It's Matt."

"Matt?"

Oh, God, no. Completely separating herself from Luke, who was sitting up beside her, Francesca stood. "What?"

"You need to come to the hospital." He named the same one they'd visited what seemed like a lifetime ago.

"It's Autumn, isn't it? What happened? Did she lose the baby? Is she okay?"

When he'd heard about Autumn's situation, the young man had cried, more for her than for himself. And he'd promised Autumn that they'd find a way to keep her baby and raise him themselves.

"I don't know." Matt was distraught. "I'm not family, so they won't tell me anything."

"Did she call you?"

"No," Matt said. "I'm sorry, Francesca, but I couldn't sit back and allow them to do this to her. She wanted to run away and I wasn't going to let her leave without me."

"What happened?"

"I picked her up around two in the morning. She had a bag packed and was waiting for me. We walked the couple of blocks to my car and I got her out of town as fast as I could."

This was taking far too long. Luke was already getting dressed. She could feel his intent stare. And his strength.

Thank God he was there.

"What happened?" she asked again. She didn't mean to snap. Hoped he was too upset to notice.

"I wish I could tell you, but I'm just not sure. One minute we're on the highway heading toward Hoover Dam by ourselves, not another car in sight, and all of a sudden, there's this car trying to run me over the edge. Somehow I managed to keep us on the road, and then the next thing I knew, I was lying on the side with a trucker standing over me and Autumn was lying a few feet away."

"How are you?" she asked. Her tongue felt glued to the roof of her mouth. Luke held up his keys, pointed toward the door.

"A broken wrist and some scrapes and bruises."

"And Autumn?"

"I don't know." He started to cry. "All they'll tell me is that she's alive."

"Okay, you stay put," Francesca said, pulling on her sweats and sliding her feet into a pair of shoes, all with the phone still held to her ear as she followed Luke out the door. "We're on our way. Just keep talking to me."

"Okay."

But he didn't talk. He just sobbed. Francesca tried to think of something to take his mind off the tension created by not knowing if the woman he loved was dying. And to take her mind off the same thing.

"Do you think you were followed from Autumn's apartment?"

"I didn't think so." He sounded like he was about to cry again. "But I'm just a kid, Ms. Witting. What do I know about jerks who kill innocent girls and leave them in the desert to be eaten by animals?''

Autumn lost the baby. And probably the chance to ever have another one. But she was going to live. Matt, having finally been allowed to see her, assured the bruised and battered girl that if she couldn't have children, they'd just adopt.

With a smile that lit her eyes despite her swollen and discolored face, she told him she'd like that.

''I'm so thankful it's all over,'' she said, with a tired smile for the three people in her room.

Sitting in the far corner, Luke didn't have the heart to tell them that it was far from over.

If, as he suspected, Amadeo Esposito had been behind Autumn's ''accident,'' she was in more danger than ever. In addition to everything else, the casino owner now had a failed murder attempt to cover up.

And Luke had the challenge of his life ahead of him.

''Hi, *cara*— Oh! Francesca!''

Gasping, Francesca whirled from the bed toward the deep voice behind her. Autumn's gaze was filled with fear—and a distaste that alerted Luke more than any words could have done. Matt stared at the man in the doorway, clearly confused.

Luke got up and took a step forward, reminding himself that he lived on the right side of the law.

''What are you doing here?'' The woman who spoke was Francesca, but the voice wasn't hers.

''I'm the emergency contact on Autumn's chart. I

flew in as soon as I heard. Frannie, love, I had no idea you were back in—"

"Get out." Her voice might have been trembling, but there wasn't even a hint of weakness. "Now."

The man moved forward. His face gained a hint of confidence when he saw Autumn in the bed.

"But…"

Francesca and Luke stepped toward him at the same time.

"I said get out."

"You might as well go, Antonio," Autumn said, her voice weak with fatigue and, at the same time, strangely competent. "She knows everything."

Luke could have removed the man. Badly wanted to. But the women he'd grown to love were handling things fine on their own. They deserved this chance.

"You have no place here, Antonio. You don't deserve to breathe the air we breathe. Now, get out before I call Security."

With a quick glance at Luke, the man shoved both hands in the pockets of dress slacks that were unmistakably silk. "I'll go for now, but we need to talk, Frannie. I have the right to explain—"

Still exhibiting no sign of weakness, Francesca took another step forward. "You have no rights. Period." For a woman who'd spent the past couple of hours alternating between crying and sitting virtually comatose as she waited to hear the extent of her sister's injuries, she was certainly finding an impressive store of strength. "There will be no further conversation, no further contact. I never want to be in the same city with you again if there's any way I can avoid it.''

Antonio Gillespie obviously didn't get his walking papers often. The man appeared to be gritting his teeth. "I loved you, Francesca. I really—''

''Get out!'' Luke had never heard someone yell so effectively without even raising her voice.

Luke almost grinned when, without another word or even a backward look, the man turned and left.

Someday he'd tell Francesca how proud he was of her.

It all happened so fast, Luke wasn't sure if he'd been instrumental in making it happen or if fate had finally taken pity on them and guided all the details into place. A police chief had retired since Mary Samuel's death. Another officer suddenly remembered seeing that case misfiled. Jackson's detective turned over copies of all the evidence he'd submitted years before. And the truck driver who'd been taking a dangerous shortcut on a lonely stretch of Nevada highway had not only witnessed but prevented what would've been the untimely death of two innocent young kids.

Less than twenty-four hours after the accident, Luke accompanied a group of city and state police officers through the back service doors of the Bonaparte resort. Half an hour after that, they escorted a handcuffed Esposito out the same way. There wasn't a lot of fanfare. No press. Just a spitting old man who'd finally found out that life eventually exacted payment from even the most powerful.

Luke didn't watch them put the old man in the back of a squad car. It was a sight he had no desire to see. Instead, he found a quiet place in a back hall and called Francesca at the hospital to let her know what had happened.

"I've come to realize something, sitting here this past day," she told him. She sounded weary, but oddly peaceful, as well. Luke envied her that.

"What?" he asked. He could use a realization or two. Anything that would help him make sense of everything that had happened.

"That life is only here and now," she said, the clarity of her voice traveling through to him. "That we can't rob the future to pay for the past."

Smart words. True words. And Luke had absolutely no idea how to transform great philosophy into practical applications. The past always made demands of the future, and sometimes it completely shaped what was to come.

# 24

Luke pulled the Jag into the drive around in front of his house that evening rather than parking it in the garage. He wasn't sure why. Except that the garage felt too permanent. Too closed in.

He wasn't looking forward to the hours ahead.

"Luke?" His mother's voice was shrill, calling to him from the living room when he came in the door.

"Yeah, I'm here."

He wanted to go up to his suite of rooms. Get out of his suit. Take a long shower. Drink a bottle of whiskey.

He walked into the living room. She was sitting on the couch, shredding a tissue. As he watched, she pulled another from the box beside her, wiped her eyes, and proceeded to shred that one, as well.

"The Allens called. They told me someone from the casino called them and said that Amadeo had been arrested. They wondered if I'd heard from you. They're on their way over."

Luke picked up the phone. Dialed. Told his parents' friends that he was home.

"Is it true?" Carol asked, glancing up at him with the skittish look of a frightened kitten.

"Yeah, it's true." He should sit. Rub her shoulder.

Give her the kind of understanding his father would have done. Hands in his pockets, he strode to the bay window that looked out over the front yard.

"Why, Luke?" She'd started to cry in earnest, her voice raised. "You have to *do* something. Help him. Bring him home."

Bring home the man who'd betrayed him? Betrayed all of them? The man was going to sell Luke a seventeen-year-old runaway's baby! And not even tell him about it. Luke could've gone to jail.

"Do I, Mom?" He whirled, facing her. "Why? Why do I have to do that?" He just couldn't talk to her the way Marshall would have. He wasn't his father. Sometimes the things his mother said and did— and didn't do—made him angry. It didn't seem to matter that she was sick. He still got mad.

"He lied to us, Mother," Luke said, pacing in front of her, so filled with tension he could feel the pressure pulsing along the sides of his neck. "He was using *me*. He's a criminal and a thief. You know Francesca's little sister? The runaway? He…"

Luke paced. He yelled. He told her everything. About Autumn. His son. The car accident. About Jackson, who was going to serve time in prison. And the dead girl in the desert. He told his mother he loved her. And that he hated how living with her made him feel—so trapped he'd lost any chance at a future. And all through the telling, he hated himself for losing it with her, a sick woman.

"Are you finished?" The words were issued in a shaky, too-high voice. He loved her and was there to care for her, yet he'd shaken her whole world and hadn't even given her a pill.

"Yes."

"Okay." She pulled at the tissue, shredded and pulled again. "First. Your father always taught you that nothing valuable or good…comes easy."

"Actually—" he stared at her bent head "—*you* were always saying that."

She didn't seem to have heard him. "So if something's hard," she said, enunciating carefully, "then you'd be remiss not to look for the possible good that might be coming from it."

He sighed. He just didn't have the patience for this tonight. He moved toward the door.

"Where are you going?" She was whining now.

"To call the Allens."

"There's a phone right here."

He came back, picked up the receiver.

"Call them, Luke. I understand, but I'd like you to listen to me first."

If he could listen to her he wouldn't need to call them. He could play the next couple of hours by rote. She'd get more and more agitated, her words more and more irrational, her need for reassurance more and more cloying, impossible to fill.

He put down the receiver. Slumped on the couch, his head in his hands.

"Son? How would you ever know truth if you didn't also know deception?"

How? Well, by definition…

"How would you recognize its value if you'd never gone without?"

He didn't have an answer to that.

"Do you trust me, Luke? Do you believe that what I tell you is the truth?"

When she was herself. "Of course."

"And Francesca? Do you think she would deceive you?"

No. But this wasn't about Francesca.

"*How* do you know?" He heard a tissue coming from the box. Out of the corner of his eye, he could see little white pieces float down to her lap.

"Because I know how it feels not to trust," he said irritably.

"There's something about the Everson men that you may not know, Luke," she said.

He could tell by the frailness of her voice that she was on the verge of a breakdown. Luke waited.

"For generations, the Everson men have been one-woman men. I realize that there's no scientific explanation for this phenomenon, but all of you, from your great-great-grandfather on down, have shared the trait."

She was shredding faster and faster. Talking faster, too. Luke had to concentrate to notice the signs at all. "It's evidenced in your father's steadfastness in the face of my illness."

He wanted to tell her that she wasn't ill. That she'd been a joy to his father.

And for the first time, Luke understood, deep in his heart, that this was the exact truth. When his father looked at his mother, he saw the soul and spirit of the woman he loved, not her illness. And all his life, being with her had brought him joy.

"Everson men cannot give their hearts lightly," she said, starting to cry again. "Nor can they force love where it does not exist. They cannot settle for less than the strongest and truest love. And most important, when they find that love, they can't walk away from it. Ever."

"Love is an overrated illusion," Luke muttered.

"No," she sniffled. She pulled out a new tissue, took a breath that ended in a broken sob. "Las Vegas is filled with illusion. You know that. You've always known that. It's why you hate it so much. But it serves its purpose—" she took a shuddery breath "—because its falseness also shows you what's real. Do you know what I mean? Love isn't the illusion, it's the one thing that's real. And it shows the illusion for what it is."

A world that was spinning wildly out of control stood still.

"If you continue trying to walk away, Luke, that's your choice, but your father raised you to be smarter than that." The sentence was hard to decipher as Carol was crying steadily now.

"No, Mom," Luke said, drawing her into his arms, "not just Dad. You raised me to be smarter, as well. Why didn't I realize how much you did for me—still do for me?"

"You…were five years old…a baby…when I got sick. It's all you knew…."

"Shh." He rubbed her back as she cried. "It's not all I know now. I love you, Mom."

Her sobs grew to wails. "I love you, too, Luke. Now…please…get me a pill…and call the Allens."

"I'm not leaving you like this."

"Yes!" she hollered, her eyes wide as she looked up at him. "Yes! You have to!" She was screaming so shrilly the sound hurt his ears. "You'll hate me forever if you don't go!"

He tried to calm her down. But when her frantic cries of "Go now!" crescendoed, Luke collected her pills and called Betty Allen.

Francesca was sitting at a Monopoly nickel video machine in one of the Strip's more upscale resorts on Thursday evening. Matteo was with Autumn. The girl was due to be released from the hospital the next morning.

It was too late to make any arrangements that evening, and Francesca was too tired to pack. But too wound up to rest. She watched the video reels spin, listened as the machine chimed railroad sounds. She'd hit the bonus round. Had to pick a railroad— a path that would determine the success of her journey.

"I'd take Short Line."

Turning, she saw Luke, still in dress slacks and shirt, with sleeves rolled up his forearms.

"How did you know where to find me?"

"Easy—you're predictable. When you're worn out, you either play at the Bonaparte or here, and I took a chance that the Bonaparte wasn't it."

His presence was a comfort she wouldn't have sought. His knowing her so well, a solace she couldn't have imagined.

"The Short Line, huh?" she asked, looking back down at the screen.

"Yeah."

"Why? Who wants a short journey?"

"So how about the Pennsylvania? I hear it's a beautiful state."

"And cold."

"B&O?"

"It makes me think of body odor."

"Guess that leaves Reading."

"Okay, so what can I read into the fact that you're here?"

"That it might be nice to take a walk on the Strip."

She stood, yanked her T-shirt down over the waistband of her denim skirt, grabbed her black leather bag.

"You're on the bonus round!" Luke said, glancing at the flashing machine. "Aren't you going to choose?"

"I already chose," she told him.

"You've got over a thousand credits there, with the potential to win a lot more."

"Those aren't the credits I want to win, Luke," she told him in all seriousness. Standing there in the middle of a busy casino, money clanking and machines ringing around them, she smiled up at him. "I have all the money I need, and the ability to make more."

"I can't believe you're just going to walk away! Why play if you don't care about the win?"

"Oh, I care about winning," she said, her gaze

steadfast. "I play slots for the escape, the diversion. But the win I want isn't on that machine."

His expression changed, his eyes filling with an intimacy that thrilled her. "So where's the win you want?"

"Odds are, it's out there," she pointed to the door. "I'll find it somewhere during a walk along the Strip."

They talked about practical things for a while. Francesca had called her mother after Autumn's accident and Kay had agreed to turn guardianship of her youngest daughter over to her eldest. She was coming out for a visit over the Labor Day weekend.

Matteo had agreed with Francesca that Autumn had to at least finish high school before they contemplated marriage. And he, in the meantime, was going to get his degree and a job that would support her and the family they'd one day have. Although she protested having to wait so long to get married, Autumn didn't appear too upset by the plan. On the contrary, she couldn't seem to stop grinning. Or proclaiming to Matt and Francesca that she was the luckiest girl alive.

They all understood that there'd be issues for them to deal with in the future. But this time around, they'd have each other.

Because Matt's family still needed him, they were all going to stay in Las Vegas. Francesca thought maybe she'd try her hand at children's portrait photography. But she had a feeling there were more stories waiting to be told....

"You want to see something?" Francesca asked as they passed the Fashion Show Mall on Las Vegas Boulevard.

"Sure."

She reached into her bag. Took out a stack of photos and handed them to him. "Meet Gian…"

He stopped under lights that made the Boulevard as bright as day even late at night. Studied each photo as though the child was his own.

People passed, in large groups and small, all ages, including children. And Luke stood with her at a cement embankment and looked at every single picture she had of the baby she'd loved so desperately and lost so tragically.

She didn't realize there were tears on her face until, with a gentle thumb, he wiped them away.

"I opened the packet at the hospital this afternoon," she told him. "Autumn wanted to see him. Both of the babies she gave up were boys. And now, with losing this one…"

"I love you, you know that?" Luke said, loudly enough to be heard amid the noise of the busy street, and softly enough to touch her heart.

"I love you, too."

"I can't promise I won't make mistakes, be a jerk, make you unhappy, but I *can* promise that, no matter what, I'll always do my best to be honest with you."

"And I promise you the same thing."

"I'm a little shaky in the trust department."

"Well, they say that having something in common is good for a relationship."

"Then I guess we have that going for us."

"Maybe." Francesca turned her head to meet his gaze, only vaguely aware of the people and traffic and lights and noise surrounding them. "You know, it occurs to me that trust isn't so much about total honesty as it is about faith. No one's perfect."

"I'm not sure I follow you."

"I find that I have faith in you to do your best. I *trust* you to do that."

With a hand against her cheek, Luke stared down at her. His eyes took on a suspicious sheen in the glow of the streetlight beside them.

"The joke's really on me, isn't it?" he murmured. "You came into my life, exactly what I needed, and I've been too full of myself to see it. But all along, I trusted you, didn't I?"

"I think so."

"Yeah." He nodded, leaned down and kissed her. And kissed her. Until someone bumped into them and they silently moved on down the walk. Hand in hand. Taking in the night. The sights. The sounds. And each other.

"You need to have another child."

"Maybe. Someday." Not anytime soon. She had a lot of healing to do before she'd be ready to face the months of worry that would accompany another attempt. The nights and days of worry, the panic every time she laid her baby down to sleep.

"Marry me?"

She wanted to. She really wanted to.

"You want children," she told him. "I don't know if…" She let her words trail off.

"I was going to adopt, anyway," he reminded her. "If we need to, we'll do that."

"It's not the birth that worries me, it's afterward when…"

"So we ask for an older child who's already made it past the infant stage."

"I have to stay in Las Vegas. I promised Autumn."

"I do, too. I'm a package deal, complete with a mother and the home she can't leave."

"What will you do here?" She was stalling; she knew that.

He shrugged. "I can always work for one of the other casinos," he said, "but when I was talking to Don Brown, I started to think about setting up an agency like his, here in this town."

She nodded. She could see him being happy in business for himself. Helping people. Protecting them.

An overweight man bumped into Luke in his hurry to get past them. "Marry me?" Luke said, his gaze never wavering from her.

"Okay."

"Now."

"What?" A couple jostled her, arms around each other, seemingly oblivious to everyone else in the world.

"Before the world spins again and some other crazy thing happens. I want to know that, whatever lies ahead, I'll have you there, facing it with me."

"But we can't just get married! We need a license. A ceremony."

He took her by the shoulders, turned her to look up the Strip, a road of brightly colored and blinking lights that offered practically everything a person could want. "We're in Las Vegas, honey. Pick a chapel."

She did.

*"A splendid read...Coffey weaves a swift, absorbing tale..."*
—**Publishers Weekly** *on* **Triple Threat**

# Jan Coffey

Two decades ago the mass suicide of the members of a New Mexico cult shocked the nation. Miraculously, four people managed to get away. But now three of them are dead and it appears that none of them will escape the tragedy that took so many innocent lives.

The past is closing in and there is nowhere to run....

**"An intense, compelling story that will keep most readers guessing until the very end."**
—*Library Journal* on *Twice Burned*

*Available in July 2004 wherever paperbacks are sold.*

# Fourth Victim

**MIRA®**